G000136116

BELLING'S WAR

By the same author

The Unseen War, Book Guild Publishing, 2007

BELLING'S WAR

Noble Frankland

Book Guild Publishing
Sussex, England

First published in Great Britain in 2008 by
The Book Guild
Pavilion View
19 New Road
Brighton, BN1 1UF

Copyright © Noble Frankland 2008

The right of Noble Frankland to be identified as the author of
this work has been asserted by him in accordance with the
Copyright, Designs and Patents Act 1988.

All rights reserved. No part of this publication may be
reproduced, transmitted, or stored in a retrieval system, in any
form or by any means, without permission in writing from the
publisher, nor be otherwise circulated in any form of binding
or cover other than that in which it is published and without a
similar condition being imposed on the subsequent purchaser.

All characters in this publication are fictitious and any resemblance
to real people, alive or dead, is purely coincidental.

Typesetting in Baskerville by
Keyboard Services, Luton, Bedfordshire

Printed and bound in Great Britain by
CPI Antony Rowe, Chippenham, Wiltshire

A catalogue record for this book is available from
The British Library

ISBN 978 1 84624 277 9

Chapter 1

Every schoolboy and every schoolgirl knows, or perhaps it would be more realistic to say, ought to know, that the fair land of Atlanta lies some 700 miles off the eastern coast of South America, its northern tip being roughly opposite Rio de Janeiro and its southern, Buenos Aires. The Island of Atlanta is just over 1,300 miles in length and its average width is about 350 miles. At the last census, it had a population of 59 million.

Many of these schoolchildren will also know that recently the formerly stable Kingdom of Atlanta has passed through turbulent times. The King, whose family had reigned in unbroken succession for eight hundred years, was thrown out to make way for a democratic republic under the leadership of Paul Reynolds.

Paul Reynolds had made his name on TV. He had hosted a weekly discussion programme that attracted a vast audience – some said, virtually the entire nation. His extreme and youthful good looks, his ready wit and natural touch made him a star and projected him into politics. The Idealist Party, which had been out of office since before the generation now entering their mid-twenties was born, elected him to be their leader and he brought the chips home.

On a ticket of reform, modernisation and the liberation of the Hurnots from the Bogos in Treskania, the Idealist Party won an overwhelming majority in the National Assembly. Paul Reynolds became the Chief Minister, the monarchy and the Senate were abolished and an invasion of Treskania was undertaken. The people rejoiced. True, they knew little of the West African Republic of Treskania, but it was generally understood the Bogos were carrying out a genocidal persecution of the Hurnots in that country. Moreover, the public had become bored with the years of stable government provided by the Realists, whose policy was one of non-intervention in Treskania and the promotion of prosperity in Atlanta. People longed for something more positive, more up to date, more exciting, and that was what Paul Reynolds and his Idealist Party offered.

Treskania, however, turned out to be a much tougher and altogether more complicated nut to crack than had been foreseen. Nor did the Idealist Ministers appointed by Paul Reynolds prove to be as idealistic as he or the public had expected. The invasion of Treskania made no headway and produced a catastrophic naval disaster when one of Atlanta's aircraft carriers was sunk in mysterious circumstances. The last straw was the defection of the Crown Prince who, for reasons that not everyone could understand, was the commander of the Expeditionary Force. Instead of joining battle with the Treskans, he formed an alliance with them and used his forces to head off an invasion of Treskania by her southern neighbour, Sudka.

The war had been conspicuously bungled and none of Paul Reynolds's much vaunted reforms and measures of modernisation seemed to have much effect on everyday life. In Atlantan politics it was scapegoat time. Reynolds disappeared, whither no one seemed to know. There was an ugly scuffle for power between some of the so-called 'heavyweight' Ministers and then Mr Belling, who controlled the police, declared himself the national Leader.

To most Atlantans this was a great relief. Mr Belling stood out as a man of action, a man who knew his mind and one who could enforce his will. He was the man to fill the power vacuum that followed Reynolds's disappearance. He would impose order where chaos had been gaining the upper hand; he would restore Atlantan self-respect where disillusion and humiliation had set in. He would crush the iniquitous coalition of the Crown Prince and the President in Treskania. He would bring the ex-King, who was at the bottom of all the trouble, to justice.

Mr Belling, indeed, initiated his Leadership with Napoleonic speed and thoroughness. To repair the loss of troops who had gone down with the sunken carrier and those who had deserted with the Crown Prince, he mobilised the Militia and set them on a course of battle training. To replace the Navy that had largely gone over to the Crown Prince, he laid down four fast carriers of the latest design together with the requisite support vessels. He ordered the production of the Swift, which was generally regarded as the most advanced military aircraft in the world, to proceed at top priority. He reorganised, retrained and indoctrinated the police, now known as Belling's Police, to ensure the stability of the country and a proper degree of political conformity amongst the population. To repair the economic damage caused by the withdrawal of the National Bank of Atlanta to a Portugese base, he introduced price and currency controls. Nor were his decrees confined to these and similar major issues. His writs ran all the way down to detailed and minor matters, such as even the proper adjective for Atlanta. Hitherto, the King's subjects had been called indifferently Atlantics or Atlantans. Such vagueness was not to Mr Belling's taste. In future the citizens of the Republic would be called exclusively Atlantans. There would be no two ways about that as there would be no two ways about so many other things. Thus it was that the former Royal Atlantic Air Academy became the Atlantan Air Academy.

* * *

3

The first Belling course at the Atlantan Air Academy was now approaching graduation. The cadets had undergone eighteen months of exacting training in the air and on the ground. Each man had completed a hundred and fifty hours of flying, ninety of them solo. Each had sat fourteen written exams ranging from navigation and meteorology to engineering and organisation and each had been tested one hundred per cent physically fit. Of the hundred and twenty original entrants, eighty–two had qualified and four of these had been selected for fast-streaming to the Swift squadron cadres. Now there were only two remaining steps before the granting of commissions: the civics paper and the passing out parade.

The civics paper, to which two hours were allotted, proved to have only one question: *How would you describe the Atlantan system of government to a foreigner who knew nothing of the country?* At the passing out parade, the salute was to be taken by Mr Belling himself.

For the final few weeks of the course the four fast-stream cadets were moved from the dormitories that slept twenty-five or more men apiece, into the greater luxury and personal spaciousness of the starred-cadet accommodation. Each room had a carpet, an adjoining bathroom and each man had a bedside chest of drawers. But, though these men had the same status and enjoyed the same privileges, they were, of course, individually very different types and now they were segregated in a room of their own they had ample opportunity for realising this.

Gerry Eggleton was the tallest, the oldest and physically the strongest of them. He was twenty-six years of age and, before joining the Air Force, had served as a Belling's Policeman. Although he had just passed a formidable array of Academy exams with marks more or less as good as any of the other three, he was the least well educated of the party. He had left school at sixteen and led a pretty

4

aimless sort of life working as a hotel porter, a waiter in restaurants and that sort of thing until he saw Mr Belling, the Minister of Internal Affairs as he then was, broadcasting an appeal to young men, inviting them to join a special police force that he was creating to ensure the stability of the newly declared Republic. In addition to the attraction of a smart uniform, there was the advantage of a high rate of pay, which was thirty per cent more than that of a private soldier or an existing policeman. Another advantage was that the only qualifications required seemed to be physical fitness and a willingness to swear allegiance to the Republic as personified by the Minister, Mr Belling. Gerry Eggleton had stepped forward and been enlisted. Since then he had sighted higher things and joined the Air Force.

Bill Marshall, who was twenty-one, was a graduate of East University where he had read mechanical engineering. He was seen by the rest as the brainiest of the bunch. He had none of the outward-going manner of Eggleton, being essentially a private sort of person. He was often to be seen in the corner of the room, ears closed and eyes focused, reading technical literature or what he declared to be serious novels. Otherwise he tended to listen to what the others said, saying little or nothing himself.

Henry Wilding was a somewhat spotty youth who, had he not had exceptionally good eyesight, would certainly have worn horn-rimmed spectacles. He was only nineteen and his previous experience of life was substantially restricted to the six months he had spent in a northern branch of the Bank of Atlanta as a probationary clerk. He had done well at school, where his best suits had been mathematics and, rather surprisingly, cricket, at which he had been very effective both as a batsman and a slow bowler. He had been attracted to the Air Force simply by having been taken by his father to watch a flying display when he was seventeen. Until then he had never thought about it.

John Rankin was twenty. He had gone up to West University as a student sponsored by the Navy on a short history course lasting a year. He had then gone to sea as an ordinary seaman on a missile destroyer and had intended after that to enter the Naval Academy. His aim was to qualify as a carrier-borne naval pilot but his superiors decided that he should be seconded to the Air Force Academy. The loss of all three of Atlanta's carriers, one by sinking and two by desertion, together with delays in the development of the naval version of the Swift aircraft, meant that, for the time-being, there was a much reduced demand for naval pilots. Aspirants therefore tended to be diverted to the Air Force. Rankin was not thought by his comrades to be as clever as Marshall, but he was the most widely travelled of them, having been on sea-going duty for ten months, during which time he had been ashore in such places as Lisbon, Bahia, Sydney, Toulon and Portsmouth.

Despite the differences between these four young men in character, outlook and experience, they got on surprisingly well. Perhaps this was because they had it in common that they had all done exceptionally well on the Academy course and were now all heading in the same direction towards a Swift squadron. Eggleton, however, who was generally confident and authoritative, was a bit worried about the civics paper, the results of which were yet to be announced.

'So, what did you put?' Rankin asked him.

'Well,' said Eggleton, 'I put that the Atlantan system of government was designed to eliminate corruption, dissension and inefficiency. I wrote that these faults were the trademarks of the old regime in which there had been quarrels between Ministers resulting in delays, bungles and the passing of bucks instead of the making of bold and correct decisions. That, I said, was what you got under a hereditary King, whose power derived from his birth and not his ability or the will of the people. I said we had eliminated those faults by the installation of a single Leader with the universal support of the people.'

'I shouldn't think the beaks would find much wrong with that,' Rankin assured him.

'Yes, but I'm afraid they might,' Eggleton responded. 'When you come to think of it, the worst bungles happened after we had got rid of the King; they happened while Reynolds was in power and he seems to have been elected by the will of the people anyway.'

'Historically, that may all be so,' Rankin said, 'but I don't think the question was about history. I think it was about politics, about correct politics. What you put may not be very historical, but I think it will be welcomed as politically very correct.'

'Trouble is,' Eggleton persisted, 'I don't really believe what I put. I don't really think it was down to the King. It was Reynolds who made the bungle and I'm not sure our Leader was appointed by the will of the people.'

'Oh come on,' Rankin said. 'I'm not sure what sank the carrier. My father says the official version can't be true but we're not here to write essays about what we think is true. We're here to get through the course.'

Bill Marshall put his book down at this. 'What does your father think did sink the carrier then?' he enquired.

'I don't really know,' Rankin replied. 'He just says the official version can't be true. He simply doesn't believe it was done by an enemy aircraft. He says Treskania has no aircraft with that capacity.'

'Gosh,' said Marshall, 'that's a thought, but I suppose he ought to know having been an officer on a carrier and now working in the Navy Ministry.'

'Well yes, I think he does,' Rankin confirmed.

'Gosh,' Marshall repeated and returned to his book.

Eggleton continued to look gloomy and confused which disquieted his friends. They were used to his confident ebullience and didn't like to see him like this.

'Cheer up Gerry,' Rankin urged him. 'You'll find it turns out OK. What about our orders for this evening?'

That did the trick. Gerry Eggleton returned to normal. He announced they would all go down the *Palais de Dance*. That old fashioned place, he said, was ideal. It was large, there would be ample quantities of girls and it was near South Park. There was nowhere better.

'OK, well give us the drill,' Marshall suggested.

'Right,' said Eggleton, who loved this sort of thing. 'Each of you takes a rubber with him. We walk into the hall and go round the edge of the dance floor. We don't bother with the girls on it, but we look carefully at those in the seats around it and the ones at the bar. It's best to note the ones with halter-neck dresses. They're much the handiest for this sort of thing I can tell you. Bare backs, halter fronts, that's what you want.'

Henry Wilding had heard this sort of thing from Eggleton before, but he still found it crude and rather embarrassing. But he didn't say so because he thought it would make him look silly and he did quite fancy the idea of the halter-necks.

'Then you choose one and get her on the dance floor,' Eggleton continued. 'Grip her by the bottom and ram your prick into her stomach to make sure she knows what your plan is.'

Wilding felt rather disgusted, but he couldn't help continuing to listen.

'If she pulls your hand up and backs off you, you just say you don't like the tune and return her to where she came from. But if she leaves your hand where it is and

8

presses up against you, you're on. You go round a couple of times and then you say it's awfully hot and wouldn't it be nice to have a little walk in the Park. If she says she's not hot and it's quite nice and cool in the hall, you return her to the seats and start again. If she thinks it is hot and a little air would be nice, you set off for the Park. As soon as you're reasonably out of sight, you slip you hand into the side of her halter-neck and check out her breasts. If that's OK, you do the rest in the Park.'

'And you find that always works?' Rankin enquired.

'Oh yes, always,' Eggleton boasted. 'It's just a matter of practice and judgement.'

Rankin didn't believe a word of this but he found it amusing and was glad that it cheered up his friend. The others were glad too because none of them liked to see Gerry Eggleton down. He was the sort of man who ought to be up and he generally was. All the same, young Wilding was very disappointed. When they got to the *Palais de Dance* there wasn't a halter-neck to be seen. He asked a girl about that and she said, 'Oh, those went out last year. No one would wear one nowadays.'

Chapter 2

Across the South Atlantic from Atlanta, there lies, on the west coast of Africa, the Republic of Treskania straddling the equator. Here too recent times had been full of turmoil. Treskania, since the eighteenth century, had been an Atlantan colony but, in the aftermath of the Second World War, such appendages of empire had sheered off and gained their independence. As in several of the former European colonies, so also in Treskania, liberation did not bring orderly government and the rule of law. In fact, it brought a state of chaos not far removed from anarchy, which it seemed would last for ever. Eventually a state of open warfare broke out between the two rival elements of the population, the Bogos on the one hand and the Hurnots on the other.

The Bogos, who probably emanated from the South America of pre-Spanish and Portugese days, are a hardy warrior-like people, active and able in many aspects of life. The Hurnots belong to a tribal culture and are notoriously easy-going and naturally lazy. In the colonial days, Atlantan rule had more or less succeeded in protecting them against Bogo exploitation but with liberation that safety net was removed and the Bogos took advantage of the opportunity. Instead of uniting to resist Bogo domination, the Hurnots fell to internecine tribal disputes and warfare, fighting, at one moment, against each other and, at another, against the Bogos. In consequence the country degenerated into a pitiful condition where famine, disease and lawlessness were the orders of the day.

World opinion saw the Bogos as responsible for this deplorable situation and the International Peace Organisation (IPO) passed a series of resolutions condemning them for what was described as genocide. It was, however, not until Paul Reynolds came to power in Atlanta that anything was done in response to these resolutions and by the time he launched the war to rescue the Hurnots they were no longer in need of it. President Tamu had come to power in Treskania and, seemingly unnoticed by the eye of world opinion, had inaugurated a system of government that was firm, fair and resolute. The civil war was ended and the rights of the Hurnot population were guaranteed. Machinery to settle their tribal disputes was established and, where it failed, the warring parties were separated by military force controlled from the centre.

The legacy of the past decades of rivalry and warfare was, nevertheless, a severe one, but at least the work of reconstruction had begun and the tribal Hurnots were returning to their traditional pursuit of agricultural activity.

It was in these circumstances that the Atlantan invasion of Treskania collapsed, but this was not for the reasons that might have been expected. Nor, for that matter, had the invasion been for the reasons that were declared. Paul Reynolds publicly proclaimed that it was to rescue the Hurnots, but the 'heavyweights' in his Cabinet had secretly intended it as a means of gaining control of the oil fields some four to five hundred miles inland from Bogotown where the invasion had made its landfall.

Atlanta possessed a powerful Navy and a potentially effective Air Force, but only a small regular Army. Any hope of capturing the Treskan oil fields depended upon its spearhead, the King's Royal Regiment. This was an elite formation and so balanced as to constitute an independent striking force. It was commanded by the popular and militarily competent Crown Prince. Paul Reynolds and his Ministers would have liked to replace him with one of their own men, but they dared not do so for fear of causing a mutiny amongst the men who were their one and only hope of victory. Moreover, the Crown Prince had been instructed by his father the King to carry out the orders of the Republican government unless they involved operations that were contrary to international law or were of such a nature as to be operationally impossible.

The King, indeed, had been remarkably tolerant of the government that had overthrown him. He was imbued with the belief that he ruled only with the will of the people and that his role was to advise and to warn but not to govern. He rather changed his mind, however, when Paul Reynolds's government put out a warrant for his arrest and threatened to try him for treason and, even more so, when he discovered that one of Atlanta's aircraft carriers had been sunk with over four thousand men on board, not by enemy action as was publicly announced, but as a result of a botched trial of strength between the Ministers for the Air Force and the Navy.

Having fled the country and found a safe haven in Wales, the King revoked his injunction to the Crown Prince, who in any case had now found himself in a perilous position. The loss of the carrier denied him the reinforcements on which he had been depending and he judged that his orders to advance immediately on the oil fields were simply not feasible. He therefore withdrew his force to a small perimeter which he believed could be defended until some means of evacuating it could be found. Here, he was pinned down by a vastly superior force of Treskan troops.

But the Treskan troops were also in a perilous position. Their commander recognised that he could not break the Crown Prince's defensive line by a frontal assault and that his only obvious recourse was to crumble it by gradual attrition. In that, he would, no doubt, eventually have succeeded because the Crown Prince would in the end have run out of ammunition and other supplies. He had been disavowed by his own government and declared a traitor. No assistance would come to him from Atlanta. His had become an army without a base. Even so, the Treskans knew they had not the time in which to exploit this position. They were imminently threatened with a massive invasion over their southern border by the unfriendly Republic of Sudka. General Attagu, the commander of the Treskan Army, was, in fact, in no better a position than the Crown Prince, and he knew it.

This stalemate induced the two opposing commanders to call a cease-fire so that the wounded could be collected and treated. In the course of the discussions to give effect to this decision, the Crown Prince and General Attagu conceived a mutual respect and admiration for one another and the Crown Prince came to realise that the grounds of the war were bogus. His own intelligence activities had convinced him that, far from oppressing the Hurnots, the government of President Tamu was bent upon securing their welfare.

So, disavowed by his government, isolated on a beachhead without a line of retreat and aware that the object of the war was the oil fields and not the protection of the Hurnots, the Crown Prince undertook to place his forces at the disposal of General Attagu to stiffen Treskania's resistance to the Sudkan invasion of the southern frontier.

The first result of this astonishing development was the even more astonishing Treskan victory in what leapt to instant fame as the Battle of the Frontier. Twenty thousand Treskan troops and about nine thousand men of the Atlantan King's Royal Regiment annihilated an invading Sudkan force of more than forty-five thousand men.

General Attagu and President Tamu were the first to recognise that this brilliant feat of arms was chiefly due to the Crown Prince who, under the cover of darkness, had moved his troops by sea from their bridgehead near Bogotown to a landing point behind the Sudkan frontier with Treskania and then, also under cover of darkness, launched an assault force along an axis between the two masses of Sudkan troops. This hit the forward formations in the rear and led the reserve forces behind to believe the Treskans had broken clean through the mass of their army to the front. Confusion led to panic and David slew Goliath.

Military correspondents highlighted the similarity of this operation to General MacArthur's landing at Inchon in the Korean War and indeed the Crown Prince had studied that action in his student days. He was therefore alert to the decisive influence that sea power could exercise in such situations. The Battle of the Frontier could not have been won had not the Crown Prince been able to exploit the support of a substantial fleet lying off the Treskan coast.

Thus, the Atlantan invasion of Treskania having been aborted and the seemingly overwhelming threat from Sudka defeated, President Tamu and his people could breathe more freely. But a breathing space was all that had been achieved, for it was obvious that the Belling government in Atlanta was set upon the destruction of the Crown Prince and his Regiment as also upon the seizure of the Treskan oil fields.

The true potential of these oil fields had only been discovered within the last ten years but, now that it was discovered, they were seen to be a prize almost beyond belief. The quality of the oil, its accessibility and its amount were on a Saudi Arabian scale, but, weighed down by their domestic problems, the Treskans had so far been unable to exploit these vast possibilities. Nor did they possess the technical resources to do much about them. They had, however, started negotiations with Brazil, aimed at an oil concord. Brazil commanded the engineering skills and the shipping to extract and move the oil; Treskania owned it. If the two positions could be adjusted, one to fit the other, both countries would have a great prize in sight, unless, that is, Atlanta upset the apple cart by getting there first.

To frustrate, or somehow divert, Atlanta's aggressive intentions towards their oil fields had indeed become the principal aim of Treskania's foreign policy and, as part of that aim, President Tamu had invited the King of Atlanta to take up residence in Treskania. The presence in Kesa, the Treskan capital, of the father of the commander so largely responsible for the great victory in the Battle of the Frontier would obviously be welcome to the Treskan people and a tie of friendship between him and the Treskan government might, in the event of his restoration to his throne, become a trump card in President Tamu's hand.

The King received this invitation in North Wales where, for the past several months, he had taken refuge as an incognito guest of Miss ap Llewellyn in Dolgellau Hall. He decided to respond by sending an emissary to Kesa charged with the responsibility of working out all the arrangements needed before the offer could be positively accepted. It was, after all, not quite a straightforward matter. There were risks on both sides. The King's presence in Kesa would certainly act as a red rag to a bull upon Mr Belling and therefore, far from parrying the threat to the oil fields, might intensify it. The King wanted to be sure that President Tamu had taken this fully into account. Then, on the King's side, there was the consideration that by moving to Kesa he might give substance to Belling's claim that he was a traitor, even allying himself to the hostile state of Treskania. Such were some of the cons. But there were also many pros. The emissary would need to discuss and balance these in consultation with the authorities in Kesa.

For such a task, it might be thought, a diplomat well versed in African affairs was required and that, indeed, might have been seen as a sensible view. But the King could not adopt it. He had no experienced diplomats to hand. His 'court' at Dolgellau Hall did not extend beyond his Private Secretary, his Valet, and Nicholas Hardy and Laura Blick, to whom might be added for certain purposes his hostess, Miss ap Llewellyn. He did not wish to be separated from his Private Secretary, Count Connors, upon whom he depended heavily for day-to-day advice. His Valet would not be seen in Kesa with quite the same trust that he enjoyed from the King, and Miss ap Llewellyn, resourceful and full of character though she was, would also not be seen there as a suitable person. That left only Nick Hardy and his girl friend Laura Blick. The King and Count Connors decided on Nick Hardy.

'The King has it in mind to appoint you as his special emissary to the Treskan government,' Count Connors told Nick. 'He wants you to prepare the way for His Majesty's removal to Kesa.'

'Surely that's a bit above my capacities,' a very surprised Nick replied.

'We think not,' Count Connors insisted. 'You carried out a very successful mission to the Crown Prince at the time he was coming to an agreement with General Attagu and you brought back invaluable information about the complex situation then prevailing in Treskania.'

'Yes,' said Nick, 'but you told me what to say to the Crown Prince almost down to the last syllable and the Crown Prince told me what I was to say to you. So really I didn't do much at all.'

16

'We thought you did very well,' Count Connors persisted. 'Mind you,' he added, 'the King won't order you to go. He'll invite you and then you must decide. Of course we'll give you a written brief covering all the points we think ought to be investigated.'

'I really think this is a job for someone with greater and wider experience than I've had,' Nick went on. 'After all, the only first hand experience I've had of public affairs was as a fairly junior official in the Ministry for the Air Force. That's hardly a qualification for being a, a, more or less an ambassador.'

'No doubt the King could find a more experienced man for the job from somewhere,' Count Connors said, 'but he could not find a more loyal one or one more prepared to take risks for a cause he believes in. He fully recognises the risks you and Miss Blick took when you warned the Navy Ministry and she warned the Air Force Ministry of what proved to be the disastrous consequences of the rivalry between the two Ministers. He knows you both narrowly escaped arrest for what your then superiors saw as breaches of the State Secrets Act. He respects your courage and your integrity.'

'But what we did *was* a breach of the State Secrets Act,' Nick averred.

'Indeed it was,' Count Connors agreed. 'But what you and Miss Blick did was certainly for the higher purpose of the public interest.'

'Yes, well that was how we judged it at the time,' Nick conceded.

'Exactly,' said Count Connors. 'So may I tell the King that if he invites you to go to Kesa as his special emissary, you would be disposed to accept the mission?'

Nick scratched his head.

'Well yes I suppose so,' he said. 'You haven't really got an alternative have you?'

'Oh yes we have,' Count Connors responded. 'We could have sent Miss Blick.'

'It was either me or you,' Nick said as he told Laura about what Count Connors had asked him to do. 'So,' he added, 'this blasted business of supporting the King means we're going to be parted again. I think it's bloody miserable.'

'You'll survive,' Laura said, rather coldly, Nick thought.

'You don't seem to mind much,' he complained.

'Of course I mind,' she said. 'But it won't be forever and I suppose it won't be quite at once, will it?'

'I think it'll be pretty soon,' he told her. 'They seem to be in quite a hurry.'

'Oh dear,' said Laura and then, going up an octave, 'D'you know Miss ap Llewellyn said an extraordinary thing to me this morning.'

Did she?' Nick asked. 'What did she say?'

'She said, had we ever thought of getting married?'

'Not her business,' Nick said. 'I wonder what put that into her head.'

'She probably wants another spare room,' Laura suggested. 'If I've told the Housekeeper once, I've told her a hundred times that we are used to sharing a room, but she just says, "Miss ap Llewellyn has given you two rooms" and flounces off.'

'I suppose it's not worth getting married just to save Miss ap Llewellyn a room,' Nick said.

'No,' Laura assented, 'but I suppose there might be other reasons to make it worth thinking about.'

18

Chapter 3

Count Connors's attachment to the King was deep and abiding and, if that were possible, had been further intensified by the hazardous experiences they had been through together when making their escape from Atlanta. On their extraordinary voyage to Lisbon, their prospects had hung in an alarming balance between capture and probable execution on the one hand, and drowning somewhere along the way on the other. They knew they had got away with it by the very skin of their teeth. And it was not as though either man had been remotely prepared for such a horrifying episode. Count Connors came of a privileged court family which, until the recent revolution, had lived more or less in a glass case. As for the King, his grandfather, Arthur VIII, had died within a few months of his birth and his father had then acceded to the throne. He himself had been the heir to the throne or King for virtually the whole of his life. His upbringing and education had undoubtedly helped to make him a conscientious and dignified monarch; it had done nothing to prepare him for the exigencies he had recently encountered nor, indeed, for those that now lay ahead. After twenty-two years on the throne, King Arthur IX had been reduced to the devices of a fugitive.

Perhaps it was his acute awareness of the pathos attached to the fall of the mighty that inspired Count Connors, within his now limited means, to take every possible step to protect the King from the buffets of the outside world, to do everything he could contrive to provide for his comfort and peace of mind. That was why he so particularly urged the King to send an emissary to Kesa before going there himself. Nor was Nick to confine himself to the big diplomatic and strategic issues. He was also to look into all manner of minor matters. He was, for example, to take careful note of the service provided by Air Direct on his flight to Kesa.

Air Direct was a new British airline which specialised in getting people from A to B without changes at C. Nick was told to book a flight on Air Direct from Cardiff to Kesa. If he was sufficiently impressed, Count Connors might well advise the King to use that means of getting there himself. So, from the moment that he drove off from Dolgellau Hall to Cardiff airport, Nick was testing the water for the King.

The procedure at the airport was impressively thorough. Nick's luggage was carefully X-rayed and he was exhaustively searched. Sitting in the departure lounge, he watched two members of the aircrew pass through and enter the aircraft. He surmised these would be the Second Pilot (three rings on his arm) and the Flight Engineer (two rings). Shortly after that, five girls followed in smart light blue uniforms. These were obviously air hostesses. After another interval, an officer with four rings on his arm went through. He was clearly the Captain. Nick noticed he was carrying a quite substantial black briefcase. This was not opened. Presumably it had been checked somewhere further back. All the same, Nick made a note that this was a potential gap in the security. But perhaps, he thought, not a very serious one. If the Captain couldn't be trusted, one had better stay permanently at home.

The flight was excellent in every respect except, Nick reckoned, one. The aircraft was quiet and comfortable. The food and drinks were good, but no information was given about the route flown or, indeed, about the outside world in general until just before the landing at Kesa airport, when the Captain announced that the local temperature was 31°C and that everyone should have their passports ready for inspection. Nick thought they had missed a trick there. For all he knew, they might have flown to Canada and not to Africa. Even so, he realised that air passengers don't take much interest in their route or anything else about the flight rather as sardines don't take much notice of the tins into which they are consigned. Air passengers, he knew, read magazines, watched TV or slept. But he did wonder how the King would regard this matter. The King was tremendously interested in details of many sorts and often unexpected ones. Nick pocketed his notes and got his passport ready. He considered he had done a pretty thorough job so far.

And so he had, except for one observation he had missed. He had not noticed that, while he was watching developments in the departure lounge at Cardiff, there was another man doing exactly the same thing with exactly the same exactitude.

* * *

The Director of Security Services had submitted various plans to Mr Belling for the assassination of King Arthur IX. Belling had long since decided that the King must be eliminated and the political judgement upon which that decision had rested had been reinforced by the personal affront the Leader had felt when the King slipped through the hands of his police and escaped via Portugal to a refuge in Wales.

However, assassination was not now what Belling sought. He believed much political capital could be accumulated from a public trial of the King, who would be shown to be a traitor, even to the extent of having allied himself to an enemy power. There would be much more to be gained from this than from a secret assassination. Moreover, Mr Belling, the head of a civilised government, ought not to appear to the world as the assassin of the King. The deed would have to be attributed to some other source and the propaganda value of such a stroke would be sacrificed. Such was the strongly emphasised opinion of Dr Offenbeck, the Leader's special adviser. Of course the King should be put to death, but it should be done in a proper legalistic sort of way.

The Director of Security Services, Major Silk, had accordingly brought forward a plan for the kidnapping of the King preparatory to a public trial in Atlanta City. He already had an agent in Wales who had successfully secured a job as an under-gardener at Dolgellau Hall. From newspaper reports in the Treskan press, he had learned of President Tamu's invitation to the King to move to Kesa. From a general inference, he had assumed that this would be accepted and that the King would probably fly to Kesa. As he had been required by the British government to remain incognito and, as such, to keep the lowest possible profile, it was more than likely he would fly from Cardiff rather than Heathrow or Gatwick. If so, it was virtually certain he would go by Air Direct, since Air Direct was the only airline operating a service to Kesa without an intermediate change.

Major Silk had compiled a dossier on Air Direct. This showed it was a small business operating from provincial airports. At Cardiff, it had seven aircraft, all of which were twin-engined Boeing Luxairs. In their Air Direct configuration, these aircraft seated a maximum of a hundred and fifty passengers and they operated a weekly service from Cardiff to Capetown with a stop at Kesa. The company did not directly employ its own aircrew, but took advantage of the considerable unemployment existing in that profession. This enabled them to charter the services of qualified Captains, Second Pilots and Flight Engineers on short-term contracts.

All this intelligence had been collected by the under-gardener at Dolgellau Hall, A4A, to Major Silk, but Arthur Johnson to Miss ap Llewellyn and the others at the Hall. A4A was a highly trained detective in Belling's Police and already, at the age of twenty-nine, in the upper echelon of that force. To Miss ap Llewellyn, he had presented himself as having been born in Ludlow and educated at the secondary school there. He had always had gardening as his main interest and he had been employed by the National Trust at Bodnant, that Mecca of the art, but only in a rather menial role. He now wished to work at a higher level which was why he had sought an interview with Mr James Finch, the head and, at that time the only, gardener at Dolgellau Hall.

Mr Finch, who had turned sixty-nine, was very pleased to meet this enthusiastic and able-bodied young man. Things were getting a bit out of hand in the garden and he found the ground seemed to be getting further and further away from his reach. He had also become almost afraid of the old fashioned motor mower with its dangerously exposed chain belts and rotating cogwheels and blades. He had been looking out for an assistant for over a year but no one suitable had come to light. Arthur Johnson's appearance was almost too good to be true. He had a certificate of qualification from the Horticultural College at Shrewsbury, an ID card with his national health and his national insurance number, and a letter of recommendation from the National Trust. Mr Finch had no means of knowing that all these documents had been produced, not in England or Wales, but in Atlanta. He told Miss ap Llewellyn that he thought Arthur Johnson would do very well and she was delighted to take him onto her staff and to accommodate him in a two-bedroomed cottage nearby which belonged to her. This had just been vacated by her chauffeur, whose wife had recently produced a second child.

The under-gardener had no duties within the Hall, but he was welcomed to its staff dining room for all his meals. Everyone liked him. He was cheerful, polite, good looking and hard working. It was here, in the staff dining room, that he came across the three maids who cleaned the house, made the beds, polished the silver and so on. They were all local girls who lived in Dolgellau or thereabouts. They came in each morning and usually went home after lunch, unless there was an evening function, in which case they stayed on until later. Arthur Johnson observed these girls with great care.

Two of them were Welsh and very good lookers they were. Both had luxuriant black hair, dark eyes and gorgeous figures. About twenty-two or three, Arthur Johnson guessed. They were full of the joys of life, constantly laughing at the jokes that characterised the staff dining room and soon raining down little pushes and punches upon the new under-gardener. Gwyneth and Marian were tremendous fun.

The third girl was quite different. She was younger and, compared to Gwyneth and Marian, who were in full bloom, she was only in early bud. Janet Hoskins was her name. She was English and sprang from Leamington Spa. When she was fourteen her parents moved to Dolgellau where her father had bought a garden machinery business. That was five years ago. Janet had now been doing mornings at Dolgellau Hall for just over a year. She liked the work and got on well with Gwyneth and Marian, but she was still withdrawn and obviously unsure of herself. Compared to them, she was quite plain and, while they usually dressed in the tightest of jeans, a fashion that had returned after several years in the wilderness, she generally appeared in a somewhat ill-fitting dress.

24

Arthur Johnson decided that neither Gwyneth nor Marian would do. They were sure to have steady boyfriends. Janet might not, and it was upon her that he now concentrated his attention. He diagnosed she was still much under the thumb of her parents, especially her mother. One of her commonest remarks was, 'I don't know what my Mum would think of that.' So Johnson decided to start, not with Janet but with her parents. He pointed out to Mr Finch that the motor mower ought to be replaced with a more modern machine.

'What sort had you in mind?' Mr Finch asked.

'Well,' said Arthur, 'I'd thought of a Smith's Multicut.'

'They'd be big money those would,' Mr Finch observed.

'Yes, they do cost,' Arthur conceded. 'I think they're about twenty-one thousand.'

'That's a lot of money for a mowing machine,' Mr Finch objected. 'You'd expect a car for that.'

'Well, you wouldn't get much of a car for twenty-one thousand, not today you wouldn't,' Arthur suggested. 'But I'll tell you what,' he went on, 'a Multicut would pay for itself in no time at all. I've reckoned it takes me six and a half mowing hours to do the lawns. With a Multicut I could do them in an hour and a half. I'm sure of that.'

'So a Multicut would save us five hours a shot you think,' Mr Finch said.

'I'm sure of it. And when you come to think of that, five hours less a mow, say thirty times a year, put into my wages told in per hour, well that's big money too.'

'You could be right at that,' Mr Finch decided. 'But I'll have to talk to Miss ap Llewellyn about it. It's her money you know.'

'Oh yes, of course it is,' Arthur readily agreed. 'Of course that's right. So we'll have to see what she decides. Of course it's up to her. If she gives the go-ahead, I could make enquiries at Mr Hoskins's.'

There was no difficulty with Miss ap Llewellyn. What Mr Finch advised she accepted. Arthur was given the go-ahead to look into a Multicut.

He walked into Hoskins Garden Machinery off the square in Dolgellau. The display was quite modest. There were some electrically driven hand-held rotary mowers at about a hundred to a hundred and fifty pounds each and a couple of combined tractors and mowers at around seven hundred and fifty pounds. He took a look at these and then approached the counter where he found a pleasant looking middle aged lady. Probably Janet's mother he thought.

'I'm from the Hall,' he said. 'Miss ap Llewellyn's looking for a new mower.'

'Oh yes,' said the lady. 'You'll be the new under-gardener then. Mr Johnson?'

'That's right,' Arthur told her.

'Our Janet mentioned that you'd come.'

So she was her mother.

'Yes, well I wondered if you did any Smith's machines.'

'I'm afraid we don't have any such in stock. They're mostly quite expensive and there's not much demand for that class of thing here.'

'Yes they are quite expensive,' Arthur agreed, 'but perhaps you could order one in for me.'

'Well, I'm not sure about that, but if you'll bear with me, I'll ask my husband.'

Mrs Hoskins withdrew to the back area and Arthur was left cooling his heels for what seemed a long time. He began to fear his mission was going to be abortive. But at last Mr Hoskins appeared with a hopeful looking bunch of brochures under his arm.

'It's Mr Johnson from the Hall is it?' he enquired in the most respectful tone.

'It is.'

26

'And you mentioned a Multicut for Miss ap Llewellyn.'

'That's right. It's a Multicut that would do the job best for her I reckon.'

'Smith's do make a very good class of machines,' Mr Hoskins said. 'And the lawns up at the Hall are extensive. A Multicut wouldn't be wasted on them. Three mowing decks. Grass collection. Hydraulic deck lifts and the decks fold when not in use. See here,' he continued taking one of the brochures from under his arm, 'this is it.'

Arthur turned the glossy pages of the brochure which showed the machine with a pretty girl in the saddle but had little technical information and nothing about the price.

Mr Hoskins read his mind.

'Here's the specifications,' he said, handing over a plain white sheet with a numbered diagram of the Multicut in black and white. 'I could arrange for you to try one if you like, but we'd have to go down to Cardiff to do that. They have a demonstration machine there.'

'There's no need for that,' Arthur said. 'I've been down there and tried one. It's definitely what we want.'

'But you didn't buy it there,' Mr Hoskins wondered.

'No,' said Arthur. 'I could have done, but I think it's always best to buy locally if you can. For one thing you get better after-sales service that way.'

'That's quite true,' Mr Hoskins agreed. 'I could get one for you and then we'd look after it for servicing and that.'

'Excellent,' Arthur said. 'That's what I had hoped.'

'It's twenty-two thousand seven fifty inclusive of tax,' Mr Hoskins had to say. 'A shocking amount of tax really,' he added. 'But I could get it without any delivery charge.'

'Good, that would be helpful,' Arthur said.

The deal was now sealed by the signing of an order and the promise of a cheque for the deposit of two thousand and seventy-five pounds to follow by post. Arthur signed the document, 'Arthur Johnson on behalf of Miss ap Llewellyn, Dolgellau Hall'.

'It's very good of you to give me the business,' Mr Hoskins declared, offering Arthur his hand.

'I'm sure it'll turn out well for Miss ap Llewellyn,' Arthur said. 'And that's the main thing.'

'That's right, I hope it will,' Mr Hoskins affirmed.

Chapter 4

The Multicut mowing machine was a great success up at the Hall. In fact it was quite a sensation. Mr Hoskins brought it along on his flat-sided lorry and it was gingerly backed off down three carefully located boards, Mr Hoskins pushing and Arthur Johnson steering. Then, before an audience of Miss ap Llewellyn, the King, Count Connors, the King's Valet, Nick Harding, Laura Blick, the Housekeeper, the three maids, Mr Finch and Mr Hoskins, it was started up and driven to the far end of the main lawn. Here, in little more than its own length, Arthur swung it round, lowered its blades and set it off on its maiden mow. It purred along and crossed the huge expanse of grass in what seemed no time at all. It swung round again and re-crossed the lawn, creating two beautiful stripes of evenly mown ground without a stalk to be seen. The congregation now processed up this splendid swathe, led by Miss ap Llewellyn and the King. Arthur Johnson was the hero of the hour. Never before had an inaugural mow been accompanied by such a ceremony.

Mr Hoskins drove back to Dolgellau in the happiest frame of mind.

'Lucky at last,' he exclaimed to his wife. 'There'll be at least three hundred a year for the servicing and I shouldn't be surprised if they don't come back for more machines like hedge cutters and perhaps a tractor. Poor old Mr Finch has let things get a bit out of date, but young Arthur means to put that right. What a bit of luck him coming to us. Such a nice young man too.'

'I reckon he's got eyes for Janet,' Mrs Hoskins remarked.

'Well what if he has?' her husband said. 'She could do a lot worse.'

'Oh yes I dare say,' Mrs Hoskins went on, 'but it's not that. It's just that she's too young to decide now.'

'She's nineteen isn't she?' Mr Hoskins asserted, 'and I don't see there's any deciding to be done. Just because he said she's a nice girl doesn't mean he's going to marry her does it?'

Mrs Hoskins seemed to ignore this and continued her own line of thought.

'She likes him you know,' she said. 'She told me she thought he was chivalrous. Now I've never heard her say anything like that about a man before.'

'Or about anything else I should think,' Mr Hoskins observed. 'I doubt she knows what chivalrous means.'

But Janet did know what chivalrous meant and she found that Arthur Johnson fitted the bill exactly. He was forever opening doors for her. He always got up when she came into the room and now he'd taken to bringing her a flower from the garden and pinning it onto her dress. She felt somehow exalted and walked about with a lighter step. She took more trouble with her hair and began to apply lipstick, though only after she was out of the shop in Dolgellau. And he took such an interest in her, even down to the details of her work. When she cleaned the bedrooms, did she do out the wardrobes? What sort of clothes did the King have hanging up in them?

She had not been accustomed to opening the wardrobes, but now she began to do so. She thought Arthur would be amused and interested to hear what was in them and she was quite right about that. He listened most intently when she told him there were three white uniforms and four khaki drill tropical suits in the King's wardrobe. Had

30

she noticed any tropical clothes in any of the other rooms? He asked. Yes she had. There were two tropical suits in Mr Hardy's room, not that he often slept there. She thought he usually slept in Miss Blick's room.

'You wouldn't want me to spy on them would you?' she said.

'No of course not,' Arthur assured her. 'There's no question of spying. It's just that I like to know about things and people. Natural curiosity you might call it, but as harmless as the driven snow.'

Janet thought the driven snow could be quite harmful but all she said was, 'Yes, of course.'

'All the same,' Arthur continued, 'you needn't bother with telling people about the things I like to know about. They might get the wrong impression.'

'I see,' she said.

He realised she was a bit uneasy in her mind about these things he wanted to know. They were walking along the old railway line from Dolgellau to Barmouth where there was nobody about. So, instead of trying further assurances of his above-boardedness, he slipped his arm round her waist. He felt her give a slight start but then she seemed to settle down and they walked on.

'Curious how disused railway lines are haunted,' he said.

'What d'yer mean?' she asked.

'Well, I don't know,' he said, 'but you can almost smell the railway smell – you know the smoke – and hear the click click clickety click as the wheels go over the rail joints.'

'My Dad said they were diesels,' she told him. 'He can remember them when he was a little boy.'

'But your father didn't live here when he was a boy.'

'No, he lived in Leamington Spa, but there were trains there, when he was a boy.'

'I'm sure there were. But I was thinking of the trains

that came along this line, on the very ground on which we are now walking.'

'I suppose one train would be much like another,' she said.

'You silly thing,' he said, giving her a little hug. 'There were all sorts of different kinds.'

'Anyway, there's none here now,' she remarked.

'Fortunately not,' he agreed, giving her a light kiss on the cheek.

After that they stopped from time to time for little hugs and kisses, but only very gentle, almost innocent, ones.

Arthur reflected to himself that he had perhaps gone a little too fast on questions about what was in the King's bedroom and so on. He sensed that he needed more control over her before trying anything further, but he realised he might not have much time. The King would obviously be going to Kesa, but he needed to know when and by what means and he needed to know this with sufficient time in hand for the necessary arrangements to be made.

'I thought it would be nice to go up to Lake Cregennan,' he said. 'I believe it's very pretty.'

'It's National Trust,' she said. 'It's up a steep hill.'

'But it could still be very pretty,' he persisted. 'What say we run up there tomorrow afternoon? Be as good a way of spending a Sunday afternoon as I can think of.'

'It'd be very pleasant I'm sure,' she said.

'Right, I'll call for you at two-thirty on my motor cycle and we'll spin up there.'

Janet gave a lot of thought as to what she should wear for the spin up to Lake Cregennan. She had never been on the back of a motor bike before and was afraid a skirt might be a bit awkward. On the other hand, she felt her rather baggy slacks were not romantic. In the end she settled on a summer dress with a full skirt. She reckoned she would be able to keep it under control by clamping it with her knees. She put the dress on and turned her bedroom chair round back to front. She squatted down on it, spreading her legs on either side of its back. The result was satisfactory. She leant forward and embraced the back of the chair, pretending it was Arthur's back. She began to look forward to the next afternoon with some excitement.

Arthur zoomed up on his motor bike on the dot of two-thirty. Janet had been watching the road from her bedroom window, but decided not to come down at once. Mr Hoskins was affability itself.

Mrs Hoskins said, 'Mind out on the roads. There's all sorts of lunatics out on them on Sundays. You watch out.'

'Oh I will,' Arthur assured her. 'I'm a very careful driver. Don't you worry.'

Mrs Hoskins did rather worry, but she edited her thoughts down to a repeated, 'Well, you watch out.'

Janet now put in an apparently casual appearance, hoping her raised heartbeat was not observable to her parents or Arthur. She climbed onto the back of the bike, adjusting her skirt with what she thought was much aplomb. They moved off at a sedate speed through the Square and out of the town on the road to Lake Cregennan. Clinging on with one hand, Janet extracted her lipstick with the other and did up her lips.

Arthur parked the bike in the National Trust car park and they walked down hand in hand past a clump of trees to the edge of the Lake. The air was soft and balmy and the lightest of breezes barely disturbed the surface of the water. Behind them lay the sea. In front and to both sides, great mountains rose smoothly but steeply.

'Let's walk round to the other side,' Arthur suggested.

They meandered along, now locked together by mutually extended arms round each other's waists. Presently they came to a little hollow, shaped almost as an armchair with a reclining back.

'This would be a nice place to sit,' Arthur said.

They settled down on the pleasantly yielding ground.

'It's lovely,' Janet said, stroking the close-cropped grass. 'You'd think you'd been over it with your mower.'

'The sheep do a better job than I could,' he said.

She laughed and threw her head back against his hand which had come to rest on the back of her neck. Then they sat in silence, breathing in the gorgeous sea air and watching birds skimming across the lake. There hadn't been a car in the car park and there wasn't a soul in sight. It seemed the National Trust had provided this beautiful and tranquil place exclusively for the delectation of Arthur and Janet.

'It's lovely,' she said.

It's time he thought. He grabbed the back of her head and began a real kiss, twisting and turning his lips against hers and gradually forcing her mouth open so their tongues could meet. He felt pleasure merging with duty for, up to now, his actions had all been calculated purely on the basis of what he knew, from his experience of women, was the way to get them under his control. That he still wanted to do, but this girl, whom he had thought so immature and naïve, had real fire in her. Her reaction was almost frightening in its intensity. It seemed a pent up wish stowed away for years had suddenly been released. They lay back against the rising ground behind them and he moved his hand up against her breasts, feeling their fullness through the thin material of her dress.

At last the kiss broke up and they sat up again, she, slightly turned away from him and he, still holding her with both hands by her breasts.

'Do you ever come across letters or anything of that sort in the bedrooms in the Hall?' he cautiously enquired.

At first she didn't reply and then, dreamily, 'I don't really know.'

He kept on playing with her breasts and began to undo the buttons down the front of her dress.

'I really would like to know how long they're all going to stay,' he resumed. 'You make a garden for the pleasure of the people who live in the house. A good gardener always likes to know whose going to be there and who isn't.'

He wasn't sure she even heard this proposition. She seemed totally preoccupied with what his hands were doing but, as they became yet more adventurous, she suddenly came to.

'I don't know if I ought to be allowing you to do this,' she said.

'Of course you should. It's only natural,' he explained. 'It's the most natural thing in the world.'

He now had one hand well up under her skirt.

'Everybody does it.'

'D'you think Gwen and Marian do it?' she asked. 'I mean, go as far as this.'

'You bet they do and a good deal more too,' he said. 'They're mature girls; they won't be letting the grass grow under their feet.'

Janet wondered how long it would be till she was thought of as a mature girl. She decided perhaps she was getting mature now. She let go of Arthur's wrist and allowed his hand to continue its stroking between her legs. Yes, she was sure she was getting mature and just for the moment she forgot her promise to her mother that she would always be a 'good girl'. Even when she remembered it, she found she wasn't quite sure of exactly what being a 'good girl' meant. Perhaps it only meant not having babies till you were married.

'You see I really would quite like to know if the King,

or Mr Hardy, or Count Connors, or any of them have any plans for going away,' he said.

'Spose you could ask them,' she half said and half gasped.

'Oh no, that wouldn't be my place. They wouldn't understand at all,' he pointed out.

When they got back to Dolgellau, Arthur was invited in to high tea by Mrs Hoskins. Her invitation sounded rather less than spontaneous. He guessed Mr Hoskins had told her to offer this hospitality and, indeed, Mr Hoskins did take the opportunity to impress upon Arthur the need to book the mower in for service in good time. To allow plenty of time for parts to come through if any were needed and to make sure the machine was ready for work by the next spring, he explained. As it was still only August, this did seem rather over-cautious, but Mr Hoskins was a careful man. And very considerate too. He wanted to be sure Arthur was fully in the picture about the various other machines he could supply and which might be so helpful up at the Hall. Arthur duly took courteous note of all this advice and promised to consult Mr Finch about it. Mr Hoskins continued to form a very good impression of Arthur, whom he considered to be an excellent class of young man.

Arthur, however, devoted his principal efforts to Mrs Hoskins.

'Janet mentioned you had been looking out for a *Phoebe* apricot tree,' he said to her.

'Oh I have,' said Mrs Hoskins. 'I've been trying for one these past two years or more, but there seems to be nowhere you can get them.'

'Well they are very special,' Arthur observed. 'And they're hard to graft, but I've managed several for Miss ap Llewellyn. They rather laugh at me about it and call me 'apricot fingers', but I have succeeded with several –

36

more than we need at the Hall. If you'd like one I could easily bring one down for you.'

'And you think Miss ap Llewellyn wouldn't mind,' Mrs Hoskins wondered.

'I'm sure she wouldn't,' Arthur assured her. 'I've got more than enough for what's wanted at the Hall.'

'Well that would be nice, if you're sure,' Mrs Hoskins said.

'I'll bring one down tomorrow if you like,' Arthur offered.

'Would that do in August?' Mr Hoskins put in.

'Yes, it'll be fine,' Arthur told him. 'They're in fibre planting pots so it won't mind moving.'

Of course it won't, he thought to himself. Even Arthur Johnson knew crab apples were quite tough. The *Phoebe* apricot would be quite OK till Mrs Hoskins discovered it was a crab apple. But that wouldn't be till next spring and by then she and her husband and Janet would know that other things were not what they thought they were.

'Praps you'd have a look at our fruit trees and advise on where we ought to plant the *Phoebe*,' Mrs Hoskins suggested.

'I'd be delighted,' the generous gardener volunteered.

Arthur was pretty satisfied by his afternoon's work and, after all these weeks without a woman, Janet was a real bonus with more to come, he thought. Yes, there would have to be more, he decided. She was coming round, but she wasn't there yet. He could tell she was still very uneasy about getting the information he needed from the bedrooms in the Hall. If only he knew how long he'd got he could pace her accordingly. But it was only from her he could find out how long he had got. So he would have to take the risk of rushing her on, perhaps faster than he would normally judge prudent, especially as she was so very

37

immature. He would fix to take her on another bike ride after he had delivered the *Phoebe*.

Janet was uneasy in her mind. She found it odd that Arthur couldn't ask Miss ap Llewellyn how long her guests were staying. She herself found Miss ap Llewellyn quite easy to talk to. So, why couldn't Arthur? He was so straight and upright, so why not? He would have his reasons though, and perhaps she was silly to be so jumpy about finding out how long these people were staying. There really couldn't be any harm in it could there? And yet...

When Arthur arrived at Hoskins's Garden Machinery with the 'apricot tree' strapped to the side pannier of his motor bike, the weather was much more favourable to the tree than to his projected second visit to Lake Cregennan. It was pouring Welsh rain, as Welsh rain is inclined to do.

'Well,' said Mrs Hoskins, 'you'll not be going up to the Lake in this.'

'No,' Arthur replied, 'I think not, but it's just perfect for planting the *Phoebe*.'

'It's a lovely little darling,' Mrs Hoskins exclaimed, viewing the treasure as Arthur released it from its transporter.

He carried it through the showroom and out into the back garden where he planted it in the place appointed the day before. Mrs Hoskins was quite carried away and skipped about like a girl. The *Phoebe* was something she had so longed to have and now here it was; she had got it. Janet looked on with a somewhat more detached air. She was bothered by the rain. Would the evening out with Arthur now be cancelled?

'I don't think it'll lift today,' he said glancing up at the lowering cloud. 'But I know a nice café with a good roof on it where we could have a cream tea.'

'You could do worse than that,' Mrs Hoskins remarked. 'You'd enjoy that wouldn't you Janet?' she added.

'Sounds smashing,' Janet said.

Enveloped in her father's raincoat, she got on the bike behind Arthur and they set forth against the driving rain. After a mile or two he pulled up.

'Cream teas are fattening,' he announced, 'and if we carry on much further we'll both get soaked. I vote we give up the idea.'

'I'm pretty soaked already,' Janet told him.

'Tell you what,' he said, 'we'll go up to my cottage and have toast and honey for tea. Would you like that?'

Janet, who really had got quite wet, thought she would. So they turned round and drove back and up the hill towards Dolgellau Hall and to the cottage about half a mile from the Hall.

'Dear me,' Arthur said, 'you have caught the rain. It's got in through the collar. I'll light a fire and you can dry off while I make some toast.'

The warmth of the fire was a great comfort to Janet for, not only had she got very wet, but she was cold. With the rain, a drop of twenty degrees in temperature had come. The hot buttered toast and soothing honey were delicious and a feeling of cosseted luxury began to pervade her senses. It seemed only natural that Arthur's hand should slip down inside the front of her dress.

'Good grief,' he said, 'you're wet through and through. You'd better take your things off and we'll get them dry.'

'Oh, I think they'll soon dry in this warmth,' she said.

'It's not a good idea to dry your clothes on yourself,' Arthur suggested. 'You can get rheumatic fever off that.'

'Go on, you can't,' she said.

'Oh yes you can, he insisted. 'It's true, you can.'

'Well, I can't undress here,' she said. 'It wouldn't be proper.'

39

'You could go upstairs,' he suggested, 'but there's no fires up there and it'd be cold. What's the harm? My eye would only see what my hand can already feel,' he went on, giving her breasts a rub and a squeeze.

'Are you sure no one will come?' she enquired.

'Quite sure,' he said, 'and if they do, they'll not be let in.'

Rather tentatively, she pulled her dress up and took it off over her head. Arthur hung it on the back of a chair and said it would soon be dry.

'What about the rest?' he asked.

'I don't think it's wet,' she said.

Arthur felt her bra and pants.

'No, perhaps not,' he agreed as he engaged her in a deep kiss.

'I've got just the thing,' he said as he emerged. 'It's great for toning up the skin and very relaxing.'

'What is it?' a very breathless Janet asked.

'It's oil of Lebanon,' he told her. 'I'll fetch it.'

As he went up stairs to fetch the sensual oil, he remembered his training and said to himself, 'Steady boy, steady, keep control of yourself and watch out you don't rush her too fast.'

He returned with the bottle and a large bath towel. He spread the latter in front of the fire and invited Janet to lie on it face down. She obediently complied. He slipped the straps of her bra off her shoulders and applied a little oil. Very gently he began to spread this and rub it in on her shoulder blades and the back of her neck. Meeting no resistance, he unhooked the bra and extended his operations down along her spine.

'Are you liking it?' he enquired.

'Yea, it's gorgeous,' she said, turning her body slightly to and fro.

'Trouble is it does stain clothing,' he warned and then slipped off her pants.

40

'Ummmm,' she muttered as he massaged her buttocks and the backs of her thighs.

She was coming along very nicely. He could tell she was going out of control but he could feel he too was heading in the same direction, which he knew he ought not to be, but was.

'Turn over now,' he said.

She did so, seemingly as a reflex rather than as a decision. He ran his oiled hands over her breasts, under her armpits, down over her stomach and onto her pubic hair. Her eyes were closed and there was a slight beatific sort of smile on her lips, and at first she appeared not to notice that his ministrations had ceased for a moment or so. When she did, she opened her eyes and beheld Arthur, now stark naked, standing astride over her. She saw the thick crop of black hair that covered his chest and then gave way to a thin line leading down to another great mass of hair around what she had thought would be limp and hanging down. She now saw it was stiff and huge and upstanding. It was nothing like what she had seen on her little brother in his bath. It was awesome.

She felt this was submission, but it was not the sort of submission she had given her mother. This submission was a form of power. She knew that what had happened to Arthur was because of her. She recognised that it was her attraction that had set him off and she rejoiced. And she knew that whatever came next was what she wanted.

And Arthur knew that too, but he also knew there might be second thoughts later and that he must not run the risk of these. He lay down beside her, but instead of taking what so easily could now have been his, he drew her hand to his erection and showed it how to stroke. Then, having achieved his release, he regained his control and became a Belling's Policeman once more. Gradually, Janet became Mrs Hoskins's daughter again.

41

'I've got to be careful not to get pregnant,' she said.

'This can't get you pregnant,' Arthur promised. 'That's for sure.'

'I know,' she said, 'but there might be more and that might.'

'Never,' Arthur assured her. 'Never. You can trust me absolutely. You know that don't you?'

'Yes I think so,' Janet assented.

'I've never done anything like this with a girl before,' Arthur lied. 'It's just you're so attractive, such a gorgeous girl, that I really can't help it. And, you know, it's quite natural and so long as we're careful and sensible no harm can come of it.'

'All the same, I don't know what my Mum would think of it,' Janet reflected.

'Well,' he said, 'there's no need to trouble her with what's only between us, what's our secret, our harmless secret.'

'No of course not,' she agreed. 'But I'll have to say something.'

'Certainly you will. But all you need say is we had a nice cream tea and the rain never stopped. She'll be quite pleased to hear that.'

Janet thought this was a good idea. It didn't seem deceitful to her at all. It was only to spare her mother unnecessary worry about things her generation couldn't understand anyway.

'Funny about those tropical clothes,' Arthur said. 'Must mean they're going somewhere tropical, but I wonder when. Can't be a holiday or he wouldn't be taking uniforms. I wish I knew when they planned to go.'

Janet still lay on the bath towel, basking in the warmth of the fire and reflecting on the glories of being a mature girl. Being completely naked seemed quite all right and it would only be the same as Gwen and Marian did.

'Does it matter all that much?' she asked.

'No, it doesn't really matter at all,' Arthur said. 'It's just I'd like to know. There might be air tickets or notes in their pocket diaries or things like that. You could easily find out.'

'I don't see how,' Janet complained.

'When they go out to play tennis they leave their ordinary clothes in their rooms don't they?' he suggested. 'Well, you could just take a quick look then. There'd be no harm in it and I'd know you loved me because you'd done a little thing like that just because I wanted to know.'

'Well,' said Janet, 'if you really want to know and there's no harm in it, I suppose I could just take a look.'

Chapter 5

Mr Belling never complained about the amount of work he had to do. He loved work though, of course, some aspects of it were less enjoyable than others. On this particular morning there were two items on his agenda that were unlikely to give him much pleasure and a third to which he looked forward with happy expectation. The first two items were interviews with his Chief of Air Staff and then his Chief of Naval Staff. These meetings were usually tedious and frustrating. Service officers were all the same; they were forever talking about the worst case that might arise and their programmes were usually behind schedule. The third item was a report by his Director of Security Services, Major Silk. Major Silk was a man after his own heart. No problem was too great for him and no pedantic scruples stood between him and the achievement of whatever the aim might be.

The Air Chief came first. Unfortunately, problems with the development of the Swift aircraft were proving more intractable than anticipated. It would now be impossible to bring the aircraft into operational squadron service for at least another eighteen months to two years.

'How can that be?' the Leader demanded. 'The prototypes flew more than two years ago. What's holding up production models?'

'Mainly two things,' the Air Chief explained. 'We're getting excessive engine vibration at between three quarter and full boost and we're having problems with the identification and suppression radar.'

'Problems, problems,' Mr Belling barked. 'Can't the Air Force ever get anything right?'

'We do our best, Leader,' the Air Chief said, 'but the Swift is a very advanced aircraft. When we get it right, it'll give us the most advanced warplane in the world.'

'But it seems you can't get it right.'

'I'm confident we can get it right. It's only a matter of time,' the Air Chief claimed.

'Time, time. How much time do you think I've got? How much time do you think Treskania needs to pick itself up? While you take your time, we'll miss the decisive moment.'

'I venture to think not, sir. With three operational squadrons of Swifts we'll be able to control the air over Treskania to such a degree as to enable us to neutralise their armed forces and destroy their naval power; the naval power of the Crown Prince, I mean. Give me eighteen months, or two years at the most, and that's what I'll give you.'

'Time, promises, they make me sick. They make me wish I'd never approved this damned Swift programme. It would have been better to build some aircraft that could actually fly.'

'We could of course have built up our conventional air strength,' the Air Chief conceded, 'but it might not have availed us much against the naval aircraft under the Crown Prince's control, especially, sir, if Brazil was to play a combatant role.'

'Blast the Crown Prince and damn Brazil,' the Leader shouted.

The Air Chief was quite used to this sort of thing. He reckoned the Leader's tantrums were worse in their bark than in their bite – at least as far as the Swift was concerned. The Leader would see that, having got as far as this with the Swift, there was no alternative to going on with it. The Air Chief felt his Swift programme and his own neck were safe, at least for the time being.

'Things are going well at the Air Academy,' he said. We've got four fast stream graduates of exceptional quality and seventy-eight others qualified at above average. These men are the future of the Air Force, the indispensable element in our future air superiority.'

The discussion turned to the passing out parade and the exact procedure that the Leader wished to be followed. Mr Belling's humour improved and the meeting ended on reasonably agreeable terms.

The Chief of the Naval Staff was the next in. Construction of the four fast carriers was proceeding on schedule, but there were two problems that caused the Chief concern. There would be, Mr Belling thought to himself, but before pronouncing on them he decided to wait to see what they were. Costs were proving to be higher than expected. The high quality metals required had to be imported from abroad and, since China had embarked on a major expansion of her fleet, the world demand was pressing hard upon the potential supply. Metal prices were rising sharply and the carrier programme would now need to be re-financed. The second problem was manning. The output of the Naval Academy would suffice to fill the requirement for junior officers but, after the mass desertion of the old fleet, there was a grave lack of senior officers and ratings. The Chief thought he would have to call for the introduction of a measure of naval conscription to meet the latter requirement and the recruitment of senior officers of the merchant marine, the former.

He had expected this news would throw the Leader into a rage and he now thought he had miscalculated in not facing up to the realities sooner. He knew in his heart he had been weak in not drawing attention to them earlier. Rather than face the wrath of the Leader, he had sheltered behind the nebulous myth that somehow these difficulties would go away. Now they had come home to roost. He was therefore both surprised and very relieved when the Leader seemed to digest the situation with equanimity. He asked a few questions and then declared that he would reflect on what the Chief had reported and consider what should best be done to secure the future.

The pleasant part of the morning was now at hand. Major Silk came in.

'Perhaps you would like first to hear about progress with project Arthur,' he said.

This, in the parlance employed in conversations between the Director of Security Services and the Leader, meant the plan to kidnap the King.

'Yes, certainly. I attach great importance to this project,' the Leader replied.

'You will remember,' Major Silk began, 'that information supplied by A4A gave us advance notice that Nicholas Hardy was about to fly to Kesa by Air Direct from Cardiff. We surmised that he was going as a representative of the King to prepare for the latter's removal to Kesa. We now have further information from the same source confirming this surmise and today I have learned the date, the flight number and the time of the King's departure.'

'That's very impressive,' Mr Belling said. 'What's the category of reliability of this?'

'It's category A1, Leader,' Major Silk informed him. 'A4A is bonking the maid who makes up the King's bed and does his room out. She has seen the King's air tickets and also those of Count Connors. The information is completely reliable.'

'Excellent,' Mr Belling pronounced. 'Knowledge is power, so how do you propose we use this power?'

'I anticipated you might ask that,' Major Silk said, breaking into a smile for the first time.

He explained that two of his other agents were now on station in Wales. A4B, a female agent, had obtained employment as a cleaner in Air Direct's offices at Cardiff airport. There was an acute shortage of cleaners in affluent Wales and she had had little difficulty in getting the job. Also, as she was unusually willing to work unsocial hours, she had excellent opportunities for collecting flight information. She was keeping A4A informed about the crews listed for the various flights to Kesa and would certainly inform him of those nominated for the flight taking the King at least two days before it took off. A4C was also now standing by in Cardiff. He was a fully qualified airline Captain with four thousand hours on Boeing Luxairs, having been employed by Atlanta Airways to fly them before he was recruited to Belling's Police. He was now equipped with an Air Direct Captain's uniform, with which he had been fitted by the official tailors in Cardiff.

'We plan to stand down the allotted Captain for the relevant flight and substitute A4C, who will fly the King to Atlanta City Airport instead of Kesa,' Major Silk told the Leader.

'That sounds excellent,' the Leader said, 'but surely it will be very difficult to achieve.'

'Well, it will be difficult,' Major Silk admitted, 'but we're confident it can be done. A4A is a first class man, very ingenious, extremely cautious and very sound. He's one of my best men and I place a great deal of trust in him. He thinks it can be done and his view of the thing is something we can take very seriously. He has worked out a detailed plan for switching the Captains and I think it will work, unless of course, something quite unforeseen happens.'

'And if something unforeseen does happen,' the Leader asked, 'what then? If the plan miscarries and the King gets to Kesa our chances of catching him will be seriously reduced. In Wales we have him more or less at our mercy. In Kesa it will be much more difficult. He'll probably be allotted an official residence and be provided with a bodyguard.'

'That's exactly my view,' Major Silk agreed. 'I think it's of paramount importance that he doesn't get to Kesa. But if our plan to fly him here miscarries, we have to face the fact that we will have missed the chance of eliminating him while he's still in Wales. Compared to the problems that would face us in Kesa, it would be relatively easy to eliminate him in Wales. He goes about in Dolgellau on foot and sometimes even quite alone. We could arrange an accident, but that would deny us the value of a public trial. Knowing the importance you attach to that, I have placed my bets on a kidnapping as opposed to an assassination.'

'Quite so,' said the Leader, 'and you're right. There will be big political advantages to be gained from a public trial and a legal execution. An assassination would not produce any of these and might even be something of an embarrassment. But of course if he escapes to Kesa, well, that would be the worst case.'

'So we have to decide,' Major Silk suggested, 'between, on the one hand, playing safe against the worst case and arranging an accident in Wales and, on the other, of going for the political advantage of a public trial and putting our trust in A4A's kidnap plan.'

'We'll go for A4A's kidnap plan,' the Leader ruled.

Chapter 6

Major Silk's confidence in A4A was by no means wholly misplaced. Arthur Johnson had gone about his work systematically, patiently and ingeniously. He had taken endless pains to discover the necessary facts, to confirm them and to learn as much as he could about all the surrounding factors in case they might prove to be of importance. He was also meticulous in keeping all his information up to date. Janet, of course, had been one of his principal informants.

After their cream tea expedition, she had taken to dropping in at the cottage every day after lunch at the Hall for 'oiling', as they termed it, although Arthur had given up bothering with the oil which, he said, tasted nasty. Having shown Janet how she could be protected against the danger of getting pregnant, he was, however, now able to take her the whole way. At first he proceeded cautiously and only completed the act after much rubbing, squeezing and licking. But Janet proved to be a quick learner and he found that not much more than a few words of endearment and the odd caress were needed as the prelude to the ramrodding that released his tension and reinforced her submission without too much waste of time.

Thus each day, when these necessaries had been completed, Arthur obtained an update on developments in the Hall. That was how he had discovered that Nicholas Hardy was flying to Kesa, the date of the King's proposed flight there and many other interesting things. Janet, indeed, was turning into a tolerably good detective herself.

'Mr Hardy's back from Kesa,' she remarked one afternoon after the 'oiling' had been completed.

'Now that's very interesting,' her lover responded. 'I've not seen him about.'

'I haven't either,' Janet said, 'but he's back all the same.'

'How d'yer know?'

'Cos when I went to make Miss Blick's bed I found his pyjamas trodden into the bottom of it and her nightie under the pillow without a crease in it. And silk does crease you know.'

'Very observant I'm sure, but how did you know the pyjamas belonged to Mr Hardy?'

'Cos girl's pyjamas don't have that opening at the front. Wouldn't be much use to them would it?'

'No not much, but you don't suppose Mr Hardy is the only man in the world with a pair of pyjamas do you?'

'I'm not as green as you think,' Janet protested. 'There was a handkerchief in the breast pocket and it had the monogram "NH" on it. I don't suppose there are all that many men Miss Blick has it off with who have the initials "NH".'

Janet's deduction had proved to be spot on. Arthur saw Mr Hardy strolling in the garden with the King and Count Connors the next morning.

Janet was proving to be an excellent informant and Arthur congratulated himself on the control he had gained over her. She no longer said anything about not wanting to spy and that sort of thing. She simply came to be 'oiled' and then spouted out the information without hesitation. Now, however, there was a difficulty. Arthur was beginning to find the ram-rodding rather boring. Janet had stoked his lust, but she no longer satisfied it and that began to expose the Achilles Heel of an otherwise accomplished agent.

Arthur couldn't help noticing Marian's startling figure

which, in her tight jeans and T-shirts, she usually displayed to striking advantage. He noticed too that she always laughed at his jokes and often touched his arm or gave him a bit of a push in a playful sort of way. He hadn't thought all that much about it and had assumed she had a steady boyfriend. But then a chance encounter opened up other possibilities. After lunch one day when Janet had not come to the cottage and gone straight home because, as she put it, it was her monthly time, Arthur had gone to the gooseberry beds to weed them. There he happened to come across Marian. Miss ap Llewellyn had given her permission to pick some gooseberries for herself. There were a few jokes about stealing fruit and obstructing gardeners in the course of their duty and young gardeners who stood about flirting with girls instead of getting on with their work. As Marian stooped to pick the fruit Arthur could see right into her cleavage and he saw too that she took no pains to obstruct his view.

'What's your favourite flower?' he enquired.

'Tulips I think,' she said, standing up straight and locking her fingers behind her head. 'Yes tulips I think, but unfortunately they're all over now.'

Arthur's eyes were riveted on the T-shirt now drawn tightly across her uplifted breasts which stood out as though asking to be touched.

'They're not all over,' he said. 'There's such things as autumn tulips.'

'I haven't seen any hereabouts,' she said, swinging round and giving him a profile of her breasts.

She's flaunting, he thought to himself.

He said, 'I'm bringing some on behind the cottage. Like to see?'

'Love to,' she responded.

She hooked her arm through the handle of her basket and they set off for the cottage. The swing of her hips and the slight movement of her breasts under the T-shirt were alluring. They went into the cottage.

'You have it nice and tidy here,' she said.

'Let's not bother with the tulips,' he said, putting his hands on her hips and drawing her close against himself.

They had a long deep kiss.

'I like your motorbike,' she announced. 'My boyfriend had one just like it.'

'Had one?' Arthur enquired. 'Doesn't he still have it?'

'I don't really know,' she told him, 'we've split up you see.'

'What a shame,' he said, swinging her round and cupping her breasts in his hands.

She pressed her bottom against his crotch and he knew he'd got the green light. He pulled up her T-shirt over her head and undid her bra. She pushed her hand down inside the front of his trousers and everything began to go swimmingly for them.

Or it would have done had not Janet had some second thoughts. The pain she had felt earlier in the day had gone and she began to feel she had been rather abrupt when she told Arthur she was not coming to the cottage today. Of course, they couldn't do the full works for the next four or five days but she could still have been a comfort to him. She had been selfish and inconsiderate. She should have known how much he would miss her and really she had been quite rude about not coming. She would go up to the cottage and make amends as best she could.

She met her mother on the stairs.

'Feeling better dearie?' she said.

'Much, thanks. I'm just off for a walk.'

'Good idea. That'll do you good. Don't be late back for supper.'

Janet strode off out of the town and towards the cottage at a brisk pace.

When she got there she found the front door was locked. She was afraid Arthur must be out, or perhaps he had gone in by the back. She would go round to see. As she passed the window of the sitting room on the side of the little house, she peered in and beheld the most dreadful sight. There, on the very rug on which she had so often lain down to be 'oiled', she saw Arthur and Marian. Both were completely naked. He lay on his stomach; she on her back with one arm round his neck and the other cast out to her left side. His left arm lay folded to form two sides of a triangle at his side and the other was thrown across Marian's chest, his hand resting on her left breast, which it slightly compressed. Her hair was spread out on the floor upwards from her head and her pubic triangle was lit by the sinking rays of the evening sun. His right knee was pushed in between the tops of her legs. He and she were deeply asleep. Clothing, male and female, lay around in mixed heaps at random. The comparison of his strong athletic, angular and hairy body with its prominent muscles and her smooth voluptuous female curves formed the perfect representation of sex in repose, the aftermath of action. It was, in truth, a beautiful sight.

But to Janet it was horrible and shocking. She turned abruptly away, letting out a low moan. So he had not really loved her at all. All the endearments had been lies, all the cuddles fake. It must have been Marian he loved all along. She was simply a credulous dupe. She felt utterly felled and humiliated. She couldn't get home fast enough. She would never go near the Hall again. Never, never! But then suddenly she stopped in her tracks as though hydraulic brakes had been applied to her footsteps.

If he had loved Marian all along, why had he made love to her? Why had he taken so much trouble? Of course it was to get her to tell him about the goings on

54

in the bedrooms at the Hall. But surely those couldn't have been important enough to justify all that fake lovemaking when, for real, he was having Marian all the time. He had said it was only to satisfy his curiosity and that it didn't really matter who was going away and who wasn't, and yet he was that keen to know. It struck her like a hammer blow. He was a liar and a cheat. There was something criminal at the bottom of his curiosity and he had used her to further his wicked plans, whatever they might be. But he wasn't going to get away with it. She would go straight up to the Hall and tell on him. She would make him pay for it. He would find she wasn't the mouse he had thought. He would find he was the mouse and she the cat. She turned and broke into a run up to the Hall.

Now, quite out of breath, she burst in through the front door without a thought of her proper access through the back. There, uncomfortably perched on one of the hall chairs and clutching a tennis racket, she saw Miss Blick.

'Oh Miss Blick, Miss Blick, I've got something terrible to tell you.'

'What on earth's happened to you, Janet. Has there been an accident?'

'No, not an accident, Miss. Something much worse.'

'Well now calm down Janet. Whatever it is I'll try to help. We'll go up to my room and you'll tell me all about it. It may not be as bad as you think.'

'Oh it is, Miss. It's worse. I mean it's worse than you think.'

'Well come on then. I can't help till I know what it is.'

Laura put her arm round Janet's shoulders and they went up to her room.

Janet sat on the edge of the bed and burst into tears. Gradually she calmed down a bit and began to explain herself.

'He's been spying on you, Miss, and on the King and Lord Connors and on Mr Hardy.'

'Who's been spying?' Laura asked. 'What do you mean?'

'I mean Arthur Johnson. He's been spying on you all and I think he's up to no good.'

'Arthur Johnson doesn't work in the house. He's in the garden.'

'I know, but he's been finding it out from me.'

'Finding it out from you? What do you mean?'

He's been getting me to tell him, tell him what I see in the bedrooms.'

'And what have you seen in the bedrooms?'

'Well things like Mr Hardy's air tickets to Kesa and the King's and Mr Connors's and Mr Hardy's pyjamas in...'

'I see,' said Laura. 'And he asked you to look for these things and tell him.'

'Yes that's what he did. He said there could be no harm in it. It was just that he liked to know things and so I told him what I noticed. I meant no harm, but now I think it was wrong and that he's up to no good. So now I'm telling you.'

'You've done quite right to tell me, but what made you change your mind? Have you fallen out with Arthur Johnson?'

'Oh yes Miss, I have. I thought he loved me. He said he did, but now I know he doesn't. I've seen him with Marian, if you understand what I mean.'

'Yes I think I do.'

'They had nothing on, nothing at all.'

'No, well that does happen sometimes. But now tell me this. I need to get it quite clear. Arthur Johnson knew Mr Hardy was flying to Kesa before he went?'

'Yes Miss, and he knew the day he came back.'

'Right. And he knows the day the King and Count Connors will be flying to Kesa?'

'Yes Miss, he does, because I told him. I saw the tickets. I meant no harm and I only told him because...'

Janet broke down again into violent sobs.

'Now listen Janet,' Laura said. 'This is very important so listen very carefully. You must say nothing to anybody about what you've told me and especially you must say nothing to Arthur Johnson about telling me. Leave it all to me and trust me to do whatever is needed to put all this right. But I should steer clear of Arthur Johnson in future.'

'Oh I will Miss. I'll have nothing more to do with him.'

'That's right Janet. But just tell him you've gone off him. Don't say anything about why. He'll ask you, but don't tell him.'

'Say nothing to anybody about it,' Janet recited.

'That's right Janet. Nothing to anybody.'

Chapter 7

Captain Murdoch had been flying Air Direct Luxairs for just over two years and had been very glad to get onto their books. His previous appointment with France Airways had been terminated when they axed some of their routes. He was also a happy man for another reason. He had recently married and had just returned from his honeymoon. Now he was about to resume flying duties. He was detailed to fly Abel Harry Tommy Zero2 tomorrow on the Kesa/Capetown route. This was Flight Number 6615 and the time off was 09.15 hours. That meant he must embark at 8.00 am which, in turn, meant he must leave home at 7.15. So he set his alarm clock for 5.45. He wanted to have time in hand before driving off to work.

The Murdochs were an unusual couple. They had not slept with each other until after they were married. They had scruples about these matters and took the marriage vows very seriously. But now that they were married, they were making up for lost time with a vengeance and they probably spent more time making love than most married, even than most recently married, couples. This was the principal reason for which they set their alarm so early on this, the morning of the Kesa/Capetown flight.

They were, in fact, well advanced in their preparations for a farewell copulation when the telephone beside the bed rang. Damn, they both exclaimed simultaneously.

'May I speak to Captain Murdoch?' asked a voice from the other end.

'Speaking,' the Captain reluctantly answered.

'This is Air Direct Operational Control,' said the voice. 'I'm ringing from Cardiff to say that Flight 6615 has been postponed. Severe electrical storms are predicted to the north and west of Kesa. Operational Control has decided that in these conditions the descent to Kesa Airport would be hazardous. Flight 6615 has therefore been postponed until tomorrow morning. Departure to be at 09.15. You are to standby for that but until then you may stand down.'

'OK, instructions understood. Will do,' Captain Murdoch said.

'What was it then?' his wife asked.

'The flight's off till tomorrow. I'm stood down. Dodgy weather apparently,' he told her.

'Great,' she said, getting back into a good position.

'Strange though,' he reflected. 'The route prediction we got yesterday evening was good. Strange there should have been such a change so suddenly. I wonder if I should have made more enquiries. I hope there's no mistake. Perhaps I'd better ring back and get to the bottom of it.'

'For crying out loud,' she said. 'He said you were stood down, so stood down you are.'

'It was a she,' he corrected her.

'OK, well here's another she who wants you to stand up,' she said as she massaged his erection which had somewhat wilted under the impact of the lady on the telephone.

Captain Murdoch gave up and resumed his marital activities. After that they dozed off to sleep and when they came to it was 9.30 and Abel Harry Tommy Zero2 was just turning onto the runway prior to take off for Kesa. Flight 6615 was right on schedule.

* * *

It is 7.30 a.m., the Air Direct Terminal at Cardiff Airport. Passengers booked on Flight 6615 for Kesa and Capetown are beginning to pass through Passport Control and are looking for seats in the Departure Lounge. Presently two aircrew officers appear. Those who understand the insignia of rank can tell that one is the Second Pilot and the other the Flight Engineer. The two men pass straight through and embark in Abel Harry Tommy Zero2. The girl at the embarkation desk marks her flight order sheet accordingly. The time moves on to 8.00 a.m. A man wearing grey flannel trousers and a tweed jacket arrives in the Airport Assembly Lounge. He passes through Security but, instead of proceeding to the Departure Lounge, he retires to a lavatory. A few minutes later an Air Direct Captain emerges from the same cubicle. He walks into the Departure Lounge and nods to the girl on the desk, who marks her flight order sheet. She's not so dumb that she can't recognise an Air Direct Captain. He follows his two colleagues into the concertina and embarks in Abel Harry Tommy Zero2.

'Morning gentlemen,' he says addressing the Second Pilot and the Flight Engineer.

'Morning sir,' they reply. 'But we were expecting Captain Murdoch,' says the Second Pilot.

'Yes I know. Poor chap. He must have picked up a bug on his honeymoon. They went to Singapore you know. Anyway the poor fellow woke in the middle of the night with a fever. Temperature of 104 his wife said. Air Direct started telephoning round to get a substitute. Awful job they had. It seemed no one was available. At about their fifth attempt they got onto me and so here I am. Scraping the bottom of the barrel you might say. Granville's the name. No need to panic. I've got four thousand hours as a Luxair Captain.'

'Right you are sir,' says the Second Pilot. 'All external checks completed. All OK. Pre-flight Pilot checks all completed. All OK.'

'Thanks very much,' Captain Granville acknowledges. Flight Engineer?'

'Yes sir,' the Flight Engineer comes in. 'Refuelling completed. I am about to check quantities and tank trims. Bear with me sir and I'll report again shortly.'

'Good man,' says the Captain.

* * *

Dolgellau Hall, 7.30 a.m,. Six suitcases belonging to the King and all labelled 'Colonel Anderson Flight 6615 Kesa' together with four more belonging to Count Connors and Nick Hardy, also labelled for Kesa, are piled on the lawn. Arthur Johnson had obligingly carried most of them out of the Hall in preparation for the arrival of the helicopter, which was ordered for 7.45. Laura had asked Arthur the evening before if he wouldn't mind doing this, though of course it was not part of his regular duties. He was glad to oblige. It gave him exactly the confirmation he needed, especially as his intelligence system had rather broken down since Janet got the sulks. Anyway, this proved that he hadn't missed anything important on that account. He had got all the information he needed and fucking Marian had been altogether better than doing a schoolgirl, which is what Janet more or less was, he reckoned. Now, however, he has fucked Marian for the last time. As soon as he had finished manhandling the luggage, he mounted his motorbike but, instead of heading for Shrewsbury to visit his Aunt in hospital, as he had told Miss ap Llewellyn he wanted to do when he asked her for the day off, he drove hell for leather to Cardiff airport. On the way he was overtaken by the helicopter carrying the King and his companions to the same destination.

'They're in the bag,' he says to himself.

He arrives at the airport and parks his machine in the passengers' car park. He enters the Air Direct terminal building and goes straight into a lavatory, where he puts on his make-up, a wig and dark glasses. He goes through Security and enters the Departure Lounge. He is reassured to see the King and his party there, but he chooses a seat as far away from them as possible. Tourist class passengers are called for embarkation first and Arthur goes on board when those with seats in rows A to G are summoned. He notices A4B stowing her hand luggage a couple of rows ahead of his seat. Her disguise perhaps might have been better but, dressed in smart jeans and close-fitting top, she no doubt looks different enough from the apron-clad woman who had cleaned the Air Direct offices. He likes the look of her figure and thinks perhaps he will cultivate her when they get home. Marian has considerably whetted his appetite, but, of course, for the moment he must ignore A4B.

The curtains between the tourist and club class accommodation are drawn back and he watches the club class punters taking their seats. None of them are of any interest to him, but the door leading on to the first class is open and he can see these privileged types are beginning to appear. But they come on by a separate entrance and, from his seat, he can only glimpse their lower legs and feet. He thinks he can make out, however, that there are eleven of them. They are all in for a big surprise and three of them for big trouble. He gets a great feeling of achievement, of a job well done. He begins to speculate about the promotion he is likely to get.

* * *

The Departure Lounge, 8.55 a.m. The girl on the departure desk looks down her flight order sheet. Everyone's aboard except Miss McEwan, club class, and Colonel Anderson, Mr Kramer and Mr Gerrard, first class. She has already crossed off Miss McEwan. She knows the feeder flight from Glasgow has been delayed and that Miss McEwan will not be boarding. She picks up her microphone.

'Attention please,' she broadcasts. 'This is the last call for passengers travelling by Air Direct to Kesa and Capetown by Flight 6615. Please proceed immediately to the Air Direct Departure Lounge. Your aircraft is about to depart. Thank you.'

A young man dashes in.

'My name's Gerrard,' says Nick Hardy. 'Colonel Anderson's indisposed. He and I and Mr Kramer are scrubbing.'

'I'm so sorry,' says the girl sympathetically.

She crosses off the three names. There is no need for her to do more than that. It's only if extra passengers are boarding that she has to report to the Captain. She picks up her flight deck telephone.

'They're all aboard,' she reports.

Captain Granville plugs in to the Chief Stewardess.

'Captain to Chief Stewardess,' he says. 'Close all hatches.'

A minute or so passes.

'Chief Stewardess to Captain. All hatches closed. Ready to taxi.'

The Captain thanks her and switches to his public address.

'Ladies and gentlemen, this is your Captain speaking. In a few minutes we'll be moving off from our dispersal and heading for the runway. We have a slot and we should be off in about five minutes. The weather on route is predicted good and I wish you all a very pleasant flight.'

Abel Harry Tommy Zero2 creeps backwards out of the dispersal, swings round and heads for the runway controlled by the Second Pilot. Captain Granville occupies the seat slightly behind and to his right. He has arranged that the Second Pilot will fly the aircraft to Kesa as he is slightly short on his required monthly hours and this will make

63

up the gap. The Second Pilot thinks Captain Granville is a good type. He is very considerate and looks after his subordinates. He wishes all the Air Direct Captains were like him.

'Stand by for take off,' he broadcasts.

* * *

It was a glorious morning. There wasn't a cloud in the sky and Abel Harry Tommy Zero2 glided along without so much as the slightest lurch or bump. If they had thought about it at all, the passengers might have found it hard to believe they were travelling at an airspeed of 590 mph and a height of 51,000 feet. But of course they weren't thinking about it. Several were asleep, some were watching TV and others were reading newspapers and magazines.

'It all looks good,' says Captain Granville. 'Shall we say lunch at 12.30?'

The Second Pilot and the Flight Engineer think that would be fine.

'Meanwhile coffee and biscuits to keep us awake,' the Captain suggests.

This too meets with approval.

'Captain to Chief Stewardess.'

'Chief Stewardess to Captain.'

'Could you send us up three coffees and biscuits please? When convenient, I mean.'

'Will do. It's quite convenient now.'

One of the stewardesses appears on the flight deck with three mugs of coffee, a small carton of milk, sugar and some biscuits.

'Thanks a lot,' says the captain. 'If you would put it here,' he adds, letting down a shelf table fixed to the back of the Pilot's seat. 'I'll do the honours. Milk and sugar all round?'

'Just a dash of milk for me. No sugar,' the Flight Engineer tells him.

'Milk and one sugar for me,' the Second Pilot requests.

Captain Granville obligingly responds to these orders, but he adds two small yellow tablets to the Second Pilot's sugar and then hands the mugs round. The Flight Engineer nearly takes the wrong mug but in the end they all get the right ones.

The Captain tunes in the route indicator and makes a careful mental note of the miles run from Cardiff, the miles to run to Kesa and the ETA there. He sees they are almost directly opposite Lisbon and turns to view the scene. Forty odd miles away and, at this moment almost exactly eleven miles below them, the Tagus draws a slender green thread across the land on its way to Lisbon.

'Looks good doesn't it?' says the Captain.

'Sure,' answers the Second Pilot, 'but I'm afraid I'm not feeling too good.'

The Captain gets up out of his seat and comes alongside the Second Pilot.

'Not feeling too good? What's up?'

'I don't know but something's hit me. I've got a sharp stomach pain and I think I'll have to make a dash for the toilet. I'm awfully sorry.'

'Bad luck old chap, but don't worry about it. You go back and try to have a bit of a nap. I expect that'll put you right.'

The Second Pilot nips off pretty quickly but, despite the pain, he manages to think what a nice tolerant and considerate man Captain Granville is.

Captain Granville takes the Second Pilot's place. He knows he will not be back on this trip but, for the time being, he leaves the aircraft on auto control and it pursues its course for Kesa. After a run of another four hundred miles, he calls up the Flight Engineer.

'I've got a shocker of a weather prediction,' he says. 'Very severe electric storms to the north and north-west of Kesa. We're advised to divert to Marrakesh or to fly round the storm and approach Kesa from the south-west. I'd prefer to make it to Kesa but we'd have to fly nearly a thousand extra miles to do it. Nine hundred and seventy four to be precise. It's a question of fuel. What do you say?'

Captain Granville knows perfectly well that he has more than sufficient fuel to do this manoeuvre but he thinks it prudent to play exactly by the rules and that is why he puts the matter to the Flight Engineer.

'OK Captain,' the Flight Engineer replies. 'Bear with me sir while I do the sums.'

The man takes an irritatingly long time to do them but at last he comes up with the news that they have enough fuel for the extra distance with seven hundred miles to spare. This was, give or take, the same as Captain Granville had worked out the night before. He is now sure he can complete his mission. He takes the aircraft out of auto control and alters course manually. He switches on the public address.

'Ladies and gentlemen. This is your Captain speaking. I have a report indicating turbulence on our route to Kesa so, to avoid giving you an unnecessarily rough ride, I'm altering course to take you round it, which will be more comfortable than going through it. I'm sorry to say this will delay our time of arrival at Kesa by about an hour. The weather at Kesa is good. The trouble is to the north and west of it. I'll keep you posted. Enjoy your lunch. Thank you.'

He now selects a navigation schedule from his brief-case and resets the automatic navigational system of the aircraft. After a moment or so, it indicates miles run from Cardiff, miles to run to, and ETA at, Atlanta City Airport.

66

Then he enquires after the Second Pilot. The Chief Stewardess tells him the poor man has developed what appears to be an acute case of food poisoning. He has been examined by a doctor from among the passengers and, while there is no cause for alarm, it is certain that the Second Pilot will not be fit for any further duties on this flight. In other words his condition, in Captain Granville's opinion, is fully as good as can be expected.

Chapter 8

The King's indisposition at Cardiff airport had not, of course, been unexpected and Miss ap Llewellyn's Bentley and chauffeur awaited, as he emerged from it, ready to drive him and his two companions, now reinforced by his Valet, to Heathrow. His and their real luggage was also in the car. That checked in at Cardiff Airport had been packed only with blankets to give it the right consistency and weight. At about the time Captain Granville was altering the course of Abel Harry Tommy Zero2 for Atlanta City, the King and his party were going aboard a British Airways flight to Malaga, where they were due to change to a Spanish Airways flight to Kesa. Laura Blick had been left to hold the fort at Dolgellau Hall where the King's communications centre was to remain until he had established one at Kesa.

Although she could see the sense of it, Laura rather resented this arrangement. Nick always seemed to be chosen for the more interesting and exciting work and she disliked the separations that this caused. She hinted as much to Miss ap Llewellyn and, for her pains, earned a rather interesting lecture from that remarkably well informed and sagacious lady.

'You see my dear,' she said, 'they couldn't use you as the King's representative in Kesa. It's not that they think you couldn't do it, but they know the Treskans would find it hard to accept an unmarried girl in that role.'

'But I don't see why that should be,' Laura said. 'I've done a mission for the King and, though I say it myself, it was pretty successful. I got the National Bank of Atlanta transferred to Funchal. The King wouldn't have any money if I'd failed. As it is, he has plenty of it and can afford to behave and act as a King should.'

'Quite true,' Miss ap Llewellyn agreed, 'but in that business you were dealing with Portugese and Atlantan exiles. Treskans are quite different. Girls have no independent status until they are married.'

'How very odd,' Laura protested.

'It's not really odd at all,' Miss ap Llewellyn maintained. 'It's just that the Treskans, especially the Bogos, are not only a proud people but they also have distinctive cultural traditions. They're quite different from western people and, indeed, they're very special among African people.'

'That's why you told me I ought to marry Nick is it?' Laura asked.

'Well yes, I suppose it was,' Miss ap Llewellyn told her. 'I really don't quite understand why you don't. I mean the two of you are so obviously in love, but perhaps I don't quite understand the cultural traditions of your generation. Anyway, if I was impertinent, I hope you'll forgive me.'

'I could never think of you as impertinent,' Laura said, 'but I do think my generation has a basically different view of marriage from yours. To ours, it's an option; it's by no means a necessity. Some of my contemporaries see marriage as a symbol of commitment, but others think it is no more than a redundant undertaking, a kind of contract when an understanding should be sufficient.'

'And where do you stand?' Miss ap Llewellyn enquired.

'To tell the truth, I'm not really sure,' Laura replied. 'Nick and I got together in the heat of battle so to speak. At one moment somebody was trying to push him under a tube train and at another we were both being chased by Belling's Police because we had let the cat out of the bag about the loss of that aircraft carrier. I don't think we've ever had the leisure and composure to think about marriage.'

'I can quite understand that,' Miss ap Llewellyn said. 'I had lots of time to think about marriage myself, and I thought enough about it to decide not to go in for it.'

Laura did wonder what she had gone in for but she knew well enough that was something she ought not to ask about.

'I suppose the estate was an absorbing interest,' she said. 'You were quite young when you inherited weren't you?'

'Twenty-two,' Miss ap Llewellyn informed her. 'Too young really, but my father didn't make old bones. And of course it wasn't just the privileges I inherited; I inherited the responsibilities too. Very little had been done to relieve the suffering of our people who were thrown out of work by the collapse of the slate mining industry. You see, my great great grandfather had been one of the industry's pioneers. His son developed it tremendously. It was he who built this house and bought much of the estate. My grandfather, when his day came, inherited a very profitable business. Slate mining was highly prosperous at that time and we were exporting the stuff all over the world in our own ships. But the tide had turned. Welsh slate gradually lost its pre-eminence as roofing material and, by the time of his death, my grandfather had switched a great deal of his effort into agriculture and light industry, especially electrical components. My family kept and increased its wealth, but the miners did not and my father did little about it. He had feeble health and spent his time pursuing literary and artistic interests in a dilettante sort of way. Perhaps that's why I have always regarded it as my main challenge and duty to provide alternative employment for the descendants of the men who used to work for us in the slate mines.'

'And by the look of things, you've had great success,' Laura interjected.

'I've done my best,' Miss ap Llewellyn said, 'but the truth of the matter is I've been saved by the general prosperity that has come to Wales in the last forty or fifty years. I think I can claim to have made some contribution, but it's a general trend that has saved us.'

'Well,' said Laura, 'you certainly are very popular around here. I think people appreciate how tremendously Welsh you are and how you never pass on the other side when you come across hardship, sickness or ill-luck.'

'Now that puts me in mind of something I wanted to discuss with you, my dear,' Miss ap Llewellyn remarked. 'I'm worried about Janet. Poor girl, she obviously lost her heart to that Arthur Johnson and I'm bothered about where that's going to leave her. We owe it to her that you rumbled Johnson and that was how you saved the King from what I'm convinced would in one way or another have been a fatal flight. Now we owe it to Janet to try to put her together again.'

'Exactly,' Laura agreed, 'and it's not going to be easy. She blurted out her bitterness to me in the heat of the moment, but now she's turned right in on herself. She feels she can't talk to her mother and her father still refuses to hear a word against the odious Johnson. Having been so much cosseted by her parents, she now feels isolated and guilty. She even thinks she might be pregnant.'

'D'you think she is?' Miss ap Llewellyn asked.

'I doubt it,' Laura said, 'but you can't rule it out. She's certainly been having sex with that man and we know how unscrupulous he is. But she says he always used a condom, so I hope she's OK. But she's very nervy, I think because her mother seems to have given her the impression that even touching a man can be dangerous.'

'Unless you're married to him,' Miss ap Llewellyn put in.

71

They laughed and that relieved the tension, but not, of course, the anxiety that both women felt.

'I suppose we'd better get her checked out,' Miss ap Llewellyn suggested. 'I could ask my doctor to do it. Janet might prefer that to going to her own doctor.'

After much further discussion, it was decided that Laura would put it to Janet that she ought to see a doctor, just as a precaution. Thereafter they would have a further conference to decide what best they could do to help the girl regain her balance.

'Mind you,' Miss ap Llewellyn concluded, 'I feel especially sympathetic to Janet because Johnson completely took me in. It never entered my head that he was anything other than entirely genuine. You were smarter than I was. You suspected him even before Janet let on didn't you?'

'Well yes, I did begin to have my doubts. He seemed simply too obliging to be true and he rather gave himself away over those buttercups.'

'What buttercups?' Miss ap Llewellyn asked.

'I came across him one evening when he was weeding the long border and started chatting to him. I watched him weed among a clump of buttercups getting everything out except the buttercups themselves. Mr Finch came along and said it would be best to get a fork under that lot to loosen the ground and then to pull them up gingerly to get the whole root system. Johnson said that was what he was about to do, but obviously he wasn't because, if he had, he wouldn't have weeded between them would he? He simply didn't know buttercups were weeds. If he'd really worked at Bodnant he would have wouldn't he?'

So there were a few chinks in A4A's otherwise impressive armour and armoury but, if he was aware of them at all, they were certainly not troubling him at the moment. He was enveloped in a glow of satisfaction. He could easily read between the lines of what the Captain had said. He knew the aircraft was now well and truly on course for Atlanta City. Within an hour or so he would deliver the King up to Mr Belling. He had accomplished his mission and it only remained to collect the credit. Once again he had proved to be a master of the art of manipulating women. What's more, he'd got what he needed from that little Janet and he'd had Marian on the side as well. It had been such a clever combination of business and pleasure. It could only have been done by someone irresistible to women. Now he could look forward to a bit of pleasure for its own sake. That last thought was put into his mind by A4B, whom he watched as she stretched up to her overhead locker to get something out of, or put something into, it.

Yes, she did look entirely different from the woman who had cleaned the Air Direct offices and who he had thought of merely as a good agent working under his orders and three grades below his own in rank. Twenty years younger it seemed, and how those tight jeans showed off her bottom and how they emphasised her crotch. Of course that's what jeans were supposed to do, but in A4B's case they were strikingly effective. And her upper storey was pretty good too. Perhaps not quite up to the luscious handfuls offered by Marian, but certainly worth handling all the same. He couldn't quite remember how many whiskeys he had drunk since take off, but it didn't matter; his job was done and the seat next to A4B's was unoccupied. He pressed his stewardess button and asked her to bring him a bottle of champagne and two glasses. Armed with these he moved forward to the vacant seat.

'I thought we might drink a toast,' he proposed.

'I don't think we ought to, not yet anyhow,' she said.

'Oh come on, it's in the bag now and this'll be our last chance before we land,' he persisted.

'If you're sure,' she said.

'I'm quite sure,' he asserted. 'If you'd let down your table, I'll pour you a glass.'

She did so and he sat down beside her and let his table down too.

'Bottoms up,' he proclaimed.

He emptied a glass for about every three sips she managed. Half the bottle disappeared without much delay. He put his hand on her thigh under her table and watched her closely. She remained totally impassive, so he slipped it down between her legs.

'You've done awfully well,' he said. 'I'm going to put you up for promotion when we get home. You've done extremely well.'

She made no response beyond taking another sip of the champagne. She felt his hand rubbing against her crotch and beginning to feel for her zip. 'This stuck up pig's got quite a nerve,' she thought to herself. 'Thinks he's the cat's whiskers.' But there was no doubt he would stand very well with the boss, the dreaded Major Silk, when they got home with the King in tow. It would pay to put up with him for the time being and later she could decide whether to clear out or to set about dominating and manipulating him. A4B was fully as ambitious as A4A and not much less unscrupulous. Both had been well trained as Belling's Police.

His hand was now trying to force its way inside her fly. She undid the button at the top. He thought, 'ahah, she can't resist me' and it didn't occur to him that she had undone the button simply because the pressure of his confined hand was hurting her stomach. He reckoned the privacy afforded by their two tables was sufficient to allow him to touch her up enough to get the mastery of her. Later, after they had made their reports, he would take her out to dinner and then he would have her, in his flat, or perhaps hers, or, if the weather was right, in the park. He pushed his other hand up under her top. No bra. He had thought as much when he looked her over while she was reaching up to her locker. He would have liked slightly bigger boobs, but these were neat and trim and quite good enough to be going on with till something better, something a bit more on the lines of Marian, came to hand.

'They're beauts,' he whispered in her ear.

'Keep it under the table,' she said. 'That stewardess's looking at us.'

'OK, OK,' he accepted. 'Have a feel of this,' he added, drawing her hand against his crotch.

She thought to herself she'd seen bigger and better than what this stuffed peacock had to offer.

'Cor,' she said, 'a regular tree trunk.'

'Ladies and gentlemen, this is your Captain speaking. We are now approaching Kesa Airport and I expect to touch down in about ten minutes. On behalf of Air Direct, I apologise for our late arrival and I regret to say we have a slight problem with Customs and Emigration. Nothing serious I'm informed, but we will have to delay disembarkation until officials have come on board and satisfied themselves about what I'm told are minor technicalities. After we have landed and docked at the terminal all passengers must remain seated until the officials have finished their inspection. I will then make an announcement about disembarkation. I do apologise for this inconvenience which is caused by circumstances beyond my control. Thank you.'

Almost immediately the seat belt signs illuminated and the stewardesses started walking up and down the aircraft checking them. A4A and A4B zipped up their flies and A4A returned, none too steadily, to his own seat. A stewardess collected the empty champagne bottle. There was quite a buzz amongst the passengers.

'It'll be drugs,' said one. 'They're very hot on them at Kesa. That's what it'll be, drugs.'

But another knew that was wrong.

'It's sure to be currency,' he suggested. 'There's an economic crisis in Treskania. Due to the war, and they have these currency controls. You see if I'm not right. You'll find it's currency at the bottom of this.'

'But if they've got an economic crisis, surely they would not object to people bringing the stuff in would they?' a third man submitted.

'I'll tell you what,' said a woman as they taxied off the end of the runway. 'I know Kesa Airport and this is not Kesa Airport.'

This caused general laughter, but hardly anyone bothered to look out.

'Where is it then?' a wit called out. 'Blackpool; can you see the Tower love?'

'I tell you this is not Kesa,' the woman insisted, rising from her seat to get a better view.

'Madam,' a stewardess intervened, 'you must remain seated until the Captain announces disembarkation.'

Somebody grabbed the stewardess's arm.

'There's somebody important on board isn't there?' he demanded. 'That's what they're bothered about. It's the King of Thailand isn't it?'

'I'm sure I don't know what they're bothered about sir,' the stewardess informed him, 'but I don't think we have the King of Thailand on board. If you'd just be patient sir, I'm sure we'll get everything ironed out without any trouble. Kesa's a very nice airport.'

'But this isn't Kesa,' the protesting woman repeated.

'Just be patient madam,' the stewardess asked, 'and everything'll turn out all right.'

Chapter 9

In Major Silk's opinion everything was turning out very much all right. He had been in the control tower at Atlanta City Airport since shortly after Abel Harry Tommy Zero2's take off from Cardiff. He had heard from Captain Granville that the King was on board. Later, he got a signal telling him that the aircraft had altered course for Atlanta City. At this point he had informed Mr Belling of the situation. Mr Belling immediately drove off from the Residence and he had now joined his Director of Security Services in the control tower. They instructed Captain Granville to lead his passengers to believe they were landing at Kesa. They didn't want any trouble on board until the aircraft was safely down and they had successfully arrested the King and his companions.

Before Abel Harry Tommy Zero2 landed, more than fifty Belling's Police had taken up positions in and leading up to the disembarkation concertina through which the passengers would eventually flow. Captain Granville was instructed to delay this disembarkation until after police had entered the first class cabin and secured the King. To be absolutely sure of the position, A4A was to be brought forward to identify the King, who might be wearing some sort of disguise. If so, this would easily be recognised by A4A who had seen the King at Cardiff.

The Chief Prosecutor was summoned and told to prepare to proclaim the charges against the King so that everything connected with his arrest would be legal and above board and, most important of all, done in the full

77

glare of publicity. Press and TV reporters and cameramen were already posted in the arrival lounge, where the charges would be read out. Everything was at the ready and here was the aircraft docking at the terminal. Mr Belling was on the verge of a political coup of the first magnitude.

Captain Fenton, in command of the boarding party of six Belling's Policemen, had assembled them in the mouth of the concertina and, as soon as the docking was completed and the Captain had ordered the hatch of the first class compartment to be opened, he led them on board Abel Harry Tommy Zero2. There he encountered A4A, who had been brought forward in readiness, or in some sort of readiness. Though the aircraft was now at rest, it still seemed to A4A to be pitching and banking. At any rate the floor kept tipping at crazy angles, which made it hard for him to keep his feet.

'Which is the King?' Captain Fenton demanded.

'The King?' A4A stuttered as though he had never heard of such a person.

'Yes the King,' Captain Fenton barked. 'Which is he?'

'Oh, you mean the King,' A4A managed. 'The King, well he's the King of Atlanta or that's what he ushed to be. But I've caught him right and proper. He's in the first class. He would be wouldn't he, being a King and all that? But we've got him now. He's in the first class.'

'Pull yourself together man. We're in the first class. Get yourself together and tell me which is the King.'

'He's not the King. He's Colonel Andershonn. That's what he calls himself, but he's in the first class all the same.'

'Take this man off the aircraft,' Captain Fenton ordered one of his subordinates. 'See that he's put under guard till further notice.'

The eight first class passengers were somewhat amazed

by this charade as also was the stewardess who had been looking after them. One of the company stepped forward.

'Now look here officer,' he said, 'what's the meaning of this and where are we anyway? We don't seem to be in Kesa at all, so where the hell are we and what's all this about a King? My name's Brown and I've got a valid ticket to Capetown and I've got a right to be taken there.'

'Just you pipe down,' Captain Fenton told him. 'You'll find nothing's valid till I've found out which of you is the King, or Colonel Anderson, if that's what he's calling himself. Fetch the Captain,' he commanded the stewardess.

She unlocked the door to the flight deck and Captain Granville emerged clutching his copy of the passenger manifest.

'Now then,' Captain Fenton resumed, 'which is the King, or Colonel Anderson if you prefer?'

'I don't actually know,' Captain Granville, or, if anyone preferred, A4C, replied. 'I've never actually seen him in the flesh. I've only ever seen photographs of him and those were a long time ago. A4A's up to date on him. He'd know.'

Captain Fenton's face was changing from red to purple.

'But you know he's on board,' he said.

'Oh yes, he's on board all right.'

'If you can't recognise him, how do you know?'

'Because I was told he was on board before take off at Cardiff.'

'Who told you?'

'The embarkation officer at Cardiff.'

'What exactly did he say?'

'She said they're all aboard.'

'She didn't actually say the King was aboard then.'

'No, she didn't actually mention the King, but she said they were all aboard.'

'All of what?'

'All on the passenger manifest and that includes the

King. See, Colonel Anderson here on the manifest and his companions, Mr Kramer and Mr Gerrard.'

'And this also shows the others in first class.'

'Yes, and it shows everyone booked in Club and Tourist as well.'

'Let's just stick to first class for the moment. As the Captain of an aircraft, I suppose you can count.'

'I don't quite get you, but yes, I think I can.'

'Well, then COUNT.'

'Right, well that makes eleven in first class.'

'It does, but if you also count the passengers sitting here, there are eight.'

'Yes I see that and I must say I'm surprised. There should be eleven. That's what the manifest says.'

'If a passenger or passengers are booked but don't actually embark for some reason, would the embarkation officer mention that to the Captain before take off?'

'Yes certainly she would. The Captain's manifest has to be correct. It goes back to the days when the Captain had to know the exact weight of passengers, cargo and fuel.'

'But your manifest is incorrect.'

'Yes, it seems so and I'm surprised at that.'

'I think I can explain,' the stewardess intervened. 'Most airlines follow the embarkation procedure the Captain has just explained. Air Direct does not. Last minute changes to the manifest are only mentioned to the Captain if *extra* passengers are coming on. If some fall out there is no need, under Air Direct rules, to mention it.'

Captain Granville felt an alarming rush of blood. He thought he had done his home work on Air Direct. Evidently he had overlooked this point and it had proved to be crucial, that is of course unless the King and his party had smelt a rat and emigrated into the Club or Tourist class. That was his only hope.

'D'you think it's possible the King and his party have

removed themselves from first class and melted into Club or Tourist?'

'Quite impossible,' said the stewardess, whom he was beginning to hate. 'The door at the back of first class is locked after take off and not unlocked again until the approach to landing. And during those periods when it's open the passage is under crew surveillance. Air Direct is very particular about it. We recognise that first class has paid a premium and we do not allow other passengers to invade their space and use their toilets.'

'So what it amounts to is the King, Colonel Anderson, is not on board at all,' Captain Fenton decided.

'It looks very much like it,' Captain Granville conceded.

Captain Fenton turned to his First Lieutenant and told him to take over command of the boarding party. He told him that the passengers were to be evacuated through the first class hatch. All other hatches were to remain closed. The identity of every man was to be established and cross-checked and every woman was to be checked to ensure that she was indeed a woman. He then turned on his heel and disembarked.

'Oh yes,' he added as he paused for a moment at the exit hatch, 'and put Captain Granville under arrest.'

'Women can only be checked by female officers,' the stewardess protested. 'That's international law and I don't see any female officers here.'

'We don't have international law in Atlanta,' the First Lieutenant informed her. 'We have only Atlantan law and you had better be pretty careful about observing it.'

'Atlanta. Is that where we are then?'

'That's where you are,' she was told.

She looked questioningly at Captain Granville but he failed to meet her eye.

'What do you propose to do about the passengers?' she asked.

81

They were to be directed to an information desk where, to use the First Lieutenant's words, 'they would be sorted out.'

Meanwhile, Captain Fenton approached Major Silk who, with Mr Belling, had entered the Arrival Lounge. The Director of Security Services and the Leader looked very pleased with themselves and with each other. Neither man was famous for smiling but that was what both were now doing.

'Sir,' said Captain Fenton, addressing and saluting Major Silk, 'it appears that neither the King nor any of his companions are on board the aircraft.'

Chapter 10

On hearing what Captain Fenton said to Major Silk, the Leader paused for a moment, looked across at the banks of journalists and cameramen and then turned a withering look upon Major Silk.

In a voice sounding like machine gun fire he said, 'Find the King and, if you can't, bring me a list of those responsible for this blunder. When I see that, I'll decide whether to add your name to it or not.'

So saying, he turned away, marched out of the Arrival Lounge surrounded by his aides and was driven away to the Residence at high speed. That left Major Silk and Captain Fenton to sort out the mess and save themselves if they could. They decided to hold their hands until the last passenger had been brought off the aircraft and checked, and every nook and cranny of the aircraft had been searched. When that was done and it was definitely established that the King was not there, Major Silk walked across to the press area and in a loud voice explained to them that the Captain of the aircraft had been found to be an enemy agent who had been frustrated by Atlanta's vigilant Security Service in an overt attempt to infiltrate the traitor King into the country. This man was now in custody. A second man, who had been aiding and abetting this dastardly attempt, had also been arrested. Both men would appear before the Emergency Tribunal and would receive their just desserts.

There was a positive roar of yells from the pressmen arising from them all shouting questions simultaneously.

'A grave threat to our security has been averted,' Major Silk imposed above the din, 'and once again I have to thank the men and women of Belling's Police for their vigilance and devotion to duty. That's all gentlemen, I'm glad there has been nothing more exciting for you to report. You can all sleep easily in your beds tonight. A dangerous plot has been completely frustrated.'

With a moderate degree of encouragement from the armed police in the lounge, the pressmen dispersed and went their several ways. A4C and A4A, the latter still somewhat tipsy, were driven off to Major Silk's HQ and, while Captain Fenton interrogated A4B, Major Silk spoke to the Air Direct Second Pilot and the Chief Stewardess. The Second Pilot was somewhat recovered from his severe stomach upset but was obviously in no condition to take command of an aircraft.

'You understand,' Major Silk said to him, 'that your flight was hijacked by a Treskan agent who, with the assistance of a second agent, was attempting to bring the ex-King into this country. Thanks to the efficiency of my people, the attempt failed. You will also understand that you were poisoned by this Treskan agent and were effectively put out of action.'

'Yes,' said the Second Pilot, 'that is what seems to have happened.'

'There is no 'seems' about it,' Major Silk corrected him. 'That is what happened.'

'Right,' said the Second Pilot, 'that is what happened.'

'Of course no blame attaches to you,' Major Silk went on. 'We accept responsibility for the serious inconvenience we unfortunately had to cause in order to be sure of capturing two enemy agents who posed a serious threat to the safety of our state. We will pay compensation to Air Direct and to the passengers involved. We will, if you wish, despatch a fast military aircraft to Cardiff to collect an Air Direct crew to fly this aircraft and its passengers on to Kesa and Capetown. Meanwhile we will provide you with first class accommodation in our excellent hotels.'

'That certainly seems to be a way of making the best of a bad job,' the Second Pilot accepted. 'In fact, I must say I think you are doing the right thing and I suppose some blame must attach to us for allowing a bogus Captain to get control of one of our aircraft.'

'Perhaps that is so,' Major Silk agreed, 'but I don't think we need press that point.'

'Thank you,' said the Second Pilot.

'So perhaps it would be best if you explained matters to your passengers,' Major Silk suggested. 'They need reassurance and we don't want any trouble or undesirable publicity.'

'OK, I'll do that,' the Second Pilot accepted.

Major Silk now linked up with Captain Fenton who introduced A4B.

'Ah,' said Major Silk to her, 'I suppose you know the truth of the matter.'

'Yes sir,' she replied. 'A botched attempt to kidnap the King.'

'No doubt, but,' Major Silk suggested, 'it might not be prudent to put it that way without an explanation of who was kidnapping the King. Our view is that the Treskans were trying to plant the King in Atlanta to foment dissent and we can take the credit for having frustrated them. It's a question of reassuring the public you see.'

'And not admitting failures by the Security Service,' A4B said to herself.

'Of course sir,' she said to Major Silk. 'I quite understand the importance of public confidence.'

'I think you'll find that A4B has a very good understanding of the position, I mean of our position,' Captain Fenton put in. 'I've had a good talk with her and she understands that we have our public position to defend but also that we must drop hard on those who failed us in this operation.'

'I'm glad to hear it,' Major Silk said and, turning to A4B, asked, 'Why, in your opinion, did the operation fail?'

'Chiefly due to the arrogance, over-confidence and lack of self-control of A4A,' she said. 'And secondarily, though not unimportantly, to the negligence and carelessness of A4C.'

'Enlarge on that a bit,' Major Silk asked.

'Well,' she said, 'A4A collected the intelligence about the King's travel plans from one of the maids in Dolgellau Hall whom he had seduced. That seduction, I have no doubt, was necessary and effective but then, after he'd got all that information, he had to go and seduce one of the other maids. He boasted to me about it, but the result was that he embittered the first maid who, I think, must have seen him with the second one. I don't quite know what happened then but it's pretty obvious that the embittered maid must have spilt the beans to the King, or one of his advisers. Anyway the King got wind of the fact that his projected flight to Kesa was threatened and he pulled out of it. A4A was now so besotted with the second maid that he stopped operating efficiently and failed to notice that the King had become suspicious. His basic trouble is that he can't keep his hands off girls – he had a go at me on the aeroplane – and he can't help boasting about it. In my opinion, he's simply not fit for the trust that was reposed in him. He lacks the self-discipline that's essential in a good agent. As to A4C, well, he was careless wasn't he? Negligent you might say.'

'Criminally negligent, I would say,' Major Silk added.

'Oh yes,' A4B concurred. 'It seems almost incredible that he didn't bother to check whether the King was on board or not.'

Major Silk now decided that A4B would be the star witness at the secret hearing before the Emergency Tribunal which would bring A4A and A4C to 'justice'. He also felt quite confident that in public she would hold her tongue or say what she was told to say. This position, he felt, was reinsured by the double promotion he awarded to her on the spot.

For her part, A4B went home in a happy frame of mind. She was delighted to have received this promotion and she was very pleased to have knocked the stuffing out of that strutting cock A4A, under whom she had not enjoyed knuckling. Whether she would have thought any differently about all this had she realised that A4A and A4C would be shot, is open to doubt.

Meanwhile, Major Silk and Captain Felton, now left to themselves, turned to the question of their own positions.

'It all depends on how the Leader reacts,' Major Silk said. 'He may decide to have us shot. He may decide to leave us as we are and adopt our cover story. He may decide to promote us and invent his own version of recent events. Or he may decide something else that I haven't thought of. But whatever he decides, I would not care to take a bet on it. So I think it would be prudent to assume the worst case and have a plan ready to get out just in case he does decide to have us shot.'

'Get out? You mean leave the country? That would be pretty difficult wouldn't it? And by the time we found out that he was going to have us shot, it would be too late and we'd get shot.'

'Oh come come,' Major Silk said in a soothing voice. 'We could get out through the Language School of the North. You have a good connection there and the Language School, as you know better than I, is the most effective of the Royalist "Rings" left in the country.'

An alarm bell rang in Captain Fenton's head.

'What do you mean I have a good connection at the Language School?' he said. 'What makes you think that?'

'I don't think it; I know it,' Major Silk informed him. 'I make a point of keeping tabs on all my men. Sometimes it comes in very handy to know just what's what. You needn't be coy with me. Your contact at the Language School could be exactly what we need. It may be the saving of us and you have to recognise the position we could establish with the King's men. Think of the things we could tell them. We might well do better under the King than under Belling. It's worth thinking about. On the other hand there is the principle of the bird in the hand or of the substance and the shadow. We would only go over to the King if Belling compelled it.'

'You mean if he decided to shoot us,' the by now somewhat bemused Captain Fenton deduced.

'Exactly,' Major Silk told him. 'And you needn't worry about finding that out too late. We'd know about it with plenty of notice.'

'I don't follow that,' Captain Fenton complained. 'I don't see how we could get notice.'

'It's really quite simple,' Major Silk assured him. 'The State Secretary keeps me fully informed about everything going on in the Leader's office.'

'The State Secretary? I didn't know there was one,' Captain Fenton confessed.

'Well you do now,' Major Silk said. 'His job is to keep a note of all the discussions the Leader has with his various advisers and to keep a record of all the decisions he reaches. Whenever required, he can then remind the Leader of any of these matters about which he may ask. What the Leader doesn't know is that he passes on to me a copy of all his notes.'

'Good God,' Captain Fenton exclaimed 'and how the devil did you fix that?'

'Quite simple,' Major Silk repeated. 'Just a matter of money. My grant for security work isn't subject to audit or any other kind of inspection because the nature of my work is top secret. So I've got plenty of money to distribute as I wish and no questions asked. I happen to find it appropriate to supply a monthly subsidy to the State Secretary. He also finds it quite appropriate because he has rather expensive tastes and his salary turns out to be insufficient to fund them all.'

'But aren't you taking rather a risk telling me all this?' Captain Fenton asked.

'I don't think so,' Major Silk responded. 'I don't think you'd split on me. But if you were foolish enough to do so, which I'm sure you aren't, I'd simply denounce you as an undercover Royalist with connections at the Language School. Whom do you reckon the Leader would believe; you or me?'

Mr Belling arrived back at the Residence in a very bad temper. He sent for the First Deputy Leader, Mr Leighton, and Dr Offenbeck. He opened the meeting with the abrupt statement that Major Silk would have to be shot. Mr Leighton was sure the Leader, as always, would have good grounds for what he had decided. All the same, he suggested it might be helpful if he could be told what they were. Mr Belling, obviously very reluctantly, outlined the disastrous events that had occurred at the airport. He ended with a repetition of the same verdict on Major Silk, though this time he did say he *ought* to be shot. Dr Offenbeck agreed that he obviously ought to be shot, but, tentatively and deferentially, he indicated that it might not be prudent to shoot him.

'It might leak out,' he suggested, 'and if it did, it might have a deleterious effect on the morale of Belling's Police.'

Mr Leighton re-entered the fray.

'Are there perhaps also others who ought to be shot?' he asked.

'Of course there are,' the Leader pronounced. 'Silk's agents in Wales ought to be shot.'

'Are they still in Wales?' Mr Leighton asked.

'Certainly not,' the Leader told him. 'Silk had them arrested at the airport.'

'Well then,' Dr Offenbeck muttered, 'perhaps if we had them shot we would have sufficient scapego—, sufficient blame-worthy people, to explain the failure.'

'Without in any way challenging the opinion that Silk ought to be shot,' Mr Leighton suggested, 'might it not be advisable to question him first and find out what cover plan he's arranged? He's sure to have concocted one and it might be as well if we found out what it is before proceeding further.'

'There might be something in that,' the Leader conceded. Turning to the State Secretary, he said, 'Send word to Major Silk that I wish to see him here at once.'

By this time, Major Silk had returned to his HQ with Captain Fenton and it was there that he received the Leader's summons in the form of a note from the State Secretary, together with a minute of the meeting with Mr Leighton and Dr Offenbeck, which had caused it to be sent.

'They've gone cool on the idea of shooting us,' Major Silk remarked. 'I think I'll risk it and report at the Residence.'

'I hope your press release will have bitten before you get there,' Captain Fenton said. 'It might be very awkward if it hasn't.'

'I think you'll find it bites pretty fast and pretty deep,' Major Silk assured him.

And so, indeed, it had. Major Silk's driver had considerable difficulty in getting to the Residence. A large and vociferous crowd had assembled in Government Square and masses of people were rushing down Government

Street and the other avenues leading to the Residence in a high state of excitement. There hadn't been much good news lately but now at last there was some bread and circus for the people. All over the country their TV sets and evening papers told them that a great victory had been won. Two of the most dangerous agents of Treskania, whose underground activities had posed a severe threat to national security, had been captured. A whole network of espionage would now collapse and a decisive blow in the war had been struck against the Treskan enemy. When Major Silk entered the Leader's presence in his inner sanctum, the roar of the crowd outside was noticeably audible.

Mr Belling seemed hardly to notice Major Silk's arrival. He sat, sunken in his chair, his chin resting on his chest, brooding about something not immediately obvious to the others in the room.

'What's going on out there?' Mr Leighton asked.

Major Silk told him about the great victory that had been announced on TV.

'But I had understood that these men were our agents and that they had made a bosh of capturing the King,' Mr Leighton protested.

'Well sir,' said Major Silk, 'that is how it at first seemed. But on further examination, it turns out to be otherwise.'

'So,' Dr Offenbeck reflected, 'as we have two men to shoot, you think it would be better that they should be enemy agents rather than our own.'

At this, the Leader suddenly sprang up from his chair.

'Stop blithering Offenbeck,' he shouted. 'This is the moment to apply the hammer to the anvil.'

He strode out of the room and across the saloon. He flung its double doors open and stepped onto the balcony overlooking Government Square. A huge roar went up from the dense crowd beneath, followed by repeated shouts of 'Leader, Leader, Leader.' This released in Mr Belling a theatrical style that had previously lain dormant. He raised his arms triumphantly and turned his shoulders from side to side presenting a chest-on view to the worshippers at all angles to the balcony.

'This is a huge leap towards victory,' he proclaimed, evoking a tremendous response from the crowd. 'This is the beginning of the end for the traitor King. I see the light at the end of the tunnel. Together our united people will travel relentlessly towards it and the day is not far off when we will debouch into the sunlit uplands. Be of good heart. We cannot be denied. We will prevail.'

'Well well,' Dr Offenbeck whispered to Major Silk, 'who would have believed that two failed agents could achieve such results?'

'Who indeed?' Major Silk whispered back.

'So now it'll have to be Plan B, assassination of the King,' Mr Belling told Major Silk as he returned from the balcony.

Chapter 11

Gerry Eggleton and his three friends, Bill Marshall, Henry Wilding and John Rankin had now passed out from the Air Academy in the top grade and had been commissioned as Air Captains. This was two steps above the basic commissioned rank of Air Second Lieutenant and was their reward for having achieved star ratings at the Academy. It was also symptomatic of the Air Force's urgent need to provide itself with the junior commanders required for the forthcoming squadrons of Swift aircraft. It was, however, proving easier to produce the young commanders than the aircraft. The Swift prototypes were still bedevilled by the problem of engine vibration at full power and also unexpected difficulties with identification and suppression radar. The result was that, when Eggleton and his comrades were expecting to start conversion flying on Swifts, they were restricted to simulators.

This was a great disappointment to the four musketeers. The prestige that would have attached to flying Swifts still evaded them and they were at a stage of life when that sort of prestige was the very essence of things. It was also rather unnerving to find that the much vaunted Swift was still attached to the drawing board. Perhaps it was the combination of such disappointment and doubt that led to an increasing scepticism on the part of the young men. The talk of an impending victorious war against Treskania and the official explanations of what had gone wrong with the first phase of the campaign began to look rather unconvincing. And what was the object of the war anyway?

'I'm not sure it's really our job to rescue the Hurnots from the Bogos,' Gerry Eggleton postulated.

'That's not what we're after; it's the oil fields we want. That's what my father thinks,' John Rankin contributed.

'If I really thought the war was about seizing their oil fields, I wouldn't feel happy about fighting it,' Henry Wilding said. 'That would be colonialism wouldn't it?'

'I suppose it might be,' Eggleton agreed, 'but what I don't understand is what part are we supposed to play in bringing about whatever it is they're after. I can't see what the targets would be. From what I can make out, the Treskans tend to disperse their troops and fight a sort of guerrilla war. That would not offer profitable targets for bombers.'

'The Crown Prince's troops might fight in a more concentrated form,' Rankin considered. 'I think they did in the battle against the Sudkans and, in that case, they might become possible targets for us. And of course we'll probably be required to knock out the Crown Prince's fleet. Something would have to be done to redress our own naval inferiority.'

'So what it boils down to,' Wilding said, 'is that we would be bombing our own people.'

'Well I suppose we would,' Eggleton accepted. 'But they've got themselves onto the wrong side. They're traitors.'

'But they're still our own people,' Wilding insisted.

Joining in the debate for the first time, Bill Marshall said, 'Whether they are traitors or not depends on how you look at it. They, no doubt, think *we're* traitors.'

Rankin had some further thoughts about that, but he decided the time was not yet ripe to air them.

At about the same time that a firing squad was finishing off A4A, the erstwhile gardener, Arthur Johnson, and A4C, Captain Granville, late of Air Direct, the King, whom they had sought to kidnap, was taking off from

Malaga on a Spanish Airways flight to Kesa. His party turned out to be the only occupants of the first class compartment, so it would have been easy for them to discuss the strange events that had led them to take this flight. The King, however, was not in a mood for discussion. He wanted a pause for thought and Count Connors was a courtier and friend with sufficient experience to know that, whatever his train of thought was, it must not be disturbed.

The King, in fact, was casting his mind back over the events of his reign that had culminated in the disasters that now beset Atlanta and asking himself how far he was to blame for what had happened. He felt that the general acceptance of the principle of constitutional monarchy that had existed at the time of his accession had lulled him into a false sense of its enduring validity. His whole upbringing and the attitude of those around him from the time of his growing up had assured him that constitutional monarchy was the best form of government for Atlanta and that the idea was supported by the people. Wherever he went he had been well and cordially received and, on national occasions, enthusiastically so. His duty was clear; it was to uphold the system. But of course it all depended on general acceptance of it, especially by the government, which he was bound to support, provided it had been properly elected.

Paul Reynolds had been properly elected and the King therefore had no option other than to endorse him as Chief Minister. He could advise and warn; he could encourage or discourage, but he could not dictate or, in any real sense, rule. When therefore Paul Reynolds proposed to dispense with the Crown what could the King do? There was nothing in his background or training to give him even a hint. Yet, Reynolds was destroying the constitution that it was the King's first duty to protect. Moreover this act of constitutional vandalism was only the first step in a series of calamities leading from an unjustified and disastrous war to the imposition of a police state in which there were no checks and balances to control the whims of the Leader. The fact that Reynolds had become one of the first victims of the monstrous regime he had unwittingly helped to create was immaterial beside the awful truth that the whole nation was now the victim.

Although the King found it impossible to acquit or convict himself of having failed the country, he now at least was sure that his future duty must be to use every endeavour to overthrow the Belling dictatorship. He was convinced that the restoration of the monarchy would be the most efficacious way of achieving that. Nor was this a selfish aim, he thought. It was an absolute duty. If at any stage doubts should arise in his mind about that, he would abdicate and leave the throne to the Crown Prince. Meanwhile, he must build on the alliance with Treskania and his good relations with Brazil and he must seek to draw around himself in Kesa Atlantan exiles as a nucleus of the popular support that he hoped he would eventually enjoy once again in Atlanta itself.

In these considerations and ponderings the King had given no thought to the question of his own safety, nor had he weighed the chances of Teskania weathering the storm that Belling's Atlanta was seemingly about to unleash. He was concerned only with what his own conscience dictated. Political policies and military measures were matters upon which he would have to rely upon the advice of his supporters. At times of grave crisis, as the King himself more than half-recognised, there was advantage in the Sovereign having a mind of a simple, straightforward and uncomplicated nature.

Count Connors and Nick Hardy, on the other hand, were chiefly and most immediately concerned with the

King's safety. They had guessed that Arthur Johnson's plan was to kidnap the King by hijacking Flight 6615. They did not reckon the intention had been to destroy the aircraft and so kill the King. If that had been so, they decided, Johnson would not have boarded the aircraft himself, as they knew he intended to do. Despite the disguise, they had recognised him in the Departure Lounge at Cardiff airport. So, now they had evaded the kidnap attempt, they asked themselves what Belling's next move would be. It seemed to them that, if Belling was to act sagaciously, he probably would not favour assassination. Assassination might not much appeal to public opinion and, in any case, the King was self-replacing. If Belling killed him, he would only make the Crown Prince King and, if he killed the Crown Prince, that would only make his brother, Prince Frederick, King, and so on. Moreover, Prince Frederick was still in Canada, where his father had directed him to remain till further notice. Hereditary succession, they believed, provided a certain degree of protection from assassination. But that would only apply if Belling was to act rationally. Dictators, they knew, often didn't, especially when they had been crossed. Count Connors and Nick therefore felt they could not rule out assassination; they could merely allot it a lesser likelihood than a further attempt at kidnap.

Count Connors placed most of his trust in protection. He was used to the idea of bodyguards and royal detectives. In the eight hundred years that the House of Herford had reigned, not a single member of the Royal Family had been assassinated, though a number of attempts had been foiled. Nick Hardy by no means discounted the importance of protection, but he urged upon Count Connors the greater importance of intelligence. Twice already, he pointed out, the King had been saved by intelligence. But for intelligence, the King would have been captured in his palace by Belling's Police. But for intelligence, he would have been on Flight 6615.

'We must aim to tap into Belling's intentions,' he said, 'and we may even be able to disrupt them. We already have some promising leads and now we'll be able to link up with Treskania's intelligence system.'

As the aircraft entered the circuit of Kesa Airport, the King suddenly emerged from his reverie.

'Cheer up you chaps,' he said. 'You look like a couple of undertakers. We don't want the Treskans to think we're a pack of miseries.'

Count Connors and Nick responded by assuming what they considered were their most affable looks. The aircraft came to rest in the lee of the terminal building. There were no docking facilities at Kesa and two coaches and a large car were presently to be seen speeding towards the dispersal. The Captain sent word to Count Connors to remain on board. The other passengers began to disembark and board the coaches. Presently a tall and impressive looking man entered the first class compartment and announced himself as the personal representative of President Tamu, on whose behalf he extended a warm welcome to the King. He then explained that President Tamu had originally intended to meet the King at the airport and accompany him in a motorcade to the residence that had been prepared for his use on Mandela Avenue near the Presidential Palace. On police advice, however, he had cancelled this plan and had now arranged for the King to be driven privately to his new home, where the President would call on him in the course of the evening.

This change of plan had been made necessary by the discovery of a plot by Atlantan agents to kill the King as he left the air terminal or possibly at some stage while he was in it. The Treskan Intelligence Agency had gained this intelligence by intercepting a signal from Major Silk's office in Atlanta City which, most curiously, had been enciphered in an obsolete code long since cracked by the TIA. If the immediately current code had been used, the signal could not have been read by the TIA. It seemed that the signal had been despatched in a great hurry, in so much of a hurry in fact, that this crucial mistake had been overlooked.

'Unless, of course,' Nick Hardy suggested, 'someone in Major Silk's office is boring from within and intended you to read the cipher.'

'That seems hardly likely,' the President's man said. 'We think it was an oversight because of the hurry. We think it was a last minute decision which left no time for the proper procedures.'

'Something they decided only when they realised the King was not on the Air Direct Flight,' Count Connors proposed.

'Exactly,' the President's man agreed. 'But Mr Hardy should talk to the TIA about his idea, in case there proves to be something in it.'

'Just to be sure we leave no stone unturned,' Count Connors added.

'Exactly,' the President's man repeated.

Chapter 12

It was fortunate for Mr Belling's entourage that, beside the very bad news reaching the Residency in Atlanta City, there was also some that was distinctly good. Following skilfully conducted negotiations, protocols of agreement had been signed by the Atlantan ambassadors in Estragala and Puerez and the Foreign Ministers of the two republics. The agreements provided that when the Treskanian oil fields came under Atlantan control, Estragala and Puerez would be afforded most favoured customer status. In return, Estragala and Puerez undertook to provide 'all appropriate assistance' to Atlanta in operations designed to secure control of the Treskan oil fields.

Although the phrase 'all appropriate assistance' was weaker than Mr Belling had wished, the agreement was a highly important development. Estragala, lying to the north of Treskania, with which it had a common frontier of some four hundred miles in length, provided an excellent base from which an invasion could be launched. Moreover, the Estragalian army was believed to number between fifty and seventy-five thousand men. Though not well equipped, this force could be expected to play at least a supporting role in the Atlantan invasion of Treskania. Another useful consideration was that Estragalian involvement would complicate any positive resistance on the part of the African Moral Union.

The agreement with Puerez was scarcely less important. After Brazil, Puerez possessed the most powerful of the Latin American navies. By the simple process of existing, the Puerezian Navy would tie the Brazilian Navy down and restrict its main strength to South American waters. Any reinforcement of the Brazilian Navy from un-American sources would fall foul of the United States in consequence of the Monroe Doctrine. Mr Belling had good reason to be pleased by the conclusion of these protocols, which immensely strengthened his political and military position.

But there was also the bad news. Not only had the King failed to board the aircraft at Cardiff Airport in which he was to have been flown into captivity in Atlanta, but the back-up plan to assassinate him at Kesa had also miscarried. It had become obvious that Major Silk's ingenious plans had somehow been leaked to the King's entourage. The damaging result was that the King was now installed in a closely guarded official residence in Kesa, where he would be a rallying point for the opposition to the Belling regime. It seemed to Mr Belling that there were only two possible explanations for this deplorable and exasperating situation: either Major Silk's security cipher had been cracked or there was a double agent somewhere in his organisation. Mr Belling sought Dr Offenbeck's advice.

Dr Offenbeck believed it was quite out of the question for the cipher to have been cracked. It depended on a highly sophisticated system far beyond the understanding of Treskanian intelligence, let alone the King's people in Wales. Yet the first leakage had been in Wales where the amateurs around the King would scarcely have known the difference between plain language and cipher. No, Dr Offenbeck was convinced, the cipher could not have failed; the explanation was a double agent.

Mr Belling leapt to his feet and seized Dr Offenbeck by the lapels of his coat.

'We'll find him and I'll have him skinned alive,' he screamed, 'and if we can't find him, I'll have Silk and all his cronies liquidated.'

Dr Offenbeck shrank back in alarm. He didn't like being touched and he was fearful of Mr Belling's tantrums. One never knew where they might lead.

'This is a very grave matter, Leader,' he said. 'We must find and eliminate the culprit, but I think we would be well advised to keep the whole matter under cover. It would be very damaging if it came to light that there was a leak in our security system.'

This advice had the desired effect. Mr Belling released his hold on Dr Offenbeck's coat and resumed his seat.

'That may be so,' he said. 'I'll send for Silk and give him twenty-four hours to produce the culprit or face the consequences.'

'That would be one way of dealing with the matter,' Dr Offenbeck opined, 'but I think there are others that might be preferable.'

'Such as?' Mr Belling interjected.

'And safer,' Dr Offenbeck concluded.

'What d'you mean safer?' Mr Belling asked.

'Well,' said Dr Offenbeck, 'I wish we could be sure of Silk but I'm not quite sure we can. I sometimes wonder if he hasn't got too powerful, a bit over-mighty perhaps. And it's crossed my mind that he may not be entirely loyal.'

'Not entirely loyal,' Mr Belling repeated. 'D'you mean he's the culprit?'

'Oh no, I wouldn't go as far as that,' Dr Offenbeck hastened to say, 'but I think it might be preferable to try a different avenue of approach. I suggest we have a very confidential word with Captain Fenton.'

An official government messenger, clad in the uniform of his service, arrived at Major Silk's HQ. He had come to deliver a personal message to Captain Fenton.

'OK, I'll see he gets it,' the clerk on duty in the entrance lobby told him.

'My instructions are to hand it to Captain Fenton personally,' the messenger insisted.

The clerk phoned Captain Fenton's office. There was no reply. At this moment another messenger appeared, but this one was not an official; he was a civilian courier and he wanted to hand a message to Major Silk. The clerk phoned Major Silk's office. The call was answered by Captain Fenton.

'Yes,' he said, 'Major Silk is here.'

So the official messenger and the unofficial one were taken up to Major Silk's office where, simultaneously, they handed over their respective messages. They both proved to be from the State Secretary. The one to Captain Fenton was quite short. It stated that he was required to report immediately to the Residency where the Leader wished to see him. Major Silk's was somewhat longer. A copy of the instruction to Captain Fenton preceded a detailed note of the discussion between the Leader and Dr Offenbeck that had generated it.

'Excellent,' said Major Silk, turning to Captain Fenton with a rather furtive smile. 'It's all falling into our hands.'

'I don't quite see that,' poor Captain Fenton said. 'What exactly is falling into our hands?'

'Power, my boy, power,' was the answer. 'We're getting to the point where we can decide whom to remove and when. We'll have to consider whether Leighton or Offenbeck should be our first target, but in the end it'll be you and I who rule the roost.'

'Rule the roost?' Fenton stammered. 'You mean control the government?'

'Of course,' Major Silk told him. 'Of course that's what I mean, though whether we do it under Belling or under the King is another thing we'll have to consider.'

'God,' Fenton exclaimed. 'I hadn't realised.'

'Well, you'd better start realising pretty smartly,' Major

Silk said. 'You've got an order in your hand and you'd best get on with it. The Leader won't brook delay.'

'But what am I to say?' Fenton pleaded.

Major Silk assured him it was quite simple. He must assure the Leader and Dr Offenbeck that the cipher could not have been broken. That would be easy because Offenbeck had already reached that conclusion himself. He must, of course, be very careful to cover over the fact that the signal had, in fact, been sent in an obsolete cipher that could easily be read by the Treskans or indeed almost anybody else. But that would be easy too. The official file copies in Major Silk's office would show that the signal had gone out in the most recently updated cipher, which certainly could not have been broken in Kesa. There would be no trace of the original signal and there was no one who knew of it other than Major Silk and Captain Fenton themselves. The rest would be a bit more difficult, but not unduly so. It was just a question of transferring the suspicion that the double agent was in the Silk organisation to the belief that he was in Belling's entourage. Major Silk carefully rehearsed the way in which this was to be done and then despatched Fenton post haste to the Residency.

Fenton, who was always dogged by feelings of resentment about things in general, now felt an upsurge of resentment about this situation in particular. Here he was proceeding to the Residency to plant an intrigue of Major Silk's making in the Leader's mind. He would have to stick to his brief exactly because Major Silk would receive a detailed report of what he said from the State Secretary. It was dangerous work, but it was he, and not Major Silk, who was having to do it. True, if Major Silk's plans came to fruition, there might be great advantages for him in store, but how could he be sure that Major Silk would keep in with him? Might he not dispose of him as soon as he

104

had fulfilled his purpose? He could, of course, un-Silk Silk by telling the Leader about the arrangement he had made with the State Secretary. But that would hardly be a wise thing to do at this stage and might even lead to his own destruction alongside that of Major Silk. No, he would have to go through with this business as instructed by Major Silk. All the same, he was being unfairly exploited. But then he was always being exploited. His own qualities never got proper recognition; he was always used as a tool; he was always at a disadvantage. He never got a chance of showing what he was really made of.

Coming face to face with the Leader, Dr Offenbeck and the State Secretary did, however, have the effect of suppressing these personal feelings and getting his adrenalin going. Yes, he did realise that the King had been forewarned both of the plan to fly him into captivity and of the assassination plot in Kesa airport. No, he was sure the cipher could not have been broken. It was highly sophisticated and the rolls were changed every forty-five minutes. Major Silk was meticulously careful about the use of the cipher; in fact, he was so meticulous that he was a very difficult man to serve under. There were times when Captain Fenton felt inclined to give up working for him and try something rather less exacting. Major Silk was almost maniacal about anything to do with security. Every precaution was taken four or five times over and it sometimes seemed it was overkill. Of course security was of paramount importance. He recognised that, but enough was enough and more than enough was no better than enough. Even so, it did mean that there was absolutely no question of the leakage having been due to a lapse of cipher security. The cipher could not have been read in Wales or in Kesa, except by the authorised agents who had the rolls.

'But,' the Leader asserted, 'these leakages did undoubtedly

occur as you yourself admit. So how do you account for them?'

'The only possible explanation,' Fenton replied, 'is that someone who saw the messages *en claire* leaked their contents to the enemy. In our organisation the ciphers could only have been read by Major Silk, myself and our agents at the other end, that is to say A4A in Wales and A4N in Kesa. A4A could not have leaked the signal to Kesa because he would only have seen the one to Wales. A4N could not have leaked that to Wales because he would only have seen the one to Kesa. So it seems impossible it could have been either of them and I can only state it was not Major Silk or myself.'

'So who was it?' the Leader demanded.

'Well sir,' Fenton answered, 'it's not for me to say that. These signals are repeated *en claire* to yourself, Dr Offenbeck, the State Secretary and Mr Leighton. Of course none of those could have leaked the contents but I suppose it's not impossible that a slip occurred somewhere in the office organisations of these high personages.'

'And what about Major Silk's office organisations?' Dr Offenbeck put in.

'I repeat sir,' Fenton affirmed, 'the only people who can read the ciphers in our organisation are Major Silk, myself and the agents at the other end.'

'And the cipher clerks?' Dr Offenbeck persisted.

'No sir,' Fenton declared. 'The enciphering process is automatically performed on the computerised rolls and the system is protected by an inbuilt alarm system.'

'I see,' Dr Offenbeck conceded.

'Thank you Captain Fenton,' the Leader announced. 'You may now return to your duties.'

When Fenton had departed, the Leader added, 'And now we're going to get to the bottom of this matter.'

A little more than two hours later a messenger arrived

at the Security Services HQ with a note for Major Silk. It was from the State Secretary and it contained a detailed account of Captain Fenton's statement to the Leader and the subsequent discussion between him and Dr Offenbeck.

Captain Fenton had to admit to himself that Major Silk really had been quite appreciative of his performance at the Residency under the grilling of the Leader. The subsequent discussion between the Leader and Dr Offenbeck, to which Major Silk was privy, showed that Fenton's statements had convinced the Leader and Dr Offenbeck that the intelligence leaks had been due, not to cipher breaks and certainly not to negligence or disloyalty on the part of Major Silk, but to sabotage somewhere in the organisation of the inner government. The Leader's confidence in his immediate entourage had been shaken; in particular he had been induced to cast a suspicious eye on the First Deputy Leader, Mr Leighton. A first long step towards crumbling the governmental structure had been taken. The door through which Major Silk would advance to supreme power was ajar. Captain Fenton had played a skilful part in producing this result.

But Captain Fenton was still very uneasy. He was sure he would be cheated out of his deserts. He always was and now he was beset by another anxiety of a quite different nature. He was going to supper with Beth Roberts, the A4B of his official life, but recently something else, something he had never experienced before. He had never before approached anything like intimacy with a girl. He had always been afraid he would be shown up, laughed at and rejected. Basically, this was because, in his early boyhood, he had had a series of operations on his penis which had disfigured it and failed to correct the curious angle at which it hung. This had given him the nickname of 'Shotcock' at school and later, when he got to his teens, the worse one of 'Straightjacket.' In those days, the boys

107

had an extra hour in bed on Sunday mornings which they misused by rubbing themselves up and sometimes each other. Fenton got drawn into these activities but, when aroused, his penis stood straight out horizontally instead of standing up vertically as those of the other boys did. This misfortune earned him the cruel ridicule of a kind that only young boys in a pack are capable of. He blamed his mother, he wasn't sure why, but he knew it was her fault. His younger brother had no such defect, so why did he? His mother was to blame. Who else could be?

Whenever a friendship with a girl began to blossom, he sheered off. He was afraid of being shown up and he dreaded the ridicule he felt sure would follow. With Beth however things were going along differently. She simply didn't allow him to sheer off. When he showed signs of doing so, she always countered with some innocent-sounding invitation which was impossible to refuse. She often touched his arm or put her hand on his shoulder; otherwise she had not touched him nor he, of course, her. He had felt much less threatened than in his previous experience and there was also the fact that, to his eye, she was an extraordinarily attractive girl. She was neat and slim. Her breasts were quite small and pointed, not at all like the horrid bulbous things his mother had, and she proved to be a much gentler and more feminine creature than she had appeared to be when in action as A4B. In fact, he fancied her, but he was afraid of the consequences and an instinct told him that this supper was planned as more than a mere meal. He thought of crying off, but in the end he changed into leisure clothes and set off for Beth's flat.

Beth too had changed into leisure clothes, T-shirt, short tight skirt and high-heeled shoes. Very alluring, but also rather frightening. Was she going to start kissing him and touching? He wished she would and was afraid she might. But all was well, at least for the time being. She gave him a slight peck of a kiss on the cheek and handed him a glass of white wine.

'The supper's cooking,' she said. 'It'll take about forty-five minutes. So what's your day been like?'

He told about his ordeal at the Residency and at the end of his tale complained that he'd get nothing out of it.

'I'm just being exploited,' he said. 'It's the same old story.'

'Then why do it?' Beth asked.

'Same reason as you do. It's our profession isn't it?' he countered.

'Yes I would have agreed to that,' she said, 'before...'

'Before what?' he asked, filling in the pause.

'Before I err, changed my mind,' she went on. 'Or rather had my mind changed for me.'

He didn't need to tell her he didn't understand what she was talking about. It showed on his face.

Beth explained that it had come to her that what she was doing and what he was doing was wrong and that she had realised straight away that she must give it up and persuade him to give it up too. Her new inner feeling was too strong to resist. Something inside her head had asked her why she was working for Major Silk's Security Services. The whole thing was corrupt and evil. At first she had felt that she was too deeply involved and compromised to get out of it. She, after all, had given the evidence that had got A4A and A4C shot. True, they had been engaged in an evil plot, but so had she. Yet, it was they and not she who got shot. If they deserved their fate, she did not deserve to escape it. And now the voice she heard in her head said she must at all costs give up this wicked life and start a new one. However difficult or dangerous this might be, it was what she must do.

'And so must you,' she told him.

This was not the threat he had expected, but it was a threat all the same. How could he give up his career? How would he earn his living? And, if he deserted Major Silk, he would be denounced and probably shot.

'It doesn't make sense to me,' he said. 'What would become of us? We might well end up in front of the firing squad.'

'It says in the Bible or in the Prayer Book or somewhere that Christ came into the world to save sinners,' she said. 'We're sinners all right, but if we reject the sins we've committed and apologise for them and put our trust in Christ, he will save us, even if not from the firing squad, he will save us nevertheless.'

'But nobody believes all that stuff nowadays,' he said. 'It's out of date and no one believes it any more.'

'Hundreds of millions do,' Beth insisted, 'and so do I. I know I'm not putting this very well and making a muddle of it. I don't know the chapter and verse of it, but I know it's true and I know what I must do – cost what it may.'

He was dumbfounded.

'She believes it,' he said to himself.

'You really believe it don't you?' he said to her.

'Absolutely,' she answered. 'I have no alternative. Oh gosh, it's time to get the supper out of the oven.'

While she set about this task, he started thinking. It was true their jobs did lead to dead ends and dead agents too. Perhaps the reason that no one ever gave him credit for anything he did was because what he was doing was wrong. Perhaps it wasn't all his mother's fault. Perhaps it was his own. He fancied he heard a voice in his head saying something like that. It was all extremely odd.

110

Chapter 13

With his arrival in Kesa, the King's position had been transformed. He, who had been a fugitive in Wales, living incognito in a private house and supported by no more than two courtiers, two activists and his hostess, Miss ap Llewellyn, was now an official guest of President Tamu. He was recognised by the Treskan government as the King of Atlanta and he had around him more than a hundred loyal Atlantans who, by one means or another, had found their ways to Kesa and offered their services to the King. This, from the point of view of the Restoration movement, was a distinct improvement but, as far as the King's safety was concerned, it was not. The relative security of Kesa had no doubt decisively frustrated Belling's plan to kidnap the King, but it was now evident that his intention was to assassinate him. And the security of Kesa would only last as long as Treskania was successful in fending off or defeating the Atlantan threat of invasion.

President Tamu and his Commander-in-Chief, General Attagu, were strongly of the opinion that if Belling's plans for a rejuvenated Atlantan Army and Air Force came to fruition and an invasion of Treskania was launched, probably through pro-Belling Estragala, with the naval support of Puerez, it would be impossible for Treskania to defeat it. The control of the air that the new Swift aircraft would confer on Belling's forces would, the President and the General thought, prove decisive. The guerrilla warfare that they planned to conduct would make life unpleasant for the Atlantan invaders, but it would not make it impossible for them.

The Crown Prince, who had masterminded the great Treskan victory in the Battle of the Frontier, was not as pessimistic as this, but he had to admit that war with the ill-equipped and badly commanded Sudkan army was one thing and war with the modernised, sophisticated and massive Atlantan forces would be quite another. On the other hand, he also believed that the prospects of disrupting Belling's plans before they reached maturity were good. He, President Tamu and General Attagu therefore found common ground in the strategy of disruption as opposed to that of direct confrontation.

General Attagu and the Crown Prince now applied themselves to the question of how best they might seek to disrupt Belling's invasion plans. They had the benefit of a flow of useful intelligence about developments in Atlanta, most of which came through the Language School. On the basis of that, they formed the impression that Belling was probably going to rely on the Swift aircraft to give him control of the air and the sea and that the carrier programme would be abandoned as too costly and too long in execution. It seemed that he intended to transport his invasion force in his fleet of former cruise liners, relying upon his air control to secure their safe passage and subsequent deployment. The cardinal question was, would the Swift squadrons have the capacity to secure this result? Would they have the power to neutralise or even destroy the King's substantial fleet, now up to strength with two carriers, one of which had been refitted in Bahia?

The Crown Prince was inclined to think that even the advanced Swifts would not be up to such a task. He believed the King's surface fleet would have an excellent chance of intercepting and sinking the cruise liners which, in themselves, would be soft targets. Rear-Admiral Fiskin, commanding the King's fleet, and Captain Willis, captain of the refitted carrier, were called in to give their opinions. Both believed the absence of a hostile surface enemy fleet would enable them to find and sink Belling's cruise liners. The search radar on their carriers would track them down and the four-inch guns of their frigates would be more than sufficient to polish them off.

'I have little understanding of naval matters,' General Attagu commented, 'but are you confident that your carriers and frigates could survive in the face of Swift squadrons? I understand these aircraft are very potent.'

'There must be some doubt as to the capacity of these aircraft,' Admiral Fiskin admitted. 'They have yet to prove themselves. But to answer your question, sir, I am reasonably confident that our surface force would survive in sufficient strength to eliminate the cruise liners.'

'Thank you, Admiral,' General Attagu replied, but the look on his face suggested that he was far from convinced.

The naval officers withdrew.

'I believe you have some doubt about this naval argument,' the Crown Prince suggested to General Attagu.

'It's not so much that I doubt it,' the General replied, 'as that the argument itself, on the Admiral's own admission, is a doubtful one. If what he hopes happens, we are saved; if it does not we are ruined. The alternatives are too sharply divided. I would favour a plan that had more, how shall I say? More space between the alternatives, if you understand what I mean.'

'I think I do,' the Crown Prince said. 'You want more fallback.'

'Not exactly fallback,' General Attagu told him. 'More concomitants, I would say. One, we already have. Your King's Royal Regiment is a highly mobile striking force of great efficiency and, if the Belling army comes in

113

through Estragala, there would be an opportunity for you to strike it while it is still off balance.'

'I certainly hope so,' the Crown Prince said, 'and now you have permitted me to recruit Treskans to fill gaps in my strength and indeed also to expand the force, we must have high hopes of what it may achieve. Your men are first class material and they are responding very well to the specialised training we are giving them.'

'That is all good,' General Attagu accepted, 'but it is only one of the concomitants I have in mind. The other is sabotage of the enemy war plan in gestation. I think we should talk to Mr Hardy about this. He has some interesting ideas and seems to have made some useful contacts.'

'Certainly,' the Crown Prince agreed, 'and there is also the point,' he added, 'that Mr Hardy has inside information regarding the Swift. He was employed in the Air Force Ministry and was directly concerned with its development.'

Nick was sent for but could not immediately be found. He had gone to the airport to meet Laura, who was arriving from Wales in charge of the complex radio systems that had been installed in Dolgellau Hall and were now being transferred to Kesa. His much longed for reunion with her was disrupted by the Crown Prince's summons, but of course he responded to it as quickly as he could.

General Attagu led off on the subject of the Swift. He said that intelligence indicated there were delays in bringing it to operational readiness. Technical difficulties had got in the way. He wanted to hear Nick's assessment of the situation. Nick explained that the prototypes had been pushed forward recklessly fast at the insistence of the Minister, Mr Leighton, in a bid to hit the headlines before the competitive alternatives being brought forward by the Navy could bite. The situation had been compounded by the Chief Minister's disastrous commitment to an early war against Treskania. The result was the calamitous sequence of events that ended with one of the Swifts crashing into a troop-carrying carrier, totally destroying itself and causing the carrier to blow up and sink with four thousand troops on board. It then emerged that the missile diversion radar, which should have been carried in the Swift, not only was not carried, but had not yet been brought to operational readiness. Subsequently it also emerged that engine vibration was encountered when at full boost.

'I believe it was your knowledge of these things,' the Crown Prince said, 'that caused you to abandon your appointment and join the Restoration movement.'

'That is correct, sir,' Nick told him, 'together with what came to light when my friend Laura Blick and I compared notes. She was in the Navy Ministry. We discovered unbelievably awful things, including how the Air Force Ministry allowed the Navy Ministry to proceed with the development of an aircraft which they knew was fatally flawed.'

'Ah yes, that would be the naval version of the Swift,' the Crown Prince surmised.

'Yes sir, it was. The Navy covertly obtained the design of the Air Force machine and reproduced it to make the naval version. This was rumbled in the Air Force Ministry but they allowed it to proceed knowing the main spar design was defective. The result, much to the satisfaction of Mr Leighton, was the crash of the naval prototype and the death of a distinguished test pilot. Laura Blick and I found it impossible to go on serving people like that.'

'Quite so,' the Crown Prince commented. 'Now Mr Hardy, General Attagu and I are particularly concerned to assess the prospects of the Swift. Some say it would be the decisive weapon in Belling's armoury if it could be got into squadron service in time for his anticipated invasion of Treskania. Others think it may be overrated. What do you think?'

Nick scratched his head. He had only recently begun to be aware of the awesome truth that his opinions nowadays were liable to determine the outcome of wars and the fate of nations.

'There are problems with the Swift,' he said, 'but I have no doubt they will be overcome. I understand the four fast carriers programme has been abandoned, or shortly will be. If that proves to be so, life in the Air Force Ministry will become less frenetic. The development of the Swift will become more orderly and, I am sorry to say, I believe it will come to fruition within the next six months or so. Operational models could then come off the production line at high speed. The Atlantan aeronautical industry is among the most advanced in the world. In fact, I would say it is second only to that in the United States. Now, as to Your Royal Highness's main question, I am bound to say I do not think the Swift is overrated. Its performance will be phenomenal in every respect: speed, rate of climb, range, reliability and load-carrying capacity. With its intended radar installations in working order, it would be invulnerable to anti-aircraft missiles and it would have the ability to detect and strike a pinpoint target anywhere within eight thousand miles of its base. Its one and only vulnerability would be if it were to meet an opposing aircraft of similar or, of course, superior performance. Only the United States could produce that, and I don't think we are expecting their participation in the forthcoming hostilities.'

'So in your opinion Mr Hardy,' General Attagu enquired, 'we have no defence against the Swift.'

'No sir, none,' Nick replied, 'except of course the Swift itself.'

'Meaning exactly?' the Crown Prince queried.

116

'Meaning sir,' Nick explained, 'unless we could gain control of a squadron of Swifts, naval version or otherwise.'

'I suppose it might be unfair of us to ask how you think we might set about achieving that,' the Crown Prince said.

'No sir, not really,' Nick asserted. 'I think there are very real possibilities.'

It was now the turn of the Crown Prince to scratch his head.

'Would you enlarge on that?' General Attagu asked.

Nick explained he had been sifting through the intercepts made in Wales and comparing them with signals picked up by the Treskan Intelligence Agency. In addition to that, and most important of all, contact had been made through the Language School with an official in the Navy Ministry who had seen the light about the Belling regime and was now fully prepared to help the Restoration movement. Moreover, this man had a son who had recently graduated from the Air Academy and was now earmarked as a Swift Captain. Like his father, the son was also firmly in the Royalist camp. Oddly enough, the last straw for this young man had been the peremptory shooting of A4A and A4C, neither of whom might have been expected to have much appeal to an idealist such as Air Captain John Rankin was. Indeed, he had no use and little sympathy for these disreputable characters, but he did take extreme exception to summary executions in a country that was supposed to be under the rule of law.

Not only would he shortly be in command of an operational Swift, but he belonged to a closely knit group of four comrades who had all graduated with stars at the same time. The other three would similarly soon be in command of Swifts. He had not yet broached the question of going over to the Restoration cause with his friends, but it was not beyond the realms of possibility that he

117

eventually would do so and perhaps persuade at least some of them to follow his lead.

Another piece of big news coming through the Language School showed there were cracks in Belling's Directorate of Security Services. Captain Fenton, highly placed in Major Silk's organisation, had contacted the Language School apparently with the intention of establishing a footing with the Restoration movement as an insurance against things going sour for him in the Belling camp. This was a promising development, but also a very dangerous one. If Fenton came decisively over to the Royalists, all well and good, but if he settled for Belling in the end, he might well blow the Language School's cover.

Even Major Silk himself was an unknown quantity. There was some evidence to suggest he knew of Fenton's contact with the Language School and had done nothing about it – so far. And there was the curious business of the signal about the plan to assassinate the King having been transmitted in an obsolete and easy to read cipher.

All sorts of possibilities had suggested themselves to Nick's mind and these now also gripped the minds of General Attagu and the Crown Prince. What they recognised they must do was to find which possibilities could be converted to probabilities or, better still, certainties.

Nick proposed that he should be despatched under cover to Atlanta with the aim of contacting Commander Rankin, his son, Air Captain Rankin, and, if at all possible, Captain Fenton. His *entré* would be the Language School, where he was already known, but from there on he would have to improvise as circumstances suggested.

'This would be an extremely hazardous mission,' the Crown Prince said. 'If you were to be betrayed, Belling would not hesitate to have you shot and, if things went wrong, the Rankins and Fenton might also get shot.'

'But those risks, sir, have to be compared with the

potential gains,' Nick countered. 'I believe we have a chance of gaining control of at least three operational Swifts and also of increasing the volume and quality of our intelligence as to Belling's intentions. Surely that, not to mention other advantages that might crop up, is worth the risk.'

'No doubt, no doubt,' the Crown Prince accepted, 'but the point is it would be you and not I who would be taking the risk and that is an aspect of it I don't like at all.'

'Your Royal Highness's training,' General Attagu put in, 'has evidently been that a commander should always expose himself to the same risks as those he asks his men to face. That is a precept I share but, where espionage is concerned, it is hardly a viable concept. Neither you nor I could penetrate into Atlanta under cover and, even if we could, neither of us could play the part Mr Hardy has in mind. We are the wrong age and have the wrong appearance. It would be difficult to disguise a face as well known as yours or a skin the colour of mine.'

The Crown Prince sat deep in thought for some time. Clearly a battle was taking place within his heart. At last he spoke.

'Very well,' he said, 'but we won't be rushing into this. The operation must be planned down to the last detail we are able to envisage. And you, Mr Hardy, must be trained and rehearsed to the hilt. For one thing, it will probably be best for you to go in by parachute. That would seem nowadays to be the safest entrance, but we'll have to look searchingly into that and all the other factors. Another thing is you can't go alone. You must have a trusted companion with you upon whom you can rely absolutely. At one stage or another you will be bound to need help. You must have a companion. We must select a volunteer and train him with the same thoroughness that we will devote to you. Am I not right, General?'

119

'Certainly you are, sir,' General Attagu affirmed. 'I believe this plan gives us a real chance, not so much of winning the war, but of averting it. Whatever the outcome may be, I should like now to record my profound appreciation of Mr Hardy's bold ideas and courageous offer of his services.'

'My God,' Nick thought to himself, 'they've accepted my proposals and I've got myself the job. If this doesn't teach me to hold my tongue, I'm a bigger fool than I thought I was. Going in by parachute! My God. And Laura's going to be livid.'

'Thank you very much sir,' he said. 'I'll certainly do my best.'

Chapter 14

Unfortunately for the Crown Prince, General Attagu and Nick Hardy, had they but known it, things in Belling's sphere of control were moving along more favourably and a good deal faster than their intelligence had suggested. The refitting of the five fast cruise ships as troop transports was nearing completion, well ahead of schedule. The reorganisation, expansion and retraining of the Army was proceeding rapidly and effectively. Belling would soon have fifty thousand men ready to undertake the occupation of the key points in Treskania and especially to gain control of the oil fields. Above all, the tale of woes that had beset the development of the Swift had now reached the last chapter. The nagging problems with the perfection of the radar equipment had been solved and a hundred and fifty operational sets of the equipment were now in production. New hardened bearings obtained from Sweden had been fitted to the engine mountings and these had overcome the vibration that had previously set in at full boost. Nothing now stood between the prototypes of the Swift and the production of operational models ready for squadron service.

The international situation was scarcely less favourable. Treskania had appealed to the African Moral Union to condemn Atlantan aggressive threats and to resist invasion if it came to that. The Presidents of South Africa and Egypt, after two lengthy sessions of the Union, the first in Cairo and the second in Capetown, had expressed sympathy with President Tamu in what they described as these 'very difficult times'. But they had reluctantly, though finally, resolved that the Union could not properly intervene in a dispute which, though Atlantan in origin, did undoubtedly involve two African states; Treskania and Estragala. They hoped 'moderation would prevail' and that 'compromise solutions might be found'.

Brazil had joined with Treskania and Sudka in applying to the International Peace Organisation for sanctions against Atlanta designed to curb her aggressive intentions. The Chinese delegate had declared his government's objection to any interference with Treskania's right to develop its own oil fields in its own way but he had stopped short of indicating any material way in which this objection might be expressed. The United States delegate supported the Chinese view and added that his government hoped there would be no squabbling about Treskan oil between the major oil-importing countries, such as his own, India, China, Pakistan, Germany, Italy, France and Great Britain. The Atlantan delegate declared that his government had no intention of interfering with Treskania's oil fields. The dispute between Atlanta and Treskania was solely concerned with the oppression by the Bogos of the Hurnots. The rights of the Hurnots had been guaranteed by the Atlantan government when Treskania was subject to it as a colony. His government regarded it as a sacred duty to ensure that this guarantee continued to be honoured. The Treskan delegate raised objection to this statement, but the President of the Council ruled this out of order since Treskania was an appellant and its representative's statement, in this context, was *ultra vires*.

Eventually, after many long and some impassioned speeches, it was resolved not to put the Brazilian-Treskanian-Sudkan application to a vote but instead to urge all countries to respect each other's oil interests. Most observers agreed that the Atlantan delegate had secured a significant success by dividing and diverting the critics of his country. Mr Belling saw his way clear to press ahead with plans for his war to rescue the Hurnots. Cynics took the view that the oil-importing countries would not take it amiss if Treskan oil production was massively increased, as it undoubtedly would be if the oil fields were taken over by Atlanta.

Belling was determined to strike while the iron was hot. History rewards the man who can pick the decisive hour, he kept telling Dr Offenbeck. To prove the point, he had Mr Leighton arrested and despatched to Prison Island to await the verdict of the Emergency Tribunal on a charge of having disclosed secret information to the enemy. In his place, he installed Major Silk as First Deputy Leader with continued responsibility for security and intelligence. Dr Offenbeck was dismayed. He would much have preferred to have had Major Silk shot. He feared him a good deal more than he feared Mr Leighton, but he had the prudence to hold his tongue.

The four-carrier programme was scrapped and the resources allotted to it transferred to the Swift development and the expansion of the Army. The balance was accredited to the contingency fund. The Chief of the Air Staff was ordered to go full speed ahead with the operational training of as many Swift squadrons as possible. The Chief of the Army Staff was instructed to ensure that the new Army was specially trained in rapid embarkation and disembarkation. The five cruise ships, each carrying five thousand men, would have to complete two voyages to transport the invasion force of fifty thousand men. Each passage to and fro could be accomplished in just under twenty hours. Allowing for turnaround times, there would therefore be an interval of almost two days between the arrival of the first wave and that of the second. This would obviously be a danger period which must be kept to a minimum.

The Chief of the Army Staff considered that the Treskan Army would lack the mobility or concentration to exploit this opportunity, but he reckoned the King's Royal Regiment would be a serious threat. The fact that it was a highly mobile and well balanced force meant that it might well strike a pre-emptive blow against the invading force while it was in its danger period and thoroughly off balance. He therefore suggested that the Air Force should deploy Swifts in a concentrated attack on the King's Royal Regiment timed to coincide with the landing of the first wave of the invading force in Estragala.

The Chief of the Air Staff was doubtful about the efficacy of such a plan. Troops in the field, he argued, were not a profitable target. The Air Force was likely to be far more effective if employed against lines of communication, supply dumps or, indeed, anything else that nourished the enemy's war effort. The best results, he claimed, would be obtained by using the Swifts in a strategic, as opposed to a tactical, role.

The Leader, however, ruled in favour of the Army plan and the Chief of the Air Staff unreservedly and rapidly agreed to set in motion the necessary preparations to implement it. He evidently did not wish to follow the ex-Chief of Naval Staff to Prison Island, whither the Admiral had been despatched after objecting strongly to the abandonment of the four-carrier project. Indeed, arguing with Mr Belling was not only unprofitable; it was highly dangerous, as the relatively uncrowded conditions prevailing on Prison Island testified. Hundreds of dissidents had been sent there, but only a handful of the cells were now occupied. The Emergency Tribunal and the firing squads had seen to that.

Yet, while Belling was certainly more feared than admired by those around him who helped him to govern the country, in the country at large he was riding high in the popularity stakes. His portrayal in the press and on TV as a decisive leader who would recover the country's honour in the aftermath of the humiliation of the botched war with Treskania went down well with the people. Right-wing opinion saw him as God's gift. Decadence, immorality and irresolution would be stamped out and foreigners would once again look upon Atlantans with respect. Left-wing opinion, though for quite different reasons, was equally enthusiastic. The reforming zeal which had projected the Idealists into power under Paul Reynolds had been disappointed by his achievements. True, the monarchy had been disposed of but, apart from that, not much seemed to have changed and the war to rescue the Hurnots had failed. Under Mr Belling things would move ahead. Class distinctions would be obliterated. Over-mighty Generals, Admirals, government Ministers and the like would be brought to book. The age of the common man had dawned. The previously unsuspected power and skill in timing of Mr Belling's oratory enabled him to cash in on these gut feelings in the country. What now seemed to be an inevitable victory in a renewed war with Treskania would turn him into a national hero. The prospects of the Restoration movement looked bleak indeed and, by most independent observers, had been written off. If such observers had been aware of the training now being undertaken by Nick Hardy, they would probably have dismissed it as being scarcely worth mentioning.

When Laura heard from Nick about this training and the purpose for which it was designed, she immediately determined that she would be the trusted companion who was to accompany him on the mission. Nick was horrified, but he knew better than to try to argue her out of this resolve, and the Crown Prince and General Attagu accepted her offer of service. So it was that the two lovers embarked on a course of parachute jumping, the tactics of evasion and those of impersonation. In all these arts, Laura learned at least as fast as Nick and, in parachute jumping, a good deal faster. She had the good fortune not to share his marked fear of heights. Her constant reminders to Nick that he was braver than she was, because it took more courage to do something you were afraid of than something you were not, did, however, preserve a good part of his morale.

The tension Nick was under, nevertheless, began to show through when it was eventually decided that the plan to enter by parachute was not practicable. An unscheduled approaching aircraft would be highly conspicuous on Atlanta's modernised radar-system. When Nick was told this he flew off the handle.

'You mean to say all those practice jumps I made were unnecessary,' he snapped.

'Not necessarily,' the instructor rather heartlessly told him. 'They might prove very handy in some future operation. You never know what's in store for us in these exciting times. Anyway, I think Miss Blick really enjoyed that phase of your education.'

These little awkwardnesses did not conceal from Nick and Laura, nor from those who were directing them, that the time in which to mount the undercover mission was now running out. Intelligence reports told the Crown Prince and General Attagu that operational Swifts were now coming into service, that the five troop-carrying former cruise liners were nearly ready to go and that fifty thousand men were standing by to board them. In Treskania, the King's Royal Regiment was placed on high alert and General Attagu's men were dispersed into the countryside on the approaches to the oil fields and Kesa.

Nick and Laura boarded a civil flight from Kesa to

126

Funchal disguised as South African travel agents. Thus did Treskania prepare to defend her territory by a combination of a highly mechanised pre-emptive strike by the Crown Prince's Regiment, an interior guerrilla campaign by General Attagu's army and the undercover operation upon which Nick and Laura had just embarked.

Treskan intelligence reports were not incorrect. Operational Swifts were now at last coming into service and the first batch of eighteen were already deployed on an airfield some twenty miles to the north of Atlanta City. Air Captain Gerry Eggleton, having been promoted to the rank of Air Major, had been placed in overall command of this force or, in Air Force terms, Wing. The Wing was subdivided into three Swift squadrons, each of six aircraft, commanded respectively by Air Captains Bill Marshall, Henry Wilding and John Rankin.

So, of these first eighteen operational Swifts, four would be flown by the four young men who had distinguished themselves at the Air Academy as being of outstanding quality and whose aptitude in handling these complex aircraft had been shown to be exceptionally good. The remaining fourteen aircraft would be flown by pilots of a more average sort of quality, which raised something of a question mark about how successful these Swifts would be under war conditions. The Swift, indeed, was un-user-friendly to pilots who were less than highly gifted and thoroughly trained. The price of its phenomenal performance was a high landing speed, a high stalling speed and an exceptionally heavy nose. The prudent course would have been to delay the war until a more mature level of experience had been built up among the non-starred average pilots and, no doubt, if that had been put to Mr Belling, he might well have endorsed it, for he had often spoken of the need to enter the war with a properly prepared force. The Air Force Chief, however, did not submit the matter to the Leader. He feared he might be accused of defeatism and sent in the same direction as his former naval colleague, the ex-Chief of the Naval Staff. Instead, he reported to the Leader that the first Swift Wing would be ready for war operations three months after its formation.

Air Major Eggleton was accordingly told he had twelve weeks in which to work up his somewhat mixed bag of pilots to a sufficient standard and to exercise them in the tactics of escorting troop ships, attacking enemy naval forces and seeking to neutralise a military force in the field. This latter, it was explained, would be the Crown Prince's Regiment, with the specific object of preventing it from engaging the Atlantan invading force during those vulnerable days while it was disembarking in Estragala.

These instructions somewhat blunted the euphoria of the wonderfully exciting challenge of flying Swifts, let alone the prestige of early promotion. The more Eggleton talked matters over with his three friends, the less any of them liked the prospects. They, after all, were fully conversant with the difficulties and dangers of flying Swifts. Moreover, two of them, Marshall and Rankin, expressed a marked aversion to the idea of pulverising the King's Royal Regiment, largely manned as it was by their own countrymen. Eggleton pointed out that the same consideration applied to the projected attacks on ships of the King's Navy, but he reckoned it was not their business to judge matters of that sort. He told his three subordinate commanders that they must remember they were professional Service officers whose duty it was to obey orders and not to decide what they should be. To this principle they assented or, at least, appeared to assent. Rankin realised his moment was not yet.

In Eggleton, Marshall, Wilding and Rankin, the Air

Force had undoubtedly spotted four young officers of top ability as pilots and commanders, but how far their absolute blind obedience to orders could be relied upon was perhaps a little less certain.

Chapter 15

Captain Edward Fenton was in a thorough muddle. Now that his boss, Major Silk, had been elevated to the political world as Mr Belling's First Deputy Leader, he was substantially in day-to-day control of the Security Department, but he was beginning to doubt if this was what he ought to be doing. Beth's view that the work of the Department was corrupt and wicked had seriously unsettled him. Moreover, the fact that Major Silk knew he had made a provisional sounding of the Language School meant that at any moment he might be denounced and shot. Then there was the problem of Beth herself. What she had said to him about Christ being with them hadn't really made sense to him, but he thought that was because she had only said a bit of what was in her mind. For some reason she had held back from saying the rest, and he wondered why. Also it was obvious that she was very interested in him and, though she had not embarrassed him so far by kissing and touching and that sort of thing, he was constantly fearful that she might begin to do so. He could of course solve the problem by breaking off his friendship with her but he found he could not bring himself to do so.

Up to now he had always managed to turn away from girls whenever he found they were exciting him. He would then go back to his magazines, a new edition of which he received in a plain envelope once a fortnight. These were full of colour photographs of girls in various states of nakedness in engaging positions and they provided him with his kicks. The beauty of it was that the photographs didn't find him out and couldn't laugh at him as he knew a real girl would. But now he found the photographs stopped doing anything for him; it was the flesh and blood Beth Roberts that turned him on and this evening things were coming to a head.

Once again they were waiting for the supper to cook. Beth was strangely on edge. It seemed she was on the verge of saying something terrific but couldn't quite find the words to do so. Meanwhile, she sat opposite him, her legs crossed. He could see the underside of her thigh almost to the top and, as she re-crossed her legs, he could catch a glimpse of the red triangle that was the centre of her pants. He knew she knew he had his eyes riveted on her, but he couldn't help it and she obviously didn't mind. She could have slanted her legs at an angle to him or she could have worn a longer skirt. She was leading him on and he couldn't resist being led on. Nor could he avoid developing an embarrassingly apparent erection.

His predicament evoked in Beth a strong feeling of compassion. She didn't know about the magazines, but she realised he was plagued by inhibitions. She saw how she had excited him and she saw too how sexually disabled he was. She knew his vulnerability had been exposed by her attractions and, while that very vulnerability made him curiously more attractive to her, it made him utterly miserable and pathetically stunted. Her wish to draw him out of the disgusting work of the Security Department and start a new life began to merge with her desire to release him sexually.

She sat down beside him and stroked the back of his head and neck.

'I'm making a fool of myself,' he muttered as he tried to conceal his erection behind his hand.

131

'Nothing of the kind,' she whispered, 'you're just a bit strung up.'

'It's not just that,' he said. 'I'm a bit odd you know.'

'Not to me, you're not,' she tried to reassure him. 'Just relax a bit. I think you're great.'

Tentatively he put his hands on her shoulders and pressed his cheek against hers. This was a relief for it removed eye contact and, seemingly, the need to say anything. In this apparent security, he remained silent and motionless for some time while she continued to stroke his neck.

'I'd love you to feel me a little bit,' she ventured.

She took his hand, pushed it up under her T-shirt and pressed it against her breasts. She wore no bra and he could feel her nipples hard against his palm. He said nothing but he began to breathe faster and faster as he experienced for the first time the actual feel of a real girl.

'This must be very uncomfortable,' she said, just brushing his fly with the back of her hand. 'Wouldn't it be better to let it out?'

He said nothing and only opened and closed his hand on her breast, establishing an inevitable rhythm as he did so.

She lowered his zip and got him out. Only a few strokes were needed to bring him to his climax and he fell back limp and fulfilled as he had never been fulfilled before.

She tidied him up.

'My God,' she said, 'the chicken'll be burnt.'

And so it proved to be. The bird that emerged from the oven was much reduced in size, very dry and extremely tough. But he didn't really notice. His mind was on quite a different plane.

'Anyway,' said Beth, 'it goes to show that the way to a man's heart is not necessarily through his stomach.'

'I've been thinking,' he said. 'Perhaps you're right and we ought to chuck it. Let's get out before we get caught.'

He was thinking of being with Beth somewhere where the threat of being unmasked and shot would be removed. Perhaps she would become a missionary or something of that sort and he would find something useful to do to help her.

'I suppose you might become a missionary,' he said.

'Not on your life,' she replied. 'That's not my line at all.'

'But you told me you believed in Christ and that He would always be with us.'

'Certainly I did, but that doesn't mean I want to be a missionary. For me, it's quite enough to be a follower. I have no qualifications to be a teacher.'

'But surely you want others to be brought round to believing as you do.'

'Not particularly. It's up to them. The message of the Gospels is there for anyone to read who wants to. I don't see it as my role to try to force people to read things they don't want to.'

'But you wanted me to come round to your way of thinking, to believe what you believe.'

'Yes, I did and I do, but that's quite different.'

'Why, and what's so different about it?'

She paused and seemed to be grappling with the question.

'Let's give up on the chicken,' she said. 'The truth of the matter is it's inedible.'

'Is it?' he absently asked. 'Well if you say it's inedible, I'll stop eating it.'

'I've got some home-made ice cream,' she announced. 'At least that won't be tough.'

She dished up some of it.

'It's different,' she said, 'because you and I are in the

133

same boat. We've committed very much the same sort of sins. We ought to share the same sort of repentance and my instinct is that we can help each other to bring that about. Anyway, I didn't come to that conclusion through reading the Gospels or listening to sermons. I came to it quite independently.'

Suddenly her whole countenance changed. Her cheeks coloured up, her eyes shone like headlights and her nostrils distended.

'I've got to tell you,' she almost shrieked. 'I came to the top of the stairs and there was a blinding flash like a massive short circuit. I lost my footing and tumbled down the whole flight and landed in a heap at the bottom – just there,' she said, pointing to the spot. 'I thought I had broken my neck. I thought I was dead and it was then that I heard a voice. It said, "Why do you work for evil people? Why do you do evil in the service of evil? Turn away from it and search for the good you can do. Remember I am always with you." I picked myself up. I wasn't even hurt, but no one was there. Yet I had heard the voice and the wish welled up in me to obey it.'

'Christ,' he thought, 'she's flipped her lid.'

'You think I've gone round the bend,' she said, 'and in a way I suppose you're right. I have turned away from my past and now I'm searching for the good I can do. It's not a choice; there's no alternative.'

She sat down. All the agitation and shrillness that had taken her over departed and he saw a radiance in her that he had not noticed before.

'So what do we have to do?' he asked.

'Well,' she said, 'we can't just get out. That would not be an answer to the call. We've got to try to make good the harm we've done. We must work for the overthrow of this Belling government and the restoration of true values in our leadership.'

'You mean the restoration of the monarchy,' he said.

'Well, perhaps, but not necessarily so. What we must seek to restore is the rule of law, orderly government that respects the right of individuals to hold and express their own views and, abroad, a proper appreciation of the rights and aspirations of other nations. Bringing back the King might be a way of achieving that, but it may not be the only way.'

'Restoration of the monarchy would give the whole idea a focus,' he suggested. 'A lot of woolly ideas about freedom and law and all that won't mean much to ordinary people. Offer them the King and they'll recognise something that means a better society than we've got now.'

'So you've been thinking about it,' she said.

'Not really,' he told her, 'but it must be pretty obvious by now that all that stuff about reform, modernisation and that crap that Reynolds gave out has landed the people with a lot of policemen breathing down their necks with guns in their hands.'

'Which makes it a bit surprising that you've been working so efficiently for the Belling government,' she put in.

'I suppose it does,' he conceded.

'Sorry,' she said, 'I shouldn't have said that. I'm just as guilty as you.'

'No need to apologise,' he observed. 'As you say, what we need to do is decide how we're going to put it right, or try to put it right.'

'So we're together on this,' she said.

'I don't know about the religious bit,' he warned her. 'If God is all powerful and merciful, why has he allowed things to come to this pass? For that matter, why do we have earthquakes, floods and famines?'

'I can't answer that,' she said. 'I don't think anyone can. There's a bit in St Paul about us seeing things only through a dark glass. I think it means that, in relation to

135

God, we understand about as much as a tadpole in a pond understands the nature of human life in a big city. But what we can understand is that Christ is compassionate and that He has spoken to me and what's more we can speak to Him.'

'And ask Him not to allow another earthquake,' he posited.

'No,' she insisted, 'that would not be much better than the proverbial small boy asking God to put a coin into his money box. I think all we can do is to pray for the strength to help people who are caught up in earthquakes.'

'Which begs the question doesn't it?' he said.

'Yes,' she agreed, 'but it's one thing to beg a question and quite another to answer it. It's probably best to stick to the bits we can understand.'

'Hm,' he muttered. 'I'm not sure I understand any of it.'

'Don't push it too hard,' she told him. 'Just relax and be patient. You may find things are not as difficult as you think.'

He reflected that this was very much the same as the advice she had given when, a couple of hours ago, they had begun to kiss and touch.

'OK,' he accepted. 'So we're going to stay in our posts and use our positions to undermine Belling, protect the King and play our part in bringing about his restoration or, at least, a restoration of civilised government.'

'Precisely,' she said. 'It may not be much and we can only play a small part in it, but it's something we can do, and do it we must.'

Chapter 16

Nick and Laura arrived in Funchal in the early afternoon. They went through passport control, reclaimed their luggage and were waved through customs. The traditional Portugese friendly courtesy was delightfully apparent. They took the shuttle into town and established themselves in their hotel. From there they walked to the Atlantan Consulate where they filled in application forms for visas to enable them to travel to Atlanta City. Under 'Nationality', they filled in 'South African'. Under 'Profession', they put 'Travel Agents'. Under 'Purpose of Visit', they entered 'To inspect hotels, leisure facilities and scenic amenities in Atlanta with a view to introducing organised package holidays for South African tourists'. They handed in their forms and then had a long wait before being called into an office for an interview.

'I see you have flown from Kesa,' the official said. 'What was your business there?'

'We started from Capetown and stopped over in Kesa for a couple of days just to get an idea of tourist facilities there,' Nick told him.

'And what impression did you form? The man asked.

'Nothing doing,' Nick said. 'Troops everywhere. The country seems to be on a war footing. It's no place for tourists at present.'

'Just as a matter of interest, did you get any impression of the general mood in Kesa?'

'Yes, people seemed very confident about the future. We got the impression they think they can defeat any foreign invasion just as they did the Sudkan one. But of course that's just the impression we got. We didn't speak to that many people.'

'No, of course not,' the man said, 'but that's very interesting. Now, as to your business in my country, what sort of numbers of South African tourists do you think might come under your scheme?'

'Initially it would be a matter of hundreds but, as the message gets around, we think that will grow to thousands.'

'Thousands? What makes you think South Africans would be so interested in coming to Atlanta?'

'Three reasons,' Nick said. 'One, your government has put out statements saying that it wishes to encourage tourism. Two, the currency exchange rate is very favourable to the rand. Three, tourist-wise, Atlanta is off the beaten track. Visiting it would have a novelty value for South Africans.'

The man then raised the question of what particular things in the country they would want to see. Nick said they would be looking at hotels in Atlanta City and other main towns and the historic buildings they contained. They would also want to travel to the north where the afforestation and general scenery would be of interest. Other things would occur to them once they got the feel of the country. The man seemed to see no difficulty about these ideas but he did warn them that military installations and such-like would be off bounds.

'At the moment,' he said, 'we are having to take certain military precautions to protect ourselves from the threat posed by the alliance between the former Crown Prince and the Treskan army.'

'We quite understand that,' Nick replied. 'But we don't expect these precautions would have any adverse effect upon the enjoyment of tourists.'

'That's right,' the man said. 'I don't think they would.'

'The fact that you have a strong and orderly government is a great advantage from our point of view,' Nick said. 'It means that tourists would feel safe and that's a most important point.'

'Quite so,' the man agreed. 'I don't see any difficulties in connection with your visit.'

He opened their passports and picked up a stamp. Nick and Laura exchanged quick glances expressing their relief at having jumped the first hurdle so easily. But then, with the stamp in mid-air, the man paused.

'I wonder why you didn't apply for your visas at our Consulate in Capetown,' he said. 'You would then have known that your journey would not be in vain. As it is, you might have run into difficulties here and wasted your air fare as far as Funchal. Wasn't that a bit of a risk? Why didn't you apply in Capetown?'

A chill ran down Nick's spine. They had not thought of that and he had no answer to hand. What other things had they perhaps not thought of? Was this man luring them towards putting their heads into a noose?

Laura jumped in.

'Yes,' she said, 'that does look silly but we didn't know till the last minute that we would be able to make the journey and, when we finally decided to go, there simply wasn't time to visit the Consulate in Capetown.'

'I see,' said the man, 'and how did that come about?'

'As you know,' Laura explained in the calmest of terms, 'our head office is in East London and that's where we live. When we booked our flight we had planned to go down to Capetown a couple of days beforehand, but at that point my mother was taken seriously ill, or at least we thought she was seriously ill, and we decided we ought to stay on in East London to see what happened. We only found out on the morning of our flight that what she had got was nothing worse than diverticulitis, I

139

think that's what it's called, and not, as we had first been told, acute appendicitis. So we dashed off to Collondale and caught the local flight to Capetown. That got us to the international airport just in time to catch the flight to Kesa. South Africans don't need visas for Treskania and we didn't think there would be any difficulty in getting one for Atlanta in Funchal because your government had publicised its wish to encourage tourism.'

'I suppose it was rather silly,' Nick added, 'but at the time it seemed the right thing to do.'

'And how is your mother now?' the man asked.

Laura saw the trap at once. She knew the lines between East London and Kesa were down and she suspected the man also knew that.

'I don't know,' she said. 'I tried to call from Kesa, but I couldn't get through. But I'm not too bothered. We wouldn't have started had not her doctor told us there was absolutely no need for us to worry.'

'I should have thought you could have used the J Net,' the man persisted.

'They don't have J Net in Kesa,' Laura told him.

Thump, thump. The man's stamp hit the passports in rapid succession.

'I hope you'll have a pleasant visit and bring us lots of tourists,' he concluded.

Nick and Laura had a rather uneasy dinner in their hotel. They had jumped the first hurdle but not as easily as they had at first thought. The man at the Consulate had undoubtedly been suspicious of them and, although he had stamped their visas, there was no knowing what he had said about them to Atlanta City.

'It may be,' Laura said, 'that he wasn't particularly suspicious of us. Perhaps his job is to be suspicious of everything.'

140

'Let's hope so anyway,' Nick remarked.

'We'd best just assume so,' Laura said. 'We haven't got that much of an alternative.'

Arriving in Atlanta City was a curious experience for Nick and Laura. Here was the town they knew so well but which now they must appear not to know at all. And, oh, how it was changed. The streets were seething with Belling's Police, and soldiers and airmen were everywhere. Even in the lobby of the Hotel Luxe, where they had reservations, two or three policemen were always to be seen walking up and down keeping an eye on the proceedings. That Atlanta was now a police state was horribly evident and it was not good for the nerves of the new arrivals. It required strong resolution on their part to avoid giving any impression of being under suspicion and to remember always not to know the way.

There was a note for them at Reception addressed to 'Mr and Mrs van Ploeg of South African Travel-Wide'. It was from Dr Hemway of the Atlantan Commission for Historic Buildings. He sought an interview as he was anxious to bring to the attention of Mr and Mrs van Ploeg the richness of Atlanta's architectural heritage and its potential as a tourist attraction. This was a surprise. Nick and Laura had expected a message from the Secretary of the Atlantan Yacht Club and there had been nothing in their pre-mission briefing about the Historic Buildings Commission. They decided their best course would be to receive Dr Hemway as though his visit was really concerned with tourism. All the same, they wondered how he had come to know of their arrival. The most likely source was the Consulate in Funchal, in which case, Dr Hemway might be a trap or alternatively a genuine tourism-touter. There was also the chance he might be their initial mission contact, who was taking instructions from the Language School. So, in an apparently relaxed frame of mind, but actually in one of high alertness, they duly received Dr Hemway.

Whatever his real purpose might be, there could be little doubt that Dr Hemway was a genuine expert on Atlanta's historic buildings. He proved to be a lean, white haired man of about sixty. He was dressed in a tweed coat and rather baggy grey flannel trousers. He tended to peer, rather than look out, from his silver-rimmed glasses and he carried a large canvas bag, from which, without much pause for preliminaries, he extracted a series of guide books, post cards and leaflets describing and illustrating the castles, palaces and stately homes of Atlanta. He spoke in rapid staccato tones of the buildings, displaying as he did so an astonishing grasp of architectural and social history. Even the policemen in the lobby were attracted and for some time they participated in the entertainment. Nick and Laura attended closely to all that was said and Laura took copious notes. The table at which they sat gradually disappeared under the piles of literature that Dr Hemway was so anxious to display.

'Perhaps we could find a larger table somewhere,' he at last conceded.

'We have a good big one in our room,' Laura told him.

Dr Hemway appeared to be not a very practical man. He got into rather a muddle collecting up his literature and it took one of the policemen to retrieve a booklet that had escaped onto the floor under the table. At last he and the two travel agents moved off to the lift and went up to the latter's room on the second floor. As they entered it, Dr Hemway put his finger to his mouth indicating that no one was to say anything. He then drew what looked like a small magnifying glass from his pocket and walked round the room and the adjoining bathroom.

'You're not under suspicion,' he said.

'Meaning?' Nick asked.

'My microphone detector picked nothing up,' he explained. 'If you were under suspicion, the room would have been bugged.'

'I don't understand,' Nick said. 'Why should the authorities want to bug travel agents?'

'They might *if the weather was very severe and the clouds were low*,' Dr Hemway replied.

'*If the weather was very severe the clouds would not be low*,' Nick countered.

The exact introductory passwords had been exchanged. They all shook hands; Nick and Laura had jumped their second hurdle.

'The fact that you are not under suspicion, at any rate yet, is the good news,' Dr Hemway said. 'The bad news is that things here have not been going too well. Commander Rankin believes he may be being watched and he thinks it much too risky to see you. That's why I'm taking his part. If he's right, suspicion will fall on his son and that would be a bad setback for us. Air Captain Rankin, as you know, has command of a squadron of Swifts and is a key man in the most ambitious part of our plans.'

The other piece of Dr Hemway's bad news was that the Restoration organisation in the Language School had had to be dispersed.

'We have evidence,' he explained, 'that Major Silk has rumbled it. We are surprised he has taken no action but we think he may be waiting to see who contacts it. He may reckon that more flies than he already knows about will get caught in its web. The loss of the Language School is a serious blow to us because our organisation is now much more diffuse in location and accordingly less efficient in action.'

'This is all very disappointing,' Nick said.

'Well it is,' Dr Hemway agreed, 'but all is not lost. Very much the contrary,' he continued. 'We've broken into the

Security Department and, so long as Captain Fenton can keep himself in Major Silk's good books, we can even hope to manipulate it to serve our purposes.'

He explained to his increasingly astonished audience how Beth Roberts had approached them and said that she and her superior, Captain Fenton, wanted to come over to the Restoration movement. They were both thoroughly disenchanted with the Belling regime and now wished to do everything in their power to atone for their part in supporting it. At first, it had seemed to Dr Hemway and his friends that this might be an elaborate trap but, though they could not be absolutely sure about it, they now reckoned that, on balance, it seemed to be a genuine offer and they had decided to take the risk of accepting it. So far, the indications were that their judgement had been correct. Through Fenton and Roberts, they had received a lot of valuable intelligence, including that concerning the Language School. They were now hoping for some positive results. Fenton and Roberts, indeed, had undertaken to try to restore Silk's confidence in Commander Rankin. This was of paramount importance because, if Commander Rankin could be put into the clear, Air Captain Rankin would be too.

'So what it boils down to,' Dr Hemway said, 'is that we are putting our faith in the genuineness of the Roberts/Fenton offer and we think your next contact should be with them. We hope they will advise on how you might best approach Air Captain Rankin. Of course you will understand that, if we have misjudged Roberts and Fenton, we will all be well and truly scuppered.'

'We understand that,' Laura replied. 'The question is, how do we set about meeting Fenton and Roberts?'

'That's something I'll fix with them,' Dr Hemway explained. 'I thought it right to make no arrangements till I knew you understood the risk and were willing to take it. Now that's settled, all you need to do is to await messages and then to look for the correct introductory code words which, of course, will depend on the date and time of the approach to you.'

'OK,' Nick assured him.

'The great thing,' Dr Hemway concluded, 'is that you've got into the country without arousing any suspicions. That's an essential start and it's not the easiest thing to achieve in Belling's Atlanta.'

'Rather an attractive old bloke,' Laura said. 'I liked him, but he must be a much tougher nut than he looks.'

'Let's hope we are too,' Nick commented. 'This isn't going to be exactly a milk run.'

The large luxurious double bed looked very inviting and Nick thought they might test it out – for therapeutic reasons he explained – but Laura felt later would do and that they should unpack first. Alas, they had not got very far with this preliminary when there was a thunderous knocking on their door and the shout of 'Open up. Police.'

Two disagreeable looking policemen strode into the room, both with their hands on the butts of their revolvers.

'You're under arrest,' one of them proclaimed. 'We've been watching you. We know who you are and your little game is over.'

'There's a mistake,' Nick protested. 'Who do you think we are?'

'We don't think. We know,' the nasty man said.

'Anyone can make a mistake,' Nick suggested in a conciliatory tone, 'but it might look a bit silly if you don't check and look a bit before you leap.'

'We don't need any of your lip,' the policeman countered, 'and you'd best not try anything on with us.'

He grabbed Nick's arm and the other man did likewise to Laura.

145

'You can talk to our Chief at the Police Headquarters about looking and leaping, but I can tell you he'll have something to talk to you about as well.'

Before anything more was said, Nick and Laura found themselves in a police car being driven away from the Hotel Luxe in the company of two very objectionable men. Neither of them dared to say anything to each other, but each knew what the other was thinking and both knew they were thinking the same things.

It must have been Dr Hemway who had betrayed them and Dr Hemway knew the introductory code words so Dr Hemway must have deeply penetrated the Restoration organisation. If this was not the end of the road for Nick and Laura, it looked exceedingly like it.

Chapter 17

Beth and Ed, as she had taken to calling Captain Fenton, were making good progress. For one so badly damaged and retarded, he was taking to sex rather more comfortably than Beth had expected. She had successfully guided him to copulation and he was now able to repeat the process spontaneously and without embarrassment. He felt as though a huge weight of apprehension had been lifted away and, as each act of union with Beth was accomplished, his self-assurance increased. He had always known he was exceptionally able; he now began to experience a new sense of convictions and also to find the courage of them. He had become unreservedly committed to the overthrow of the Belling regime and, though he had not been able fully to swallow Beth's religious motivation, he had recognised in her a reliable arbiter of the difference between right and wrong. For that reason, he thought there must be something in her belief in Christ. Indeed, he hoped that in the fullness of time he might be able to share it.

Meanwhile, to all appearances, Captain Fenton and A4B continued to be Belling zealots actively seeking intelligence about the enemy in general and the Restoration organisation in particular. Captain Fenton's regular reports to Major Silk, however, bore little relationship to the actual facts that came to his notice. Nor was his proposal that A4B should be infiltrated into the Swift squadrons badly received. He suggested to Major Silk that, as the Swift squadrons were a vital element in the Leader's war plans, it would

147

be desirable to keep a sharp eye on the morale of the officers. Major Silk thought the idea important enough to mention to the Leader, whereupon Mr Belling sent for Captain Fenton and asked him to explain matters.

Captain Fenton said he had been getting important information about the Swift squadrons from Commander Rankin, the father of one of the Swift commanders.

'But I had understood Commander Rankin was an unreliable, possibly a disloyal, character,' the Leader said.

'No sir,' Captain Fenton boldly retorted, 'that was due to a complete misunderstanding. Commander Rankin did express some rather rash opinions about the cutting of the carrier programme and that did cause us to watch him with particular care. What we found was a former naval officer with some pretty conventional naval opinions. But we also found a public servant totally dedicated to the support of the Leader, the prosecution of the war against Treskania and the permanent exclusion of the King. In some ways, he might seem to be rather a silly man, but as to his loyalty there is no doubt whatsoever.'

'And you said he had given you important information about the Swift squadrons,' the Leader interjected.

'Yes sir, his son commands one of the squadrons and that's the means by which we hear these things.'

'And what do you hear?'

'We hear, sir, that some of the pilots are a bit shaky in their commitment to the cause.'

'Shaky are they? Well find them and get them put in front of firing squads.'

'That's what they may deserve, sir, but I submit that such a course would not suit our best interests. It would have a damaging effect on the morale of the Swift force as a whole and, at this particular stage, that's the last thing we want.'

'But we can't have shaky pilots flying our Swifts and that's flat.'

'No sir, of course not. Certainly they must be removed from the Swift squadrons, but I think the best way to do it would be to say their flying skills have not reached the requisite standard. They could then be posted away to suitable backwaters. Controversy would be avoided and no harm would be done to the morale of the sound pilots.'

'Ingenious,' Major Silk commented. 'But how serious is this? How many pilots are at issue? How much would the Swift squadrons be weakened by their removal?'

'Quite so,' Captain Fenton resumed. 'I can't be sure on that at present. Commander Rankin's information, useful as it is, is inevitably a bit patchy. I would like to put in one of our agents so that we can get a picture that's reliable and complete.'

'Who have you in mind?' Major Silk asked.

'I was thinking of A4B,' Captain Fenton told him. 'She came well through the awful debacle of the King's flight from Cardiff. She was the only one of our people who did and, if the others had done even half as well, we'd have bagged the King without a doubt. But you may prefer someone else,' he added, knowing he was taking a risk, but feeling it was essential to sustain credability.

'I think she'd do as well as anyone I can think of,' Major Silk assented.

Things were going well for Major Silk. He was now the second most powerful man in Atlanta and, with the State Secretary firmly in his pocket and Dr Offenbeck apparently falling into line, he could see the means by which, when the moment came, he could step up to the summit. But there was one disquieting consideration. Something had got into Captain Fenton.

Captain Fenton had been an invaluable tool in Major Silk's hands. He had shown himself to be exceptionally gifted at the complex work that fell to the lot of the Department of Security Services and much of the success achieved, for which Major Silk got the credit, was due to Fenton's skill and perseverance. And he had the sovereign advantage of natural subservience. Indeed, he seemed to have no independence of thought or, where the big picture was concerned, judgement. He was, in short, a born underdog, an asset that exactly suited Major Silk. In addition, Fenton had given up a hostage by talking to the Language School and thus providing Major Silk with a ready means of eliminating him should that ever be necessary.

That was the opinion of Captain Fenton that Major Silk had formed but now he no longer adhered to it. Whatever had got into Fenton had transformed him. Suddenly, in place of his former subservience and diffidence, he exuded an air of confidence and authority, an impression that was particularly apparent when he addressed the Leader on the subject of Commander Rankin and the Swift squadrons. Major Silk now regretted the confidences that he had extended to Fenton, especially those concerning his own ultimate ambitions. Those confidences were given to an underdog from whom he believed he had nothing to fear but, now that the underdog had developed a bark of his own, such thoughts assumed a different complexion and Major Silk began to be half afraid of Captain Fenton. True, he could use the Language School gaffe to expose Fenton but, if he did, Fenton might raise counter charges and who could say which side Belling would take, especially as Fenton was nowadays increasingly in the Leader's good books. Worst of all, Fenton knew about Major Silk's little arrangement with the State Secretary. For the time being at least, Major Silk decided, he would give Fenton his head in running the Department of Security Services and go along with the advice he gave the Leader.

Captain Fenton was well pleased with the result of his interview with the Leader. His way was now clear to launch Beth into the Swift squadrons. Her official reports would enable him to remove pilots from the front line and so reduce the effectiveness of the squadrons. He hoped too that she would open avenues of negotiation leading to the fulfilment of the most ambitious part of the immediate Restoration plan, namely, the transfer of some Swift aircraft from Belling's control to that of the Crown Prince and General Attagu. He wondered if the King's agents had yet arrived in Atlanta. The successful achievement of the Swift plan would require their participation since a departure of the aircraft from Atlanta must necessarily be followed by an arrival in Treskania. Very careful coordination of the Restoration movement in Atlanta and that in Treskania would be needed.

Captain Fenton was turning these matters over in his mind when he received a report that the police had picked up two Brazilian spies known as Samuel and Kate Pearson. The Department of Security Services had known about this couple for some weeks. There was reason to believe they were photographing military installations and the converted cruise liners for the information of Brazilian Intelligence which, of course, also meant Treskanian Intelligence.

This was troublesome news for Captain Fenton. He had been hoping the two agents would slip through the hands of the police and get safely back to Brazil with their intelligence. Now he would have to face up to the awkward fact that his official efforts to apprehend them had been successful and it was difficult to see how they could be rescued from the firing squad. Such a fate for this couple would bolster his reputation with Major Silk and the Leader, just as repeated failures to catch such people would undermine his credibility and perhaps lead to his loyalty being questioned. It did, however, seem perfectly awful that people in sympathy with his own aims should be sacrificed to the firing squads so that he could maintain his position as a borer from within. He wondered what view of this moral dilemma Beth would take. Meanwhile, he had to form his own view because the two Brazilians were about to be brought before him.

'When you've brought them in,' he told the policeman, 'wait in the outer office and, if I need any help, I'll ring this bell.'

The two handcuffed spies were then marched in. Captain Fenton was rather surprised. They seemed to be Anglo-Saxon, or perhaps Nordic in appearance – not what he expected of Brazilians. But of course the great country of Brazil embraced citizens of numerous different ethnic origins, so perhaps the appearance of these two was not as surprising as he had at first thought. Their appearance, however, served only to emphasise the starkly tragic fact that Captain Fenton would have to have these strikingly attractive people shot unless some unexpected bolt from the blue turned up to reverse the course that events were now taking.

'I see from this report,' he began, 'that you deny being Samuel and Kate Pearson. This is foolish and can only serve to worsen your prospects. If you would now come to your senses and make a full confession you might be able to give us information about Brazilian spy tactics. Sometimes information of that sort can be set off in mitigation of your own offence.'

'I'm sorry,' Nick said, 'it's no use because we are not Samuel and Kate Pearson and we know nothing of Brazilian espionage.'

'By carrying on like this you're simply putting your heads on the chopping block. If you will now tell me how you were briefed, what methods you employed to get the information wanted and how much of it you have succeeded in getting, I might be able to reduce the sentence upon you. I might be able to save your lives. While you've still got your heads on your shoulders, use them. Think. See sense.'

Nick shook his head. 'I'm sorry,' he repeated, 'but I can't help you. The fact is we are not Samuel and Kate Pearson and there's no way we can become them.'

'You do realise the penalty for spying is the firing squad,' Captain Fenton told them.

'I suppose we do,' Nick answered, 'but we are not Samuel and Kate Pearson, we are not Brazilians and we are not spies. We are Mr and Mrs van Ploeg. We are travel agents representing Travel-Wide of East London, South Africa and we've come to Atlanta to prospect for possible South African tourist packages – not that your police are exactly encouraging us at the moment.'

Van Ploeg. East London. Travel-Wide. South African tourism. A series of recognitions rushed through Captain Fenton's mind. Could it be that this couple really were not Brazilian and were in fact the agents so eagerly awaited from Kesa? He glanced at his watch. The first group of introductory code words was still valid.

'*If the weather was very severe and the clouds were low,* what would you do?' he asked.

This indicated to Nick and Laura that Atlantan Intelligence had rumbled their mission. Dr Hemway had known the introductory code and so did this intelligence official. If they gave the correct response, they would be confirming that they were Treskan agents. As, however, they already had given it to Dr Hemway, there might not be much point in withholding it from this man. Even so, Nick instinctively felt they ought not to give the response. It was their duty to try every means of protecting the King's interests and those of the Treskan government. He

153

began to think that the best course might be to admit to being Pearson. He glanced at Laura. Her slight shake of the head suggested to him that she too thought they ought to withhold the response. Whatever they did, they were likely to be shot and, if they had to be shot, it might be more helpful to the cause and confusing to Belling's if they were shot as Brazilians.

'I don't know,' he said. 'I don't quite understand you.'

'You're making things very difficult,' Captain Fenton said. 'You say you're not the Pearsons. Are you sure your are the van Ploegs?'

As he put this question, he leant forward and fixed Nick in an intense eye to eye contact. As he relinquished it, he noticed a hotel key tab sticking out of Nick's breast pocket with the number 287 stamped on it.

'What's that key?' he demanded.

'It's our hotel room at the Luxe,' Nick told him.

'That's rather interesting,' Captain Fenton said.

He opened a file and turned over some documents and then stopped at one and studied it carefully.

'Very interesting indeed,' he added. 'That would be room 87 on the second floor.'

'That's correct,' Nick confirmed.

Captain Fenton pressed the bell button on his desk and the nasty policeman came in.

'Sir,' he said.

'My information is that Samuel and Kate Pearson booked into room 787 at the Hotel Luxe.'

'Yes sir, that is so,' the man agreed.

'In which room did you arrest them?'

'Room 787 sir.'

'So how come they have the key to room 287?'

'I can't say sir. We arrested them in room 787.'

'What do you say to that?' Captain Fenton asked, turning to Nick.

154

'Your officer is wrong, 'Nick answered. 'We were in room 287 and that's where we were arrested.'

'This is ridiculous,' Captain Fenton said. 'There's five floors difference between the two rooms. Surely you can't have muddled up the second and seventh floors,' he put to the policeman.

'I suppose you might,' Nick suggested. 'The lift has an express and a local button. If you press express, the first stop is the sixth floor. If you press local, it goes up floor by floor. And the girl's recorded voice is very unclear. I think it perfectly possible you could hear "second" when actually she said "seventh," especially if you thought you were on local, because the seventh floor would be the second stop.'

The policeman's face had turned very red, which was enough to tell Captain Fenton that Nick's explanation must be correct. Feeling confident that the Pearsons would have taken a rapid departure after the police raid, he told the policeman to get along to the Luxe and see who he could find in room 787. The wretched man needed no second invitation to withdraw.

'Mr van Ploeg and Mrs van Ploeg, we owe you a profound apology,' Captain Fenton said.' 'You have been the victims of a stupid error. I will do whatever I can to repair the damage. I can but hope you will meet no further difficulties during your stay in my country. I'll give you this card,' he continued, 'just in case there is any trouble. If you show it, you will be brought to me and I will be able and willing to help you.'

Nick and Laura looked at the card. It bore the inscription 'Captain Edward Fenton. Department of Security. Republic of Atlanta'. They recognised that this was the man whom their own intelligence believed had come over to the Restoration movement. If only he had given his name earlier. What a lot of trouble would have been saved and there would have been no need to suspect Dr Hemway of betraying them.

'We'd have got on much better if we'd known who you were sooner,' Laura said.

'By the way,' she continued, '*If the weather was very severe the clouds would not be low.*'

Chapter 18

Beth Roberts, alias A4B, now had the additional title of Mrs Greene. As such, she had been invited by the Chief of the Air Staff to take up the post of Domestic Inspector of the Swift squadrons. The Chief of the Air Staff had been instructed to make this appointment by Major Silk. He had not been asked to give an opinion as to the necessity or otherwise of such an appointment; he had merely been told to make it. Mrs Greene was directed to look into all the domestic arrangements on the Swift squadrons ranging from the quality of the food, the comfort of the mess and so on, to leisure facilities and any other factors that might affect the morale of the officers. She was then to render a report to the Chief of the Air Staff. The same Mrs Greene, in her capacity as A4B, was directed by Major Silk to detect signs of disaffection in the squadrons and to list the names of officers whose loyalty might be in doubt.

Mrs Greene's appointment proved to be very popular with the Swift pilots. They were flattered to find the authorities were concerned about their comfort and welfare and Mrs Greene's appearance and personality convinced them that she was just the person to represent their interests; they found her easy to talk to, easy on the eye and easy to like. In double quick time, she was on personal terms with all the eighteen first line pilots and the pool of nine others who formed the second line that would act as replacements for the first and the nucleus of the reinforcements who would eventually fly the Second Wing, as and when the next batch of Swifts came off the production line.

These twenty-seven young officers formed the pivot upon which the Belling war plan turned. The three first line squadrons were now judged to be almost war-ready, having been rehearsed respectively in the tactics of protecting troop ships, attacking enemy naval vessels and destroying ground formations of the enemy armies. These functions were not interchangeable between the squadrons, since the skills called for in each case were different, as also were the armaments and other equipment carried in the aircraft. Similarly, the nine pilots of the pool were divided into three groups to shadow the three operational squadrons. It was therefore apparent, as A4B had been led to expect and was now able to confirm from her own observations, that the removal of even a few pilots was capable of disrupting the efficacy of the whole force.

The troopship protection patrols would have to be flown continuously for a minimum of sixty hours, or ten hours each for the six aircraft available. That would be strenuous, but anything more per aircraft would be impossible. The naval attack squadron would face a different kind of problem. A single search aircraft would detect enemy naval movements. If they were concentrated, then an attack could be launched. Probably three aircraft would be sufficient. But if the enemy dispersed, more attacks would be needed and the squadron might soon find itself severely stretched. The ground attack squadron in some ways had a simpler challenge. Assuming the Crown Prince's force could be detected in a concentrated form, it would be a relatively easy target for the Swifts, but the calculation was that it would take six of them to ensure success. In other words, five might not be enough. Added to these considerations was the expectation that serviceability of the operational aircraft would not be 100 per cent and might well be as low as 80 per cent.

Though only aware of some of these facts and probabilities, Mrs Greene did not have to be Einstein to see that the disruption of the Swift war effort could be achieved by quite small tinkerings. But these tinkerings would have to be extremely subtle. They would have to be believable to Major Silk and Mr Belling. They would have to be substantial enough to disable the Swift war capacity and yet not so large as to cause Major Silk and Mr Belling to panic.

The answer, Mrs Greene appreciated, lay in a fine balance between quantity and timing, but she, of course, was not expected to take the precise decisions on her own; they were to be produced by a council of war consisting of herself, Captain Fenton, Nick Hardy and Laura Blick. This was a much less authoritative body than had originally been planned. The hope had been that it would be possible to communicate through the Language School with the Crown Prince and General Attagu. But now, unfortunately, the under cover system of radio communications which had been provided by the Language School was no longer available, the Language School having been dispersed and a new Restoration HQ not yet established. Indeed, the arrangement of a meeting between the four operative people was not a simple matter. Captain Fenton knew that he might well be being watched by Major Silk and, though Nick and Laura seemed to be in the clear for the time being, they too might still be under some degree of suspicion and Beth Roberts, with her two feet in three different camps, was not the sort of proposition an insurance company would want to take on.

Nothing daunted, the four conspirators duly made their ways independently and at different times to a small country inn eight miles out of town and here they set to work, being interrupted only from time to time by the appearance of the landlord to take orders or to gossip.

Nick explained that the original plan for the Swifts had been to man each aircraft with three pilots, two on duty and one resting, so that flights of very long duration could be undertaken. This would have given the squadrons strength in depth. For ordinary operations the squadrons would have had the luxury of being over-manned and it would therefore have been far harder to disrupt them. This plan, however, had been abandoned while he was still working in the Air Force Ministry and the single pilot policy had been substituted as a result of a shortage of pilots with Swift capacity. In the days of the Realist government before the revolution, the Air Force had played second fiddle to the Navy and the bulk of the best air cadets in those times had been trained for carrier-borne aircraft. The defection of two of the carriers to the Crown Prince and the sinking of the third had, at a stroke, deprived Atlanta of the greater part of its best pilots. This accounted for the acute shortage of Swift-worthy pilots that the Atlantan Air Force was now encountering. Beth's fear that their plans of disruption might be brought to nothing by the recruitment of fresh pilots was, he suggested, not realistic.

In the light of this encouraging news, Beth proceeded to explain the detail of what she had discovered. As to Swift defection, she said they could rely absolutely on Air Captain Rankin. He was definitely prepared to fly his Swift to Treskania and submit to the command of the Crown Prince. Moreover, he would carry with him a full set of spare parts together with all necessary manuals. Loading up in such a manner would cause no suspicion as his squadron had been instructed to practise the transfer of its base from Atlanta to Estragala. No other pilot had yet been sounded on the question of defection and she had specifically told Air Captain Rankin not to attempt anything on that front. One false move would turn Major Silk's spotlight onto him and the Restoration movement would lose its one certain Swift recruit. She had high hopes of Air Captain Marshall with whom she had got onto particularly friendly terms and she now sought authority to target him. She believed that if he turned her down and reported her, she might be able to extricate herself by claiming to Major Silk that she had been testing Marshall's loyalty to Belling and, she added, she believed she might be able to rely on the support of Captain Fenton in such a subterfuge. This remark relaxed the tension and caused a laugh around the table.

Beth was duly authorised to try out Air Captain Marshall. If he could be persuaded to defect, two of the three front line Swift squadrons would be significantly weakened. There would also be the sovereign advantage that at least two Swifts, flown by their highly expert squadron commanders, would pass to the control of the Crown Prince and General Attagu.

Such a development would significantly change the balance of air power and it would not just be a question of two aircraft coming over to the Restoration side; it would also be that of reducing and possibly even disrupting the radar effectiveness of the remaining Atlantan force. Beth had discovered from Air Captain Rankin that the radar carried in the Swifts included a capacity to lock radar transmissions from exterior sources. Though no one other than Air Captain Rankin had thought of using this facility against other Swift aircraft, there was no doubt that it could be so used.

There remained, however, a serious problem for the Restoration war council. Nick pointed out that if the Swift squadrons were seen by Belling and Silk to have been seriously weakened they might postpone the war and await the arrival from the production lines of further reinforcements and the training of pilots to fly them. He believed it probable that fifty or sixty Swifts would become available in the next three to four months. That, of course, would not solve the problem of pilot shortage but he feared it might be possible to dredge up twenty or thirty from one source or another within eight or nine months. He therefore suggested that Beth's initial reports should be to the effect that the Swift squadrons were 100 per cent reliable so that Belling's and Silk's confidence in them could be maintained until the eleventh hour and fifty-ninth minute. Once that had been achieved, and Belling had got himself irrevocably committed to war, she would have to attempt to convince him that several of the pilots must, after all, be posted out on grounds of unreliability before operations began. This would be a tricky business to put it mildly but, if it could be brought off, the rewards might well be incalculable.

Everyone was impressed by Beth's reaction to this challenge. She told the meeting she was confident she would succeed.

'I know,' she said, 'I am doing the right thing and I believe I will be helped to achieve it.'

Nick and Laura found this rather startling, a fact that must have shown on their faces because Captain Fenton found it necessary to offer them some reassurance.

'She's not mad,' he said. 'She's perfectly rational and highly professional. She believes profoundly that Christ has called her to abandon her old life and adopt this new cause. She doesn't think Christ will tell her how to carry out her mission. She simply thinks she has been told to undertake it. Is that right?' he asked turning to Beth.

'Yes, more or less,' she said.

* * *

162

The Leader's evening conference was attended as usual by Major Silk and Dr Offenbeck, but on this particular occasion the three Chiefs of Staff had been ordered to join it. Two important developments had occurred which led Mr Belling to require their advice. One of these developments was favourable; the other was not, but the two in combination seemed to suggest that the date of launching the attack on Treskania should be brought forward.

The favourable development arose from A4B's report on morale in the Swift squadrons. The key figures, she observed, were the Wing Commander, Air Major Eggleton, and the three Squadron Commanders, Air Captains Marshall, Wilding and Rankin. These, she reported, were entirely reliable. None were politically minded but all were keen to serve the regime without reservation and impatient to demonstrate their airmanship in the forthcoming war against Treskania. The other pilots were much in awe of their commanders and it was highly unlikely that any of them would show the slightest hesitation in carrying out whatever orders they were given. In short, the Swift squadrons were reliable, although it would be necessary to keep a watchful eye on the juniors to ensure they were all staying solidly in line. A4B undertook to produce further reports on this aspect as events demanded. She therefore submitted that Mrs Greene should retain her appointment as Domestic Inspector of the Swift Squadrons for the time being. Mr Belling found this report very satisfactory and took the opportunity of congratulating the Chief of the Air Staff on the high morale of the Swift men.

The unfavourable development was an intelligence report showing Brazil to be mobilising her naval strength. Warships were being taken out of mothballs and brought into the operational fleet. Naval reservists were being called up and the Brazilian government was generally adopting an increasingly hostile attitude to Atlanta. It seemed that Brazil was planning to intervene in a war between Atlanta and Treskania, no doubt with the primary aim of protecting her oil concessions in the latter country. In view of Atlanta's naval inferiority, a junction of the Brazilian fleet with the Crown Prince's would pose a serious threat. Mr Belling's conclusion was that both developments, the favourable and the unfavourable ones, argued in favour of the same decision: an early war.

He thumped the table and declared, 'We must strike before the Brazilians are ready. The Swift squadrons are sound and our victory will be assured.'

All the same, he asked for the advice of the Chiefs of Staff. The Chief of the Air Staff went first. He said he was confident that the Air Force could fulfil its role in the forthcoming war. This, he reminded the meeting, was, first, to provide air protection for the troopships, second, to neutralise the enemy fleet either by sinking any vessels that threatened the troopships or by compelling them to stand off and, third, to strike directly at the Crown Prince's Regiment should it launch an attack on the invasion force while it was in an unbalanced and below strength situation. Though the resources available to achieve these aims were adequate, they were only just so and there was very little behind the front line in the way of reserves.

'We are having to pay the price for the years of neglect of our air strength which we incurred under the old Realist government,' he said. 'The Swift is a war-winner, but I would be much happier if we had more of them and the pilots to fly them.'

'But you're satisfied that our existing strength is adequate,' the Leader put in.

'Yes, sir, I am satisfied,' the Chief of the Air Staff assured him, 'but I would be more satisfied if we had greater reserves behind the front line.'

164

The Leader's brow contracted into a frown.

'But,' the Air Chief hastily added, 'I fully appreciate that we cannot wait for the ideal situation. We have to strike before the Brazilians arrive on the scene.'

The Chief of the Army Staff followed. He said his situation would be critical until he had established his whole invasion force in Estragala and formed it up as a battle group. He was therefore dependent on the Air Force to secure the safe passage of the troopships and to disrupt the Crown Prince's Regiment in the initial stage. After that he saw no difficulty in securing the chief centres of administration and the oil fields. The Treskanian army was little more than a guerrilla force and, while it might achieve a degree of harassment, it would be incapable of standing up to his well equipped and heavily armoured troops. The Crown Prince's Regiment was a different matter. It was a balanced force of very significant potential and he believed it had been expanded by the recruitment of Treskans to a strength of up to twenty thousand men. It was absolutely crucial, he stressed, that the Crown Prince's force should be prevented from striking while the invasion force was still building up.

The Chief of the Naval Staff, who had a great deal more political know-how than his recently disgraced predecessor, said his six submarines would be deployed along the likely routes of the enemy fleet and that his minelayers would operate in appropriate areas. Beyond that, he had to admit he could do little and that reliance must be placed on the Air Force to neutralise the enemy's naval superiority. That, he thought, might be questionable if time was allowed to enable the Brazilians to intervene.

'So that's the professional advice,' the Leader announced. 'It confirms my conviction that we must undertake this necessary war at the earliest possible date. When would that be?' he enquired, addressing himself to the Chief of the Army Staff.

'We can load and despatch the first sailing of the troopships within the next eighteen days,' he was told.

'Right,' said the Leader, 'It's war eighteen days from today.'

Neither Major Silk nor Dr Offenbeck had uttered a word and now they sat gazing at each other trying to fathom what the other might be thinking. In that moment of suspense, an Air ADC entered the room and handed a note to the Chief of the Air Staff.

'Who's that man?' the Leader demanded. 'I don't remember inviting him to attend.'

'I'm afraid it's grave news sir,' the Air Chief said. 'One of our Swifts has crashed on returning from a training flight. Air Captain Rankin and two of his subordinate pilots have been killed and the aircraft is a write-off.'

Chapter 19

The news of the Swift crash struck Mr Belling as though a bolt from the blue. For several moments he sat motionless and speechless staring vacantly ahead of him. Not a sound was uttered by any of the others attending the conference. Then there was a tap on the door and the ADC returned to the scene bearing a second note.

'It's worse than we were first told,' the Chief of the Air Staff announced. 'Four, not two, of Air Captain Rankin's subordinate pilots were on board and all have been killed.'

'Five front line Swift pilots in one aircraft,' the Leader growled. 'It's sheer lunatic madness. Am I surrounded by idiots? Who's responsible for this?'

'I'm afraid the answer to that, sir,' the Air Chief stuttered out, 'is the late Air Captain Rankin. He was the commander of the squadron; his would have been the decision.'

'Bunkum,' the Leader shouted. 'Don't these commanders have directives from above – from yourself for example?' he added glaring at the Air Chief.

'Yes sir, they do, but we have to sort out our priorities. The imminence of war and the need to get the Swift squadrons ready for action in time inevitably led to concentrated training. Air Captain Rankin will have been aiming to achieve on one flight what otherwise would have taken four. It's the time factor sir, that's what it is.'

Dr Offenbeck whispered to Major Silk, 'He's putting the blame on the Leader himself. That's not going to be good for his health.'

'What are you two whispering about?' the Leader demanded. 'If you've got something to say, say it out aloud.'

Major Silk thought to himself that this was the first indiscretion he had ever known Dr Offenbeck to make, probably the first he had ever made.

'I was just saying we ought to get straight down to the question of how this will affect the timing of our attack on Treskania,' Dr Offenbeck claimed.

'All right, well, how will it?' the Leader put to the Air Chief.

'Rankin's squadron was earmarked for the strike against the Crown Prince's Regiment,' the Air Chief said. 'We have to face the fact that, though that squadron still has five operational aircraft, it now has only one operationally trained pilot. The choice is therefore between deleting the planned attack on the King's Royal Regiment or deferring the date of the commencement of hostilities.'

'That's not a choice,' the Army Chief interrupted. 'We can't land our first wave in Estragala without the assurance that the King's Royal Regiment can be neutralised at least until we have the second wave ashore.'

It seemed to Dr Offenbeck that the situation was so grave that the Service Chiefs were facing the facts and, most unusually, telling the truth, but this time he kept the reflection to himself.

The crippling effect of the Swift crash on the Belling war plan was fully reflected in that it had on the Restoration Movement's schemes for countering it. To Beth Roberts, who had lined up Air Captain Rankin and, through him, most of the pilots in his Swift squadron on the Restoration side, it was a shattering blow. And to her it was not just a question of the lost opportunity of bringing off the coup that would have transformed the balance of air power as between Belling and General Attagu; it was also the loss of John Rankin, a man she had come to know and admire.

'I'm really not sure I can face this,' she confessed between sobs to her coadjutor and lover.

But Captain Fenton, for the first time in their relationship, now proved to be made of the sterner stuff.

'We've no alternative,' he said. 'We've got to go on. We must get our war council together and decide how to do it.'

The confidence and authority with which he spoke amazed Beth. She had not realised he had it in him. She saw in a flash that she had really changed this man for the better. By cutting away the bond of his inhibitions she had released the real character that must have lain beneath. Her own courage began to revive.

'How best d'you think we can do that?' she asked, suddenly confident that he would know the answer.

'Well,' he said, 'summoning the council will be risky. I think I'm still OK with Major Silk, but of course I'm not sure. He may be watching me – and listening. All the same, the emergency justifies the risk. We must summon the council and this time we'll get a better attendance than last time.'

He explained that he had been in touch with Mr Edgar Hindley. Hindley had been a key figure in the disbanded Language School organisation and he was now building up a new communications network. This, Captain Fenton believed, would enable him to convene a much more convincing war council than the last one.

'I'll get onto Hindley and tell him to call a meeting,' he went on. 'He'll know best whom to summon. Of course Hindley's on Belling's wanted list but we'll have to hope his lines of communication are adequately secure.'

'If they're not,' Beth said, 'he'll hand the names of all our principals to Belling and Silk on a plate.'

'True, that's true,' Edward Fenton conceded, 'but, as I've said, the emergency justifies the risk.'

And so it did. Within forty-eight hours of the Swift crash, the Restoration's informal war council, so far as could be judged quite unknown to the Belling camp, assembled in a stock room above the retail premises of Harker and Hall, the well known tailor and clothier, whose business was in Pepper Street, less than a mile from the Residence, where Belling and Silk were simultaneously conferring.

Mr Hindley opened the proceedings by giving out a detailed brief upon the order and the manner in which those attending were to disperse after the meeting. He stressed the importance of following these instructions meticulously so that each member would melt back into the *va et vien* of Pepper Street without drawing attention to themselves individually or collectively. He then expressed to Commander Rankin the profound condolences of the meeting upon the death of his son, Air Captain John Rankin. Commander Rankin made a silent and dignified gesture of acknowledgement. The council then got down to business.

Beth Roberts reported that John Rankin had been training his subordinate pilots in the art of landing a Swift without the height, speed and direction aids that were available at their main base. On the official flight plan, he had entered this as 'training for the eventuality of a landing in Estragala'. Actually, she explained, he was preparing them for a landing in Treskania, where the runways were also primitive. Evidently, on the third approach when one of the trainee pilots was presumably flying the aircraft, the nose had dipped and the recovery manoeuvre had caused it to stall with fatal results for all on board.

The deep silence which followed this pronouncement

was eventually broken by the clear, collected and precise voice of Commander Rankin. Making no allusion to his own personal loss, he said, 'So what this amounts to is that we have lost the opportunity of flying five Swifts from their side to ours and they have lost the opportunity of launching their attack on Treskania at this time. You can bet your bottom Crown they won't attack till they have the means of neutralising the Crown Prince's Regiment while they secure their base in Estragala. They may retrain one of the other Swift squadrons or they may build up a replacement one, but in either case it will take time and time is not on their side. Time will allow Miss Roberts to recruit Air Captain Marshall for the role my son certainly intended to play; time will allow our Brazilian friends to mobilise their fleet and use their sea power to reinforce our own. I look upon the tragedy that has occurred as a set-back, not as a disaster.'

A murmur of appreciation and admiration rippled across the room.

Nick was as much moved by Commander Rankin's words as was anyone else in the room, but he at once sensed the danger of leaning too much in the direction of sentiment and too little towards that of hard reasoning. Was the Commander placing too much trust in surface sea power? Was he hoping too much of the Brazilians? Might not their contribution be blunted by Puerez's sea power? Had he sufficiently estimated the dangers of trying to recruit Air Captain Marshall? Suppose the young man refused to come over to the Restoration Movement. He might then expose Beth Roberts and, if so, probably Captain Fenton himself. Two of the keystones in the Restoration arch might then be pulled out and the whole structure reduced to rubble. Had Commander Rankin reckoned such possibilities?

But it was easier to think these things than so say them.

To say them might seem to discount the courageous constancy of Commander Rankin. Moreover, by comparison with Commander Rankin and all the others in the room, he and Laura were mere visitors, mere outsiders. They did not live permanently in the shadow of the Belling regime; the others did.

Laura, who was of one mind with Nick about so much, sensed his thoughts and his hesitation.

'You may think it odd, even impertinent, that I should comment on what Commander Rankin has said,' she ventured, 'but I do think we must guard against over-optimism. If the Brazilian fleet moved into our waters and if Air Captain Marshall and perhaps several members of his squadron came over to us, the cards would be very much in our hands, especially if Puerez didn't move. But suppose Marshall doesn't come over. Suppose he denounces Beth. What then would become of the Brazilian fleet even it did come to our assistance? I know excessive pessimism could destroy our cause, but so could excessive optimism.'

Commander Rankin leapt to his feet. Laura's heart missed a beat. She had been offensive and presumptuous. She had made a fool of herself and now she would get her come-uppance. Nick would be infuriated by her gaffe.

'I think there is a lot in what Miss Blick has said,' he announced. 'I did not take sufficient notice of the other side of the coin in what I said. My training as a naval officer has led me always to believe in success, in victory. For an officer in command of a ship at sea, that may be a sound precept, but perhaps in strategic planning not always so. If you weigh my words, weigh Miss Blick's too.'

There was a second murmur of approval followed by a flurry of *sotto voce* exchanges between the members. Laura caught Nick's eye and saw that he approved and admired. She felt intensely relieved. Then Mr Hindley spoke. He had not been elected chairman, nothing had been said about that, but by the right of natural authority he was acting, and was accepted, as such.

'Perhaps if Dr Wesker gave us his thoughts, it might help us to organise ours,' he said.

Laura was thrilled. She had never previously seen Dr Wesker in the flesh though he had been familiar to her in the pre-revolutionary days on the TV screen and ever since she had been a student at university she had admired him beyond measure. And what's more, he was Nick's Uncle. Indeed, when she first met Nick, she was engrossed in one of his most famous books. A copy of it had been lying on the table in the canteen where she and Nick had exchanged their first words over a canteen lunch. In those halcyon days, Wesker had been generally regarded as Atlanta's most distinguished living historian and this was a view eagerly shared by Laura, but where she perhaps differed from what was probably the majority of those forming this general opinion, was that she had actually read the books he had written. She grabbed her shorthand notebook and took down verbatim what the great man said.

'People sometimes seem to think that I can predict the future rather as clairvoyants are supposed to do. Well, that's rubbish of course. In that sense, I can no more predict the future than any of you may be able to do. If, however, we examine the past searchingly we may get some clues as to the course of future developments. This is not a matter of prediction; it is a matter of trying to understand how history unfolds, of finding the trends. If we do our work carefully and dispassionately, we may be able to detect a trend and, if we succeed in that, it may not be unreasonable to expect that, by projecting our understanding of its past development, we may be able to arrive at an informed estimate of its future. I stress that I say only that it may not be unreasonable to expect this. As, however, we are now all

anxious to know, or to guess, what Mr Belling will do in the next weeks and months and what will be the consequences of his decisions, I suggest it is worth attempting a forward estimate on the principle I have enunciated.

So where are we at the moment? In Mr Belling we have a dictator who intends to launch an aggressive war. He needs to do this not of course for the idealistic motives he proclaims in public, the protection of the Hurnots and so on, and not fundamentally even for the materialistic aim he has in mind, the control of the Treskan oil fields. Basically he needs to do it to preserve his power base. Mr Reynolds's humiliating failure to defeat the Treskans wounded the nation's pride and gave Mr Belling his chance. He was propelled into power by Reynolds's failure and the belief that he would reverse it. Only a successful war can keep him in power. Without it, he will fall. Without it, the people will begin to notice the symptoms of economic collapse that are all around us and they will begin to resent the objectionable behaviour of Belling's Police. A successful war will turn the people's attention away from such things and focus it on the great hero who redeemed the nation. Here we may see reflections of Gustavus Adolphus, Charles XII, Louis XIV and, more strikingly, Napoleon, Hitler and Mussolini.

I think we would be foolish to expect exact reflections to appear. The best we can hope for are some general ones.'

Nick scribbled a note for Laura.

'Who was Charles XII?' it asked.

Answer, 'King of Sweden, you dolt. Possibly shot by one of his own men.'

'Does that mean someone's going to shoot Belling?'

'You dolt. That's an exact reflection.'

Laura was annoyed. She had missed some of Dr Wesker's words.

'. . . XIV had hereditary bases whereas Napoleon, Hitler and Mussolini did not. Like Mr Belling, they had to look to other *entitlements and that, one suspects, made them all the more dangerous. Louis XIV could afford to disengage. Napoleon could not. I could develop this train of thought...'*

Mr Hindley glanced at his watch.

'Perhaps...' he said.

'Quite so,' Dr Wesker responded. 'Perhaps we'd better come to some conclusions,' he added.

'First and foremost, we can understand that Mr Belling must make war. He cannot be deterred or even, for any length of time, postponed. Even in unfavourable circumstances, he will see the risk of making war as less than that of not doing so. This makes him a very dangerous customer, both to his own side and to ours. Our challenge is to find the means of bringing about his destruction, or facilitating his self-destruction, at the minimum cost to ourselves and our allies. Napoleon's self destruction came about at huge cost; that of Hitler at an astronomically greater cost. Mussolini was disposed of at somewhat less expense.

So now, if we turn to Mussolini's career, we will...'

At this point Dr Wesker's discourse was rudely interrupted by the arrival of four Belling's policemen. They thrust open the door at the rear of the stock room, sending it crashing against the wall, and advanced up the room, hands on the butts of their revolvers.

'What's going on here?' one of them shouted, glaring at Dr Wesker, who took a pace or two backwards. 'Is this a political meeting?'

'Certainly not,' Mr Hindley informed them in the calmest of calm tones. 'This is a meeting of the City of Atlanta Historical Society.'

'And what's that about?' bawled the policeman. 'Don't you get funny with me; I could get very funny with you and don't you forget it.'

'Of course not,' Mr Hindley assured the gatecrashers, 'but I don't think you can object to loyal followers of the

Leader listening to a lecture explaining the historical reasons for which he will inevitably redeem the nation and how we can contribute through steadfast loyalty.'

'Well,' said the policeman, turning to his colleagues, 'I suppose that sounds all right.'

'I don't know about redeeming,' one of them commented. 'That means paying for something and I don't think the Leader has to pay for things.'

This did not please the first policeman.

'Don't you get philosophical,' he warned his colleague, and, turning back to Mr Hindley, 'anyway we don't like meetings and you'd better close this one down.'

'As you wish,' Mr Hindley accepted, 'but perhaps you'll allow me to wind the proceedings up. I think Mr Belling would expect that.'

'Well make it snappy,' he was told.

'Right, ladies and gentlemen,' Mr Hindley announced, 'we must now conclude our meeting, but before you go your separate ways I'm sure you will agree that we have all learned to understand the historical forces that make Mr Belling's triumph inevitable and the destruction of his opponents inescapable. What you have to do, what each one of you has to do, is to work out for yourself the best contribution you can make to this glorious outcome. In view of what the police authorities say, we must not hold another meeting, but individually we can all work for the cause to the best of our abilities.'

'That's it then,' the policeman said. 'The meeting's over. Just a minute, what's this?' he added, picking up Laura's shorthand pad. 'Looks like some sort of a code.'

'Oh no,' Laura said. 'It's only ordinary shorthand. You're welcome to read it if you like.'

'I can't read this stuff,' the man said. 'It's all lines and loops. What does it say?'

'It's what the lecturer told us about Mr Belling's triumph.

I'm sure one of your colleagues could read it,' she risked. 'It's only ordinary shorthand.'

The pad was received by each man with a shake of the head.

'Better take it to Headquarters,' the redeeming man suggested.

'I'd quite like to have it back,' Laura said, 'because I was going to type up a copy and send it to the Leader. I heard him say in a speech the other day that he liked receiving letters of support from the public. I think he'd like this one; it's very supportive.'

The policeman scratched his chin and wiped the sweat off his forehead with the back of his hand.

'OK, miss, you can have your pad back.'

With feelings of considerable relief, the Historical Society of Atlanta City debouched into Pepper Street and, quickly merging with the crowds, it ceased to exist as an identifiable group.

'Just to think of it,' Mr Hindley reflected to himself, 'four Belling's Police had the whole spearhead of the Restoration Movement at their mercy in one room and they let the prize slip through their fingers. They didn't even recognise Henry Wesker. Lucky they didn't know shorthand. I must see to it that that girl is told not to put things down on paper.'

Chapter 20

It was now five days into Mr Belling's eighteen-day countdown to war. Thirteen days to go. Five days since the Swift crash. No fresh orders from Mr Belling and nothing collectively decided by the Restoration Movement. History seemed to stand still, but the first wave of the invasion force embarking on the troopships preparing to sail for Estragala did not pause to reflect on this curious state of affairs. They had no conception of it. Simultaneously, General Attagu's soldiers were dispersing to their guerrilla positions and the Crown Prince's Regiment was standing ready for a sudden thrust against the Atlantan invaders in Estragala. Neither General Attagu nor the Crown Prince knew whether or not their forces would be open to attack from Atlantan Swift aircraft and they could not estimate the chances of their surface fleet engaging the enemy troop transports before they reached Estragala. What they did know was that powerful elements of the Brazilian fleet were putting to sea prior to heading towards the waters that divided Atlanta from the African coast and that Puerez was apparently doing no more than waiting to see which way the wind would blow. What they did not know was whether or not their naval forces would be attacked by Swift aircraft. The proverbial fog of war was thicker than usual.

* * *

Mr Belling's Chiefs of Staff were becoming seriously disturbed. It was obvious to them that the date for the commencement of the war would have to be postponed. Unless the means of neutralising the Crown Prince's Regiment existed, the expedition would be exposed to destruction piecemeal as it arrived in Estragala. Time must be allowed to repair the loss that had been suffered by the Swift crash. Even before it, the margin between a sound strategic plan and a madcap adventure had been perilously slim. The three Chiefs were fully agreed about this. What troubled them was how this could be put to the Leader and which of them should put it. Day after day and now hour after hour they had waited in the hope that the Leader would see the writing on the wall and come to his senses. But now, with only thirteen days to go, he had not done so. No countermanding order had come; no order of any kind had come. Seven thousand troops had already been embarked. Another eighteen thousand would follow in the next few days and then the first wave would be ready to go.

'We'll have to say something,' the Chief of the Army Staff said.

'Perhaps we should send in a joint memorandum,' the Chief of Naval Staff suggested.

'That would be most unwise,' the Chief of the Air Staff ruled. 'It would be dangerous to put anything like that on the record. We'll have to speak to him, see if we can talk him round. As the issue is mainly the Crown Prince's Regiment, it's primarily an Army matter, so surely the Army Chief should do the talking. Of course he'd have the full backing of both of us, but he ought to take the lead.'

'Oh no, I don't see it quite like that,' the Army Chief said. 'The problem has arisen because of the Swift crash and that's undoubtedly an Air Force matter. I think the Air Chief would carry the weight. He'd have much the best chance of convincing the Leader.'

'I can see the force of that,' the Air Chief accepted,

'but the crash has not improved the Leader's opinion of the Air Force or of me. If I was to be the spokesman, that would be of its nature an irritant. Our best chance is for me to keep a low profile.'

'Possibly that is so,' the Naval Chief said, 'but I don't think I could be of much service. The Navy's hardly in the war plan.'

The three top officers sat gloomily surveying each other, weighed down, it seemed, by the weight of their gold braid.

Major Silk and Dr Offenbeck were no less anxious than the Chiefs of Staff, but for different reasons. Both would prefer to jump overboard rather than stay on a sinking ship, that is, if the ship was sinking and, so far as Silk was concerned, unless there was still time to save it after the Leader had been pushed overboard. Offenbeck thought differently. He knew he was not a front man. His aim was to be the power behind the throne. Who sat on the throne was not a matter of prime importance to him; what mattered to him was the influence he might exert upon whoever it was. He had watched Silk for some time and he didn't fancy him as his Chief. He preferred Belling, but he now couldn't fail to see that Belling seemed to be heading for disaster. Even so, he would reserve judgement and await events. Leaving a decision to the very last minute would give him the best chance of getting it right.

'Don't you think it's rather surprising that the Leader hasn't issued a new directive?' Major Silk put to Dr Offenbeck in one of their frequent consultations.

'Well, I don't know about that,' Offenbeck countered, 'but I suppose he may do.'

'Do what?' Silk asked.

'Do what you thought he should,' Offenbeck told him.

'I didn't say what he ought to do,' Silk hastily asserted. 'I just asked if it was not surprising that he hadn't.'

Offenbeck decided it might be imprudent to say 'hadn't what?' so he confined himself to 'precisely.'

'I hope he's not ill,' Silk tried out.

'I hope not,' Offenbeck responded.

Another very worried man was Air Major Eggleton. The Swift Wing he commanded had been deprived of virtually the whole of one of its squadrons. Was he now expected to perform with two squadrons what had been designed for three? No new instructions had come through and he was increasingly afraid that this was exactly what would be expected of him. It was as clear as daylight to him that the task was impossible. He had thought of asking the Base Commander for guidance but hesitated to do so. Everyone seemed to be on edge and he didn't think his position would be improved by asking questions. This seemed rather unfair because his subordinates were constantly asking him questions which he had to answer as best he could. Air Captain Marshall was being particularly tiresome. He kept asking if the air plan was going ahead or if the war would be postponed.

The only consolation Eggleton had was Mrs Greene's sympathetic understanding. She was such an awfully nice girl and so much concerned with the welfare of the Swift pilots. Everyone liked her and she was terrific for keeping up morale. Had it not been for Mr Greene, whoever he might be, Eggleton would have invited her to go dancing with him and to take a walk in the Park afterwards. Especially, she helped him to keep his temper with Marshall.

'He means no harm,' she told him. 'It's only natural he should be a bit worried. I suppose, if the truth were known, we all are a bit aren't we?'

Eggleton thought it was very understanding of her to have said that.

Whatever Major Silk might think or hope, Mr Belling certainly was not ill. In fact his mind had been in overdrive since the Swift crash. He had never doubted that the war must proceed on schedule. He didn't care to suffer the humiliation of having to shelve his plans simply because one aircraft had crashed. Nor did he think there would be profit in asking the Chiefs of Staff how to proceed. They were a feeble and basically defeatist lot. He would decide for himself what to do and now he had come to a conclusion.

In preparation for the meetings he was about to have, he had caused a large map of the South Atlantic to be pinned to an easel which stood in the centre of his office. It showed the east coast of South America and that of the west of Africa with Atlanta more or less in the centre. Treskania's northern frontier with Estragala was marked in red and that to the south with Sudka in green. Things were now ready for the interviews to begin. The State Secretary came bumbling into the office and started taking his seat at the desk in the corner which was reserved for his use. The Leader looked up.

'I don't need your attendance. There is no need to keep a record of these meetings,' he declared.

The State Secretary was surprised and mortified but he had the prudence to make no comment and he crept out of the room with his tail between his legs.

The first visitor was Colonel Kent, the officer in charge of troop embarkation.

'How many men are now embarked?' Mr Belling asked him.

'Well sir, I thought you might...'

'Don't think. Just answer the question.'

'Eight thousand four hundred at the last count, sir.'

'On how many ships?'

'On two sir. Five thousand one hundred on the first ship. That's now capacity and three thousand three hundred on the second ship. There's room there for another fifteen or sixteen hundred.'

'When will the second ship be fully loaded?'

'Later today sir.'

'And then we'll have ten thousand men ready to sail. Is that right?'

'Yes sir that's right, plus or minus a hundred.'

'Now these ten thousand men, I assume they're the spearhead troops.'

'Yes sir. They're the van of the rapid deployment group.'

'And they'll be sailing with full equipment, ammunition and so on.'

'Yes sir, they will. They have their fast armoured cars and troop carriers with them and of course their machine guns, rifles and so on, and their helicopter gunships, air recce component and their Engineer element.'

The Leader paused in thought for a minute or two.

'Right,' he went on. 'Now what about the second wave?'

'The third and fourth ships are due to start loading this evening. They're the follow-up troops and they should all be on board within three days.'

'That's another ten thousand men.'

'Yes sir, that's correct, give or take a hundred.'

'With full equipment?'

'Yes sir, with full equipment.'

'And then we come to the fifth ship. When will that start loading?'

'It'll come alongside as soon as the fourth ship casts off. That'll be three to four days from now.'

'And what troops will these be?'

'Three thousand of the second wave of the rapid deployment group, the medical corps, staff and miscellaneous rear troops.'

'So the whole of the first convoy of five ships with about twenty-five thousand men will be ready to go in not more than four days from now. You're sure of that.'

'Yes sir, I'm sure of that.'

'Good man,' said the Leader showing a trace of a smile. 'You're ahead of schedule by, let me see, by nine days.'

'Yes sir, we are. You had ordered us to embark at the greatest possible speed and we found we could do it faster than originally estimated. By bringing emergency gangways into operation we've been able to embark men in twenty columns. With two ships loading, that's forty men hitting the decks simultaneously every seven minutes. The rest of the time is taken up by equipment, supplies and so on.'

'I consider that most creditable,' the Leader said. 'What are your initials Colonel Kent?'

'G, sir.'

'Just G?'

'Yes sir, just G.'

'Very appropriate. G for good man,' said the Leader committing his first flippancy for many weeks.

He picked up a form and filled in at the top 'Colonel G. Kent'. He ran his eye down the following print which read 'is promoted to the rank of...' In the space following, he entered 'Brigadier with immediate effect'. He applied the Leader's stamp, which said, 'By special order of the Leader'.

'Here you are then,' he said, handing the document to the Colonel. 'You're promoted to Brigadier.'

'Thank you very much sir,' said the astonished officer, throwing the smartest salute he could muster.

He really was astonished because he knew he was fourteenth in seniority on the Army list of embarkation officers. He had only got this job because everything was being done at top speed and he happened to be on the spot at the right time. But whether Brigadier Kent was lucky or not, he was now thoroughly confirmed in his loyalty to the Leader.

The next man in was equally astonished. It had never

occurred to Air Major Eggleton that the Leader would summon him personally. He had seen Mr Belling when he took the salute at the passing out parade of the Air Academy and he had heard him exchange a few words with the cadet next to him in the rank, but he had never dreamed that the great man would receive him one-to-one.

'I'm very sorry about the loss of the Swift from your Wing,' the Leader began, 'but that's something we have to get over. I need some information from you about the operational capacities of the remaining force.'

'My God,' Eggleton thought to himself, 'I'm going to have to tell him we can't carry out a mission assigned to three squadrons with two. And that'll probably get me the chop.'

'Now of course your Wing can't be expected to carry out the threefold role allotted to it when we were counting on three squadrons. That's obvious. What I need to find out is what operations we can confidently undertake now.'

'The simplest solution, sir, would be to drop the ground attack plan. That was the role allotted to the squadron we've lost. But that may not be an option.'

'I don't want you to bother about options,' the Leader snapped. 'I want to hear from you about operational capacities. Let's suppose your primary role was defined as the attack upon naval vessels at sea and anything else was relegated. I mean that anything in addition to the destruction of naval units was seen as a bonus, not a necessity.'

'That would make things a lot more realistic sir,' Eggleton said.

'Let's take a look at this map,' the Leader suggested walking over to the easel.

'You can see roughly the routes our troop transports are bound to take and you'll understand we have to keep hostile naval forces away from those vicinities at the operative times.'

'Yes sir, I see that.'

'Now,' the Leader resumed, 'I don't reckon we can afford to supply close air support with the resources available. We must find other more economical ways of keeping enemy ships out of the way. My idea is that we should employ the tactics of concentrated attack on any threatening naval elements. If we can inflict sufficient damage, the enemy will either withdraw or he will disperse. In the first case, we will have achieved our object. In the second, our targets will be reduced in number because we need only search for and attack ships which threaten to come within range of our troopships. What d'you think of that?'

'That seems to be a very sound plan,' Eggleton said, not because he thought it was a sound plan, but because he thought it would be unwise to say it wasn't. 'With both squadrons devoted to attack, I'm sure we could achieve some spectacular sinkings. But of course at the moment there's a difficulty.'

'A difficulty,' the Leader said. 'What difficulty?'

'Our last recce, sir, showed the Royalist fleet cruising off the Portugese coast. Most of it, in fact, was within Portugese territorial waters and I understand that might raise a difficulty about attacking it. Our present instructions are not to embroil the Portugese.'

'Yes, that's quite right, at least for the time being, but I wasn't thinking of the Royalist fleet; I was thinking of the Brazilians.'

The Leader pointed to Bahia on the map.

'They're carrying out exercises off Bahia, working up their reserve ships and rehearsing them in manoeuvres with the main fleet. As soon as they think they're ready, they'll head east towards the routes of our troopships.

But I think we can defeat that. Suppose we launched a surprise attack with the entire strength of our Swift squadrons, could we not inflict crippling damage and, if we could, would not that send a signal to the Royalist fleet to keep away?'

'That's an audacious plan and, in my opinion, a practicable one,' Eggleton said. 'While those Brazilians are concentrated we could count on good results, especially from our attack squadron.'

'Yes,' said the Leader, 'and the effect on Royalist morale would be tremendous. But you seem to think only one of the two squadrons could be counted on to get the best results. Why should that be so?'

'The attack squadron has been training specifically on the destruction of naval vessels at sea, sir. The escort squadron, which was to have escorted the troopships, has been training basically as a mobile radar search station. Its job was to detect the approach to the danger zone of enemy ships. It would then call on the attack squadron to deal with them. The principal load of these escort aircraft would be fuel to give them the duration to fly very long patrols; the principal load of the attack aircraft would be anti-ship missiles. So you see, sir, the two squadrons are not entirely exchangeable. All the same, we could rearm the escort squadron and count on it to give a good account of itself in an attack role. I am only making the point that they would not be as efficient as the pilots who have more experience of attack tactics.'

The Leader nodded. He found young Egggleton impressive and constructive and he began even to like him.

'I take the point,' he said. 'And your immediate superior is the Base Commander. Is that right?'

'Yes sir, that's correct.'

'And the Base Commander reports to the Chief of the Air Staff.'

'Yes sir, he does.'

How very odd it was, Eggleton thought, that the Leader seemed to be working things out the wrong way round. Instead of working from the top down, he was working from the bottom up. But of course it wasn't Eggleton's place to say anything about that.

'If you now got orders to attack the Brazilian fleet as soon as possible, how soon would be possible?' the Leader posited.

'In the case of the attack squadron, sir, four hours; in that of the escort squadron, twelve hours. The aircraft would have to be reloaded.'

'You'll get a bit more notice than that,' the Leader said, 'but I want you to put preparations for the eventuality in hand straight away.'

'Sir, with the greatest respect, I have to say that I haven't the authority to do that.'

'Nonsense,' the Leader said. 'If I give you the authority, you've got the authority.'

'I'm sorry sir, but that simply wouldn't work. It would cause confusion and argument at a time when it would be just that sort of thing we'd need to avoid.'

This was very impressive stuff, the Leader thought. The man was not only clear headed; he also had courage. He couldn't imagine the Chief of the Air Staff or the Base Commander speaking his mind like this.

'I suppose you're right about that,' he said. 'I'll give the orders to the Chief of the Air Staff. Anyway, you now know what's in the pipeline. By the way Eggleton, you're not to fly on this mission yourself. I mean to keep you in hand.'

Eggleton thought the interview was over and that he was about to be dismissed.

'One more point,' the Leader said. 'Could the Pool aircraft, there are nine of them, I think, could they fly reconnaissance over Estragala?'

'Certainly they could sir. It would be very good training for them.'

This really did conclude an extraordinary meeting, the oddest and most unexpected thing that had ever happened to him, Eggleton thought. As he made his way out of the Residence, he reflected on a rather strange thing Bill Marshall had said to him. He had suggested the Leader might be losing his reason. Apart from being a dangerous thing to say, it was quite obviously wrong. But of course Marshall had not seen the Leader face to face as Eggleton now had, and very impressive he had proved to be. He would have to have a word with Marshall. There must be no unsteadiness at this juncture.

Chapter 21

The Leader's order that the two front line Swift squadrons should now be dedicated to the single purpose of attack on enemy naval forces at sea had now come through to Air Major Eggleton down the chain of command from the Chief of the Air Staff. After discussing matters with the Base Commander, Eggleton decided to amalgamate the two squadrons, but he was denied the opportunity of commanding the new formation himself by the Leader's insistence that he was not to fly on war operations. The question therefore arose as to which of the two squadron commanders, Marshall and Wilding, should be selected for this responsibility. The Base Commander thought Marshall should be chosen but Eggleton thought not. He preferred Wilding for the task.

Mashall was two years older than Wilding, he was the cleverer of the two and he had the more pronounced personality. Both had very high flying aptitude ratings, but Marshall's were the slightly higher of the two. The Base Commander was surprised by Eggletons's choice and thought it odd that no very clear reasons were given to support it. He considered it best, however, to accept the advice of the man with the immediate responsibility. So, Air Captain Wilding was given the command of the twelve operational Swifts now on standby for imminent war operations.

The reason for this was that Eggleton's confidence in Marshall had been compromised. The hint he had given that the Leader might be losing his reason was disturbing.

Nor was the impression improved when Eggleton had a word with him about his attitude. He had turned sulky and even muttered something about not being particularly keen to attack ships that were manned by fellow citizens. Eggleton wanted to keep him on board because he was an old friend from Academy days and, in any case, he could scarcely afford to part with a first rate operationally trained Swift pilot; they didn't grow on trees. He decided his best course would be to put the man in command of those Pool aircraft that were to fly the recce sorties over Estragala. That wouldn't raise any awkward questions about attacking fellow citizens and it might allow time to get him sorted out. But how should this sorting out be tackled?

It suddenly came to Eggleton that the obvious solution was Mrs Greene. She understood all about that sort of thing and was sure to be able to bring Marshall to his senses before matters got serious. So he explained the problem to Mrs Greene and, as he had expected, she was very sympathetic and willing to help.

'Bill Marshall's perfectly sound,' she had said. 'It's just that things are happening at such a pace. The poor chap's got a bit confused and he tends to feel that nobody understands him. All he really needs is a sympathetic ear. I'm sure I can help.'

'We can't have him making snide remarks about the Leader,' Eggleton explained to her, 'and he mustn't think of the Royalists as fellow citizens when in fact they're traitors.'

'No of course not,' Mrs Greene had agreed, 'but I'm sure he's sound at heart. It's just that he says silly things like that because he's personally unhappy and frustrated. I don't think they really mean anything serious. I think I can help him to get over it and he is a first class pilot is he not?'

'Certainly he is,' said Eggleton. 'That's why I want him sorted out.'

191

'Exactly,' Mrs Greene assented. 'You can rely on me.'

Eggleton felt very relieved and turned his attention back to getting the former escort aircraft rearmed with anti-ship missiles. He had been wise, he thought, not to have told the Base Commander anything of his doubts about Marshall. Had he done so, one of his best pilots might by now have been posted out of the Wing.

Though Captain Fenton had caused the meeting of the Restoration war council to be convened, neither he nor Beth Roberts had attended it. Mr Hindley had decided it would be a foolhardy risk for them to do so, especially as they were in a uniquely important position from the Restoration point of view. But, relying on Mr Hindley's improving system of secret intercommunication, it was now essential for the Restoration Movement to re-gather its momentum after the debacle of the meeting in Pepper Street. The first requirement was to bring Captain Fenton and Beth Roberts into the picture and to hear from them of any activities they might have been up to. Nick and Laura were assigned to this task because it was judged that they were less likely than most of the other members of the council to catch the eye of Belling's Police. The suggestion that they were travel agents who might bring some much needed foreign currency into Atlanta's coffers seemed to have convinced Belling's Police who were, no doubt, at least partly guided by Captain Fenton's favourable opinion of Mr and Mrs van Ploeg. Nick and Laura were glad that at last they had the opportunity of doing something useful. So far, their mission had achieved virtually nothing.

Mr and Mrs van Ploeg came quite openly into Captain Fenton's office. In the visitors' book under 'Purpose of call' they had entered, 'To consult Captain Fenton regarding access to historic buildings of potential tourist interest'. Nick explained that the war council meeting had achieved nothing of value. Henry Wesker's talk had been a mistake and largely a waste of time.

'We're not dealing with Hitler or Napoleon,' he said. 'We're dealing with Belling.' He reported that the question of tackling Air Captain Marshall had been raised, but nothing had been decided. Beth interrupted to say that this question had settled itself. She explained how she had been asked by Air Major Eggleton to talk Marshall out of his wobbly feelings about Belling and the war and how that had enabled her to discover that Marshall would be prepared to take Rankin's place and fly a Swift onto a Treskan base. What he now needed were the coordinates of the base selected, the call signs and the landing procedure.

'How do we proceed on that?' she asked.

Nick told her he had all that information and would pass it on to her for onward transmission to Marshall as soon as possible. He would also ensure that Mr Hindley would alert the authorities in Kesa via a line of communication that he had now established through Funchal.

Oddly enough these pieces of information had been exchanged in a matter of fact, even casual, way. The huge significance of what had happened was somehow too much for the four people who were considering it.

'Did you really say Marshall would definitely fly a Swift to Treskania?' Laura asked.

'Yes, I really did,' Beth told her, 'and I'm perfectly sure he means it.'

'So we've achieved our number one objective,' Laura said.

'Not quite,' Beth corrected her. 'These Swifts are very dangerous aircraft. I just pray we won't have a second disaster.'

'Have you any idea when this flight will be?' Nick asked.

'Within the next day or so,' Beth said.

She explained that Marshall had been put in charge of reconnaissance flights over Estragala and that these were about to be intensified. She thought he would simply peel off from one of these and put down in Treskania. He was waiting only to learn what were the coordinates and call signs he would have to use. And there was something further she had not yet told the meeting. Marshall's chief radar officer was going to fly on the sortie and was intending to take as much radar and radio equipment as possible with him.

'This gets better and better,' Nick said. 'And there's a valuable pointer as well. Presumably these reconnaissance flights over Estragala mean that the invasion's imminent.'

'I certainly think so,' Fenton said. 'There's another clue on top of that. Two of the troop transports have cast off from the quayside and are either on their way, or perhaps standing out to sea.'

'I'll make sure Mr Hindley hears all this,' Nick said, 'and he'll certainly convey it to Kesa at the very first opportunity. Thank goodness he's re-established his communications system. If he hadn't, I or Laura would have had to go back with the news personally and that would have been a pretty inefficient way of doing it.'

'If that's all,' Fenton said, 'we'd better break up, but let's have those coordinates a.s.a.p.'

'I'll go straight back to our hotel and telephone them to you immediately. You have my code I think,' Nick told him.

'I have indeed,' Fenton confirmed. 'Look forward to hearing from you.'

Major Silk had learned from the State Secretary, whom he was continuing to subsidise, that the Leader had held a series of meetings. His pensioner, however, was unable to report on them as he had been excluded from the room.

194

'Who did he see?' Silk asked.

'There was an Army officer. I didn't recognise him. He was quite junior,' the State Secretary replied. 'Then there was another officer. Quite a young man. Air Force, but I've not seen him before either.'

'Hm,' Silk muttered. 'Who else?'

'No one so far as I know, except that the Chief of the Army Staff came in and asked to see the Leader. I was told to tell him to come back some other time as the Leader was too busy to see him.'

'And that's all you know,' Silk grumbled.

'I'm afraid that's all I know,' the State Secretary admitted and then added, as though to mitigate the failure, 'about those particular meetings, I mean.'

Silk ordered his car and had himself driven to the Department of Security. From there, he summoned the Chief of the Army Staff to wait upon him.

'I understand you wanted to see the Leader and that unfortunately he was unable to spare the time,' Silk said to the General.

'Yes sir, but of course I understand the Leader is under heavy pressure of work for, um, the benefit of all of us.'

'Quite so, quite so, but perhaps you will now inform the First Deputy Leader what you wanted to discuss. I should think it must have been pretty urgent.'

'Well yes sir, pretty urgent. Or perhaps not exactly urgent, but important all the same. Yes, pretty important. And I was to speak with the authority of the Chief of the Air Staff as well.'

It immediately crossed Silk's mind that this might be the first sign of mutiny. It might be the very opportunity he was waiting for. After all, Belling was heading for disaster and if he was allowed to plunge the country into war without the proper military preparations and without the support of the armed forces, Silk himself might be harnessed to the catastrophe. Might this perhaps be the moment to dispose of Belling?

'Well, General, you'd better tell me what the matter is. As Deputy First Leader, I may be able to deal with it.'

'Well yes sir, thank you. Perhaps the matter's not as important as I thought, but I do think it is important all the same and so does the Chief of the Air Staff. It's just that Colonel Kent's been jumped up, I mean promoted, to Brigadier out of turn. That sort of thing makes a lot of bad blood and we think the same thing may happen to Air Major Eggleton. We are seriously disturbed about this.'

'I can't see that the promotion of two relatively junior officers can be a matter of all that much importance,' Major Silk said. 'Is that all you've really got to complain about?'

'Well yes sir, I mean actually no sir, because it's not just the actual promotions and Eggleton hasn't been promoted. But it's the procedure. Of course we're all one hundred percent behind the Leader. Our loyalty's unshakable, but we may get into an awkward position if promotions are made out of turn and without our sanction. And it's not just that; if questions of strategic and tactical importance are discussed with junior officers without our knowledge, difficulties may arise.'

'I think this is a bit of a storm in a teacup,' Major Silk said. 'I don't see much of a problem but, if you like, I could have a word with the Leader.'

'That's very good of you sir. We'd be most grateful and I'm sure that includes the Chief of the Naval Staff as well. I hope there's nothing impertinent about what I've said.'

'No, no, I'm sure the Leader will understand. In fact, if ever you do have anything to complain of, I mean really serious things, it might be helpful if you mentioned them to me. You see, I may be able to sort them, or I can explain them to the Leader. You must understand that he bears huge responsibilities and we must not burden him with anything except the biggest issues.'

'I quite understand sir,' the General said. 'I'll tell my colleagues and I'm sure they'll be as grateful as I am. There is just one other thing sir. We're getting near zero hour and we haven't got any instructions as to what action we are to take in the aftermath of losing virtually the whole of one of the Swift squadrons. There is the question of neutralising the Crown Prince's Regiment while we effect our landings and we think the decision about this can't be delayed much longer.'

'I'm sure you're right about that,' Major Silk said. 'I'll mention that to the Leader too.'

With further expressions of gratitude and loyalty, the Chief of the Army Staff withdrew and Major Silk returned to the Residence, where he was quite taken aback to find the Leader sitting in his office.

'I hear you've been having a talk with the Chief of the Army Staff,' Mr Belling said. 'What was that about?'

'Too childish really,' Major Silk promptly answered. 'He's bothered about Brigadier Kent's seniority and he'd even wanted to see you about it. I told him not to be an idiot and that he'd get the paperwork through on Kent in due course.'

'Anything else?' Belling enquired.

'No, nothing,' Silk affirmed. 'He's a bit of an old woman and all he wanted was the paperwork. I thought it best to humour him.'

197

Chapter 22

General Attagu and the Crown Prince had been meeting regularly to review developments. They had noted the intensified reconnaissance flights by Atlantan Swifts over Estragala. They had learned from Mr Hindley in Atlanta that two of Belling's troop transports had cast off from the quayside with full loads of troops and equipment and that two more were embarking more troops. They knew that one or possibly two Swift aircraft would shortly land on their longest runway near Bogotown and that these would then be at their disposal. They had heard that the Brazilian fleet would shortly set sail for the war zone to cooperate with the King's fleet at present standing by in Portugese waters. They recognised that the Atlantan attack was imminent, but they considered there was no need for them the revise their strategic plan, at any rate for the time being.

The first aim was to prevent the Atlantan troopships from reaching Estragala. If the King's fleet approached from the north and the Brazilian from the south, the hope was that the Atlantan air attack would be divided and, in each case, weakened, but whether it would be sufficiently weakened or not was a highly debatable issue. On balance, General Attagu and the Crown Prince followed the opinion of their naval advisers, which was much less optimistic than it had been earlier. They now believed that probably the Swift anti-ship potential would prevent any of their surface ships from engaging the troopships. They accepted that they must preserve their fleets in being with a view to the eventual blockade that would, they hoped, ultimately maroon the Atlantan invading force. So the expectation was that the Atlantan invasion force would reach Estragala. This would afford the Crown Prince the opportunity to strike the first wave while it was still off balance and before the second wave arrived.

Even assuming the Crown Prince's assault was effective, it seemed likely that sufficient of the invading force would succeed in regrouping and crossing the frontier into Treskania. It was deemed unlikely that it would then advance southwards towards Bogotown as this would involve crossing the Flatlands, where the ground was marshy and the roads primitive. The most likely axis of advance was eastwards, keeping to the north of the Treskan Mountains and Kesa City. Only then would it wheel to the south in the direction of the oil fields.

During this advance, General Attagu intended to subject the Atlantans to constant guerrilla attacks, a form of warfare in which his troops were particularly effective. After that, he and the Crown Prince would have to review the possibility of concentrating the Treskan forces and linking with the Crown Prince's Regiment to fight a set-piece battle.

Such was the plan of General Attagu and the Crown Prince. It had been approved by President Tamu and the King but the two heads of state had expressed some provisos. President Tamu had observed that the outbreak of hostilities, or even the imminent threat of them, would trigger a meeting of the Peace Council of the International Organisation and also of the African Moral Union. He did not wish to have to defend Treskania from a charge that it had made an unprovoked attack on Estragala. He ruled that the Crown Prince must not move into Estragala until it could be established that the movement was not unprovoked or, in other words, until there was incontrovertible evidence that Estragala was acting as a springboard for an Atlantan invasion of Treskania.

The King's proviso was somewhat less specific than President Tamu's. Nevertheless, he strongly emphasised his wish that the Atlantan troopships should not be sunk. He spoke of the need to fight the war, not only with the aim of winning it, but with that of winning the peace too. If the troopships were sunk, the loss of life would be appalling and would result in lasting bitterness and accusations of overkill. All the more would this be so if the sinkings were achieved by his own ships. After the war, when he hoped his people might be reunited, they would be divided and the chance of cordial relations between Atlanta and Treskania would be prejudiced. Were there not other ways in which the troopships might be fended off, the King had asked.

'We must respect the views of the King, we are allies,' President Tamu had said.

When General Attagu and the Crown Prince sat down to consider these provisos, they agreed that the President's was categorical and would have to be observed. Militarily, this was a handicap, but it would have to be accepted. The only room for manoeuvre was the matter of what constituted 'incontrovertible evidence'. The King's proviso would have to be respected, but this was not quite the same thing as observed.

'I think we must try to follow the King's wish by, as he put it, fending off the troopships,' the Crown Prince said. 'If we could keep them at sea, they would soon run out of supplies and they might then have no alternative other than to put back to port.'

'That might be very difficult to achieve,' General Attagu considered.

'I agree,' said the Crown Prince, 'but we should look into it. You have to realise,' he added, 'that my father has spent a good deal of his life in a glass case. He doesn't always see things quite – well, quite realistically.'

That was a mark of the confidence and mutual trust that existed between the Crown Prince and General Attagu. There were very few people to whom the Crown Prince would have ventured such an opinion and there were very few who would have received it with more sympathetic understanding than General Attagu.

At the very time that General Attagu and the Crown Prince were attempting to estimate Belling's probable next intentions, he was holding another series of meetings from which the State Secretary was excluded. Even so, the State Secretary was able to observe the comings and goings and these he faithfully reported to Major Silk. The first two visitors had spent nearly three hours alone with the Leader. One of them, the State Secretary immediately recognised, was Major-General Waymark, the overall commander of the invasion force; the other, he eventually deduced, was Commodore Wilkins, the Commodore of the Troop Transport Convoy. The second meeting lasted less than twenty minutes and the guest was the Chief of Belling's Police. The last meeting was attended by the young Air Force officer, whom the State Secretary had seen on a previous occasion, and Air Brigadier Walters, the Base Commander of the Swift Wing and other supporting aircraft. This lasted only five minutes and that was all the information the State Secretary was able to give Major Silk.

It appeared to Major Silk that the Leader was now dealing directly with the commanders of the invasion force without reference to the Chiefs of Staff, himself or, so far as he knew, to anyone else, including Dr Offenbeck. The lack of hard information was disturbing, and what had the Leader been seeing the Chief of Police about? It struck Silk that he himself might well have been the

201

subject of that meeting. Now he must surely act, not only to seize the fleeting chance of power, but to save his own skin and of course, he reminded himself, the country.

Major Silk had long thought of the various tactics he might use to dispose of Belling when the time came, but he had come to no final conclusions in advance of the crisis that now imminently confronted him. Now, he could no longer leave the options on the shelf; final conclusions were urgently needed. He would achieve the aim through the action of the armed forces. The Chiefs of Staff were already virtually in his pocket. He telephoned the Chief of the Army Staff.

'I want to see you and your colleagues very urgently. Would you all come to the Department of Security straight away?'

'I'm afraid we can't quite do that,' the very startled General said. 'We've just received a summons from the Leader to attend on him at the Residence and I think we'll have to obey that. Should we come to see you later?'

This caught Silk completely off balance.

'No,' he replied to the General, 'or rather yes. Telephone me after your meeting with the Leader and I'll see then what arrangements can be made.'

Major Silk then proceeded at full speed to the Residence and went straight up to his office there. On his desk, he found a note. It was from Belling and it said there was to be an important meeting at 17.00 hours at which Major Silk's presence was required. He shot along to Dr Offenbeck's room.

'What's going on?' he asked.

'There's a meeting at five,' Offenbeck said. 'Haven't you been asked to it?'

'Yes I have. What's it about?'

'I suppose that will come to light at five,' the exasperating Offenbeck returned.

Five o'clock had now arrived. The three Chiefs of Staff, Air Brigadier Walters, Brigadier Kent, Major Silk, Dr Offenbeck and the State Secretary had assembled in the Leader's office. The Leader himself had not yet appeared and those he had summoned watched a technician putting the finishing touches to the installation of a complicated looking piece of radio equipment. Perhaps a second examination of the scene would have suggested that they were watching each other rather more than the technician. The atmosphere was charged with a mixture of suspicion and curiosity. No one spoke a word and the silence was deep. Then the Leader came in and they all stood up.

The Leader glanced at his watch.

'Be seated gentlemen,' he said and glanced at his watch again.

'I decided,' he started, 'to plan our operations directly with the commanders concerned. This was in no way intended to imply any loss of confidence in our Chiefs of Staff, in the First Deputy Leader or any of my other advisers. I took the decision simply on the grounds of the paramount importance of secrecy. The fact is that the more often a thing is said and the more people it is said to, the greater is the chance of a leakage.'

As he spoke, the Leader met no one's eye. He looked straight ahead as though viewing a distant horizon. Had he looked at his audience he would not have failed to detect a look of sceptical disbelief. But he didn't look at them.

'As I speak,' he continued, 'a powerful force of Swift aircraft are carrying out an attack on the Brazilian fleet off Bahia. I am confidant it will have devastating effects.'

An audible and collective gasp greeted this news. The Leader glanced yet again at his watch.

'In a few moments we'll get the news from the horse's mouth,' the Leader said.

The three Chiefs of Staff looked as though they had been struck on their heads with three sledgehammers. Major Silk looked at Dr Offenbeck, who seemed to be examining the plasterwork on the ceiling.

The radio crackled.

'Victor Leader One to Highspace. Am switched to protected and scrambled talk. Over,' it said.

'That's Air Captain Wilding, the leader of the attack,' Air Brigadier Walters told the meeting.

'Highspace to Victor Leader One,' the radio said. 'Receiving you loud and clear. Proceed with your report. Over.'

'Victor Leader One to Highspace. Attack completed. All nine Swifts safe and on course for base. One carrier sunk. Two battlecruisers sunk. Five missile destroyers sunk. Numerous frigates and other craft sunk. Have detailed photocover of all strikes. Am transmitting images forthwith. ETA base 20.10 hours. Over.'

'That looks like an overwhelming victory,' the Chief of Naval Staff said.

'It does indeed,' a number of other voices around the room echoed.

Major Silk glanced at Dr Offenbeck and saw only the usual inscrutable expression.

'I bet he's been in the know all along, the cunning bastard,' Silk thought to himself.

What else did he know that Silk didn't?

'Yes,' said the Leader, 'we've blunted the Brazilian Navy, or rather stunned it I should say. I doubt if we'll hear much more of it for the time being. The other piece of news I have for you is that five troopships with twenty-five thousand men on board are now at sea and well on their way to the African mainland. We need not fear for their safety now that the Brazilians are out of contention and the King's fleet is out of range in Portugese waters. Our plans are unfolding like clockwork.'

'The whole thing's a masterstroke,' the Chief of the Air Staff said.

'Yes,' the Leader repeated, 'we've outwitted the enemy; we've got the initiative; it only remains now to exploit our advantage ruthlessly. The time has come for the Chiefs of Staff to resume their normal functions. From here on, I shall be asking the Chiefs of Staff to advise me as to the various courses of action open to us.'

'So, if I may say so,' the Chief of the Army Staff proposed, 'let us begin by congratulating the Leader upon the audacious plan with which he has initiated the campaign and the brilliant success that has crowned the opening clash of arms.'

Hear hears were repeated all over the room. Silk silently recognised that he too had been outwitted. The chance he thought he had, had gone. His priority now was his own survival.

'You will of course have recognised sir,' the Chief of the Air Staff said, addressing the Leader, 'that the Air Force will not be in a position to attack the Crown Prince's Regiment should it intervene in Estragala.'

'Certainly I have,' the Leader replied without batting an eyelid.

The Chief of the Army Staff leant forward anxiously in his chair.

'The Crown Prince's Regiment may be a serious threat during the interval between the first and second landings,' he said. 'We believe he's already up against the frontier and that he could reach our landing area quickly at a time of his choosing.'

'Have no fear,' the Leader replied. 'The Crown Prince will be powerless to intervene in the opening stages of the campaign. Our ships are not heading for Estragala; they're heading for Sudka. They will disembark their troops almost at the very point that the traitor Crown

Prince landed his before the Battle of the Frontier. This time he and his deserter troops will be hundreds of miles from the scene of the action. He expects us to come in from the north; actually we're coming in from the south. He's got it wrong and by the time he realises it we'll outnumber him by two to one.'

'Brilliant,' said the Chief of the Army Staff.

'Now,' the Leader announced, 'I wish to institute a Council of War. I will take the chair. Membership: the First Deputy Leader, the three Chiefs of Staff and others to be enlisted as we think fit at later stages.'

Instead of having gone mad, as Major Silk had thought, the Leader seemed to have gone sane.

Chapter 23

In the last few days before the Atlantan troopships sailed, General Waymark's staff had given intensive study to the Crown Prince's tactics before and during the Battle of the Frontier. In particular, they had studied all the evidence they could find regarding the landing place he had used on the Sudkan coast. They had located the stretch of rock standing sheer some ten to fifteen feet above sea level, which gave onto ten fathoms of water alongside and thus formed a natural quayside. They had therefore dispensed with the pontoons intended for use in a landing on the coast of Estragala and planned to disembark the troops directly by gangways. They believed two of their ships could be moored simultaneously and were confident that the troops could be disembarked almost as fast as they had been embarked. This was a sovereign military advantage, all the more so, as everyone believed the landing would be in Estragala, that fiction having been kept up in every quarter until the last minute.

What was even more remarkable than these expected natural advantages, was that they materialised in practice almost exactly as anticipated. Within eight hours of reaching the landing point, all five ships had been cleared and General Waymark had twenty-five thousand men ashore in Sudka within thirty miles of the Treskan frontier. Before they had formed up to advance, all the ships were out to sea again at full speed ahead for Atlanta and the embarkation of the second wave. There was no sign of any Sudkan resistance; nor had any been expected, since the Sudkan Army had

207

made little progress towards recovery after the pulverising blow inflicted on it in the Battle of the Frontier. General Waymark gave the order to advance into Treskania in a north-easterly direction so as to pick up the road and railway which ran in parallel nearly due east towards the oil fields.

After several hours of collective advance, during which no opposition was encountered, and having now reached the road to the east of the River Treska, General Waymark took the bold decision to release his mobile assault force with instructions to race for the oil fields. Had the Crown Prince's Regiment been anywhere in the vicinity, this would have been military suicide; as it was, it was no more than a slight risk.

Although the alarm bells were now ringing in Kesa, the invasion having been spotted by Treskan sentries at the road and rail bridges over the River Treska, General Attagu and the Crown Prince were incapable of any immediate response. They had been completely outwitted by Belling and were now confronted by a modern army under the command of a general who didn't hang around. If they shifted their focus from the Estragalian frontier, the second Atlantan invading force might strike from that direction. If they moved towards the oil fields, even assuming they could get there in time to do any good, they would find themselves in the desert where the enemy armour would be stronger than the Crown Prince's and the topographical conditions wholly unsuitable for General Attagu's guerrilla tactics. It required no great power of military appraisal to see that the situation was desperate.

The only plus point was that two Atlantan Swift aircraft had landed near Bogotown where they were now being examined by General Attagu's and the Crown Prince's officers.

* * *

The two Swifts had been flown by Air Captain Marshall and his second in command, Air Lieutenant Smith. All that was known of their fate in Atlanta was that they had failed to return from a reconnaissance flight over Estragala. As the last message received from them had been when they approached the Estragalian coast on their supposed return flight, it was assumed they must have crashed into the sea. As there had been no reports of technical problems, it seemed they must, by some means or other, have been shot down. This was puzzling since the four other pilots who returned safely reported they had encountered no opposition. All the same, the conclusion was that Marshall and Smith had been shot down. That meant the Treskans must have a weapon of much greater sophistication than previously believed. The immediate question was, did the King's fleet also have any such weapons?

If so, attacking it might be a great deal more hazardous than the operation just completed against the Brazilians. The Chief of the Air Staff and Air Brigadier Walters felt very unsure of their positions; three Swifts had now been lost in a matter of weeks. They couldn't afford more losses on that scale. If the King's fleet moved out of Portugese waters and into the path of the troopships, they would be confronted with an agonising problem.

Of course General Attagu and the Crown Prince knew nothing of the conclusions that had been drawn in Atlanta about the loss of the two Swifts. What, however, they now did know was that the two aircraft were packed with the full range of radar equipment used in various combinations in the Swift front line squadrons. In addition to that, the chief radar officer of the Pool Squadrons had accompanied Air Captain Marshall on the flight and he had brought with him the full range of operating and servicing manuals relevant to this complicated and very advanced apparatus. Finally, it had been explained to the Crown Prince and

General Attagu that this equipment could be operated, either air to air or surface to air, as the radar officer put it, to 'blind' the Atlantan front line Swifts. This meant their navigation systems could be blocked and they would also be unable to lock their missiles onto targets.

The two allies now fully understood the significance of information they had received in outline from Nick Hardy's signals via Mr Hindleys's covert communications system. They reckoned the five Atlantan troopships had now been at sea on their return voyage for six hours. In another four hours they would be back in port. Thereafter, they calculated on the basis of information from Nick Hardy, three or four days would be required to embark the second wave of the invasion force and the five ships would then be ready to sail.

'By God, we can do it,' the Crown Prince exclaimed.

'By God we can,' General Attagu said. 'Just.'

'We must signal Rear-Admiral Fiskin without delay,' the Crown Prince decided. 'And we must get this radar stuff out to him at high speed.'

There did not appear to be an aircraft in Treskania that could land on a carrier, apart from a few helicopters, which lacked the necessary range. Certainly a Swift could not land on a carrier. So it was decided to order Admiral Fiskin to despatch one of his carrier aircraft to Bogotown where it would pick up the radar sets and the radar officer. Meanwhile the Admiral was told to move his fleet towards the war zone forthwith.

'Now we have attended to the needs of tomorrow,' General Attagu said, 'we must tackle the problems of today.'

There could be no doubt that General Waymark would shortly be in control of the oil fields. As General Attagu and the Crown Prince flew back from Bogotown to Kesa in their helicopter, they pondered over the question of what Waymark's next move would be. The Crown Prince thought he would double back and occupy Bogotown and so secure a base for his reinforcements and supplies. General Attagu was convinced he would move north to take Kesa. It was not just the effect on morale of capturing the capital that General Attagu thought would appeal to him; he suggested that his prime object would be to control the hub of the road and rail system that Kesa represented.

'To protect Bogotown, you would have to move across the Flatlands,' he told the Crown Prince. 'Waymark would get there ahead of your Regiment. But your Regiment could get to Kesa ahead of him, that is, if you move at once.'

'That would mean leaving all the landing points open to the enemy,' the Crown Prince argued. 'It would allow them to build up an overwhelming military strength.'

'Maybe,' General Attagu conceded, 'but we can't defend all the key points simultaneously. If we defend one or even two such points, the enemy will simply choose another. I think you'll find Belling wants Kesa. Its capture would give him just the kind of victory he seeks; the kind that confers a political gloss. Remember, he's a politician, not a soldier.'

'The King's Royal Regiment will move to Kesa forthwith,' the Crown Prince signalled to his second in command.

General Attagu shifted the HQ of his troops to the Treskan Mountains south of Kesa and gave orders to distribute his guerrilla battle groups along all the likely approaches to the capital from the direction of the oil fields.

General Waymark's original intention had been to seize Bogotown and to secure control of the coast from there to Portville as soon as he had succeeded in occupying the oil fields. He now realised he could afford to change

211

his mind. An army coup in Sudka had overthrown the pro-Treskan government of Professor Adadaka and installed one of their number, Colonel Josca, as President. The new regime was solidly anti-Treskan, the officer corps, which was the source of its power, being determined to wipe out the humiliation of the terrible defeat in the Battle of the Frontier. This meant that General Waymark need now have no anxiety about the security of his right flank. Nor need he bother with Bogotown. His landing place in Sudka would serve him equally well for reinforcements and supplies. Moreover, his mobile assault force had reached and taken control of the oil fields without incurring a single casualty and with the expenditure of scarcely any ammunition. He reckoned he was now in a position to go for Treskania's jugular and that, he and the Leader at home believed, was Kesa.

Nevertheless, General Waymark had to accept a degree of caution in his forward planning. He must wait for the main part of his army to catch up with the mobile assault troops. He must then regroup north of the oil fields at the southern end of the desert and prepare to advance across it, through the Treskan Mountains and so to Kesa. If the Crown Prince's Regiment was not there, he would storm the city straight away; if it was there, he would dig in and await the arrival of the second wave. When that came to hand, he would have fifty thousand men to pit against the Crown Prince's twenty to twenty-five thousand. General Attagu's Treskan army need hardly be taken into account. It was ill-equipped, out of date and, so far, conspicuous by it absence. It would have little more than nuisance value. The Brazilian fleet was *hors de combat* and the King's fleet was showing no sign of seeking combat.

General Waymark was encouraged by his government to believe the fall of Kesa would lead to the collapse of the Tamu regime. He was therefore already planning the establishment of an emergency military government which would take its orders from his army of occupation. If that expectation proved to be over-optimistic, he would have to engage the Crown Prince's Regiment and crumble it till it ceased to be an effective fighting force. That would cost him casualties, but soldiers must expect casualties in war and they would be a small price to pay for the stunning victory that was now all but in sight.

Mr Belling was elated. His rule would now be confirmed by that most potent of mandates: victory in war. Those around him, several of whom he knew had been on the point of revolt, now hailed him as the great Leader and fell over each other in saluting him. World opinion was beginning to show the respect that Paul Reynolds had never gained. The Brazilian appeal to the Peace Council of the International Organisation had fallen flat. The Brazilian ambassador's claim that his fleet had been the victim of an unprovoked and barbarous attack was countered by the Atlantan ambassador, who invited the Council to ask themselves what the Brazilian fleet had in mind when it mobilised its reserve ships and headed for the sea lanes of the Atlantan Republic. In the debate that followed, there were some fiery speeches on both sides, but ultimately the vote was in favour of deferring judgement and a resolution was passed urging all governments to respect each other's integrity and to refrain from provocative acts.

The Treskan appeal fared scarcely better. President Tamu's representative pointed to an undoubted act of aggression on the part of an Atlantan invading force which, he claimed, was motivated by a desire to seize the Treskan oil fields. He said this was an unlawful war for an unlawful purpose, namely the theft of Treskania's undoubtedly legally owned oil fields. But the Atlantan ambassador vigorously denied these charges. He said that the invasion was not motivated by the wish to take over the oil fields. It was motivated by the moral obligation of his country to release the Hurnots from the uncivilised persecution they were suffering and which amounted to genocide. While it was true his country's forces had occupied the oil fields, this had only been done to prevent the Bogo government from setting fire to them. The Council, he said, should take note of the huge ecological disaster that had thus been averted.

The Council resolved to establish an international commission of inquiry to investigate the conditions of the Hurnots in Treskania. Meanwhile, until the commission reported, judgement of that issue must be deferred. The question of the legality or otherwise of the war, they decided, was also, to a considerable extent, dependent upon the same issue. The Council did, however, resolve to caution the government of Atlanta against associating moral obligation with military action without the most thorough consideration. The Atlantan ambassador then announced that his government welcomed this note of caution and he assured the Council that his government would readily undertake to afford any such association of moral and military matters the utmost consideration. The Council welcomed that assurance and resolved to keep developments under close observation.

The African Moral Union expressed grave concern about the situation. They deplored the presence in Treskania of Atlantan troops but they observed that two factions of the same were, in fact, at war with each other. It could be argued that the war was an Atlantan civil war and therefore not strictly the concern of the Union. As regards the involvement of Estragala and Sudka, they declined to express a view as such disputes as there might be were between sovereign African states.

On the morrow of the debates in the Peace Council of the International Organisation, Mr Belling made an

214

appearance on the balcony of the Residence. He was greeted by tremendous cheering and flag waving from a huge crowd. Church bells were rung and artillery salutes were fired from South Park. In the afternoon, the Leader decorated Air Captain Wilding with the Atlantan Gallantry Cross and the other pilots, who had taken part in the attack on the Brazilian fleet, with the War Flying Cross. He announced that General Waymark had been promoted to Field-Marshal and awarded the Order of the Republic First Class. In the evening he broadcast to the nation.

'The unshakable faith we have in our country's destiny is now being realised in victory at sea and on land. The Brazilians have been taught a lesson they'll not easily forget and, by a brilliant military stroke, Field-Marshal Waymark has placed our army in Treskania at the very threshold of overwhelming victory. Our friends, the Hurnots, will soon be set free from the oppression of years inflicted upon them by a heartless and ruthless government and we have secured the safety of the oil fields of that unhappy country from the destruction planned by Tamu and his gangster puppets. In saving Africa from an unspeakably frightful genocide and the world from an environmental disaster we are truly and nobly meeting the moral obligations that history has conferred on us.

'All true Atlantan men and women have responded to my call to action in a manner that has astonished the world and I thank you all. But it has not astonished me. It has not astonished you. We have all known what we Atlantans can achieve and now that I, your Leader, have your united support and loyalty, nothing can stop us achieving it.'

Dr Offenbeck confessed to Major Silk that he had been surprised that the Leader had gone ahead with Waymark's promotion and his national broadcast before the fall of

Kesa. He added, however, that he now realised what a bold and wise decision the Leader had made.

'By acting and speaking now,' he said to Silk, 'he has stamped his authority upon this historic passage of events. When Kesa falls, people will see that the Leader dominates, rather than merely follows, the course of history.'

Silk said to himself, '*If* Kesa falls.' To Offenbeck, he merely remarked, 'of course, that's what we all think.'

Chapter 24

If there were any people in Atlanta more worried than Air Major Eggleton, they would have been hard to find. A most extraordinary thing had happened in the Pool squadrons. It was not just that two Pool Swifts had failed to return from a reconnaissance sortie over Estragala, but that all the reserve radar sets had disappeared from their storage shed and the Pool radar officer had disappeared with them. Try as he would, Eggleton could not resist the conclusion that treachery was at the bottom of it. Had Marshall and Smith really been shot down or had they deserted? Why had the radar equipment gone missing and why had the radar officer done likewise? It was all too obvious that something totally disastrous had happened and that Eggleton was to blame for it. He had known that Marshall was wobbly but he had concealed that from the Base Commander and had relied on Mrs Greene's assurance that Marshall was sound. His own prospects were bleak indeed. He would have to make a clean breast of it to the Base Commander.

The Base Commander was appalled.

'If this gets out, he said, 'we'll both be for the high jump.'

'But it's bound to get out,' Eggleton said.

'Hold on,' the Base Commander parried. 'Who keeps the inventory of the Pool radar equipment?'

Eggleton explained that the radar officer was responsible for the inventory but that this document had also disappeared.

'Would anyone else know about the inventory?' The Base Commander pursued. 'I mean know what was on it.'

'Only the stores Corporal, I think,' Eggleton told him.

'Get him in,' the Base Commander ordered.

The stores Corporal proved to be distinctly elderly, weedy and slightly stooped. His face wore a wary expression suggesting that he was not keen on the limelight and that experience had taught him contact with the top brass was inclined to attract it.

'So you're responsible for the Pool radar inventory,' the Base Commander began.

'No sir, that's not me. That's the job of the radar officer in charge,' the man said.

'What then exactly is your job?'

'I issue the equipment against properly authorised chits.'

'Who authorises the chits?'

'Well sir, that would usually be the Pool Squadron Commander or the Wing Commander and, of course, most often the radar officer.'

'Usually. Would anyone else authorise the chits?'

'No sir, just those I've mentioned.'

'So why did you say usually?'

'I meant it just as a manner of speaking sir.'

'Well then, as a manner of exact speaking, who authorised the removal of all this equipment?'

'Well that's just it sir. No one did.'

'You mean to tell me you issued the equipment without an authorised chit.'

'No sir, I did not. It's my belief that the radar officer signed it out himself.'

'And that would be perfectly in order would it not?'

'Yes sir, perfectly. That's in his authority,'

'All right Corporal, I'm satisfied you have discharged your responsibilities correctly.'

'Thank you sir, that's why I had to report to the Wing Commander that the equipment had gone.'

'Quite so, quite so and you acted quite correctly. And you know where the equipment is now do you?'

'No sir, that's what's worrying me.'

'The Wing Commander didn't tell you?'

'No sir he didn't say anything to me about it.'

'Yes, well I think he was quite correct in that. He wasn't authorised to say where the equipment had been sent. I think that's right isn't it Eggleton?'

'Yes sir, that's quite right,' Eggleton felt he was bound to say.

'Right, well now the transaction's been safely concluded, I am in a position to put your mind at rest. I've had the stuff transferred to Base HQ. I'm not talking about the reasons for that, but that's what's happened.'

'So that's all right,' the Corporal said. 'I expect you called it in for modification.'

'I said I don't want it talked about. Do you understand that.'

'Yes sir. I'll keep it to myself.'

The Corporal executed a rather feeble sort of salute and withdrew.

'This'll be a bit risky don't you think sir?' Eggleton suggested.

'Not nearly as risky as admitting what has really happened,' the Base Commander insisted.

* * *

Another very worried man was Major Silk. He had been on the point of starting a *coup d'état* to overthrow the Leader and he had missed the bus. Had the Leader suspected anything? Probably not, it now seemed. If he had, Silk would now surely have been beyond the state of being able to worry about anything. Even so, he was on very dangerous ground. Fenton knew he had it in mind to displace the Leader when the opportunity came. In a moment of folly, he had told him so. Fenton knew much too much and now he would have to pay for the mistake his superior had made. It was rather a pity. Fenton was a very good man who had been useful in the past and might have been more so in the future, but the milk was spilt and there was no point in crying over it. Major Silk sought an interview with the Leader.

'I've been reviewing our plans for getting rid of the King,' Major Silk said.

'Indeed,' the Leader replied. 'We certainly don't seem to be having much success on that front.'

'True,' said Silk, 'but it strikes me what a boost it would be if we could bring it off at the moment of victory. It would be the icing on the cake.'

'It would,' the Leader agreed, 'but as our assassination plans have gone awry, I'm now hoping we'll capture the brute. We could then have the public trial we'd originally thought of and that really would be a boost.'

'That would be best of all,' Silk said, 'but even so, I think we need to consider why our plans to capture the King and then, if that failed, to assassinate him, aborted.'

'Treachery, of course,' the Leader declared. 'Those agents we had in Wales were traitors. They must have leaked it and they've paid the price. I think they were shot, if I remember correctly'

'So they were,' Silk reminded him, 'and deservedly so. But I'm afraid it goes deeper than that or, I should say, higher. Fenton knew and didn't report it to me.'

'Fenton!' the Leader shouted. 'I thought he was one of our best men. What didn't he report?'

'That our agents A4A, A4B and A4C were all bent. It was they who sabotaged our plan to fly the King here and now I've discovered it was Fenton who blew our airport plan to assassinate the King in Kesa.'

'When did you find this out?'

'Only last week. Had I known earlier, of course I would have told you.'

'Right,' said the Leader, 'we'll have him arrested and tried. Perhaps that'll help others in his line of business to stick to the straight and narrow.'

'If I may suggest it Leader, I think that might be unwise. If we put Fenton on trial he would say things that might be, might be, er, misunderstood, if they leaked out. I think it would be better if he had an accident, he and the girl, A4B. She's hand in glove with him and a bit more than hand, if you follow me.'

'All right,' the Leader assented. 'Do as you think best. Now, about the two Swifts we lost. They seem to think the Treskans must have some sort of an anti-aircraft weapon that we don't know about. Have you got a theory?'

'I suppose there are other possibilities,' Silk speculated, 'but they seem very unlikely. The other aircraft had no technical problems. So why did those two come to grief? It seems they must have been shot down. As you know, that's what the Chief of the Air Staff thinks and that, I take it, is what must have happened.'

'It certainly seems the most likely explanation,' the Leader said. 'As a precaution, I've given orders to speed up the second sailing of the troopships. I want them through before the King's fleet appears on the scene. We can't rule out the possibility that they have some of these weapons on board.'

Major Silk was quite satisfied with the interview. Not that he was particularly bothered about the Swift aircraft or even about the fate of Fenton and the girl. What pleased him was that the Leader had spoken to him in a trusting and even a friendly sort of way. It seemed he was safe for the time being. The point that struck Dr Offenbeck when he heard about what had passed was that Silk had found it necessary to involve the Leader in the assassination of Fenton and Miss Roberts. He no longer has the nerve to do that sort of thing on his own, Offenbeck thought. That was surely a sign that Silk was losing his grip and his confidence.

* * *

Since the disaster that had engulfed the Brazilian Navy, President Tamu had been constantly and sympathetically in touch with President de Farias of Brazil. The two were not merely allies, they were also close personal friends with very similar ideas on the role of government. No sooner had President Tamu been made aware of the significance of the arrival of the two Atlantan Swifts in Treskania than he gave orders that one of them with its radar secrets was to be handed over to the Brazilian government. Some of his advisers thought this was generosity to the point of rashness. Possession of two of the world's most advanced military aircraft was, they thought, hardly an asset to be parted with, especially when the country was confronted with a dire crisis. President Tamu, however, insisted that Brazil also was confronted with a dire crisis that had been brought to bear by her support for Treskania. He was determined that Treskania should now afford her ally every possible assistance. Air Lieutenant Smith was therefore briefed to fly his Swift to Bahia and to carry with him a set of the radar instruments of the same kind that had been flown out to the King's fleet now debouching from Portugese waters.

President de Farias received this as a wonderful act of friendship and an encouragement to press ahead with the regrouping of the surviving elements of his fleet. In a lengthy conversation with President Tamu, he offered to despatach a military contingent to Treskania. This would consist of two thousand combat soldiers. These men had no experience of battle conditions, but they were well armed and had been trained in offensive and defensive tactics. To General Attagu, this seemed like manna from heaven. He asked that the Brazilian contingent should be landed at Bogotown. Such a move, he believed, would open up new possibilities. Ultimately, he told President Tamu, it was essential to maintain control of Bogotown, Treskania's principal point of contact with the overseas world.

'Without Bogotown we would end up in Square Street,' he remarked to the Crown Prince.

'Or more likely Queer Street,' the Crown Prince observed.

President Tamu found this very amusing, which did the two men's morale no harm at all. The fact that the President could laugh at such a time, and even pass the joke on to President de Farias, reminded them of the resilience of their chief and nourished their own.

So almost at the same time that the King's fleet bore up south-westwards from Portugese waters, a Brazilian convoy of four passenger ships with an escort of two destroyers sailed from Bahia bound for Bogotown. On board were two thousand three hundred troops armed with automatic hand weapons and twenty-five of Brazil's latest heavy machine guns. One of the destroyers carried Swift radar which had been hastily installed under the tuition of Air Lieutenant Smith.

The long-term outlook did not appear quite as bleak as it had done only a few days ago. Short-term prospects, however, had grown more desperate than ever. Field-Marshal Waymark had closed on Kesa at an astonishing speed and his assault force was already close to the southern outskirts of the city. The Crown Prince had been outrun. His Regiment had to traverse much more difficult terrain than the open desert across which Waymark had come. While Waymark's officers in the van surveyed Kesa through their binoculars, the Crown Prince's Regiment was still some twenty-five miles to the north of the city.

General Attagu's response to this unexpectedly grave threat was instant, intuitive and original. He called in numbers of his guerrilla troops from the mountains and sprinkled them in various strategically placed buildings throughout the city. Further parties of guerrillas were organised to bring in supplies and evacuate casualties. The President, the King, Ministers and foreign embassies were evacuated to Pennon, a small town fifteen miles north of Kesa. General Attagu then issued an order of the day.

'Such invading troops as get into Kesa will not get out of it', it read.

Chapter 25

Field-Marshal Waymark had come up to the front himself. He wanted to be sure of the position by personal observation.

'There doesn't seem to be anything there,' the commander of the front assault formation told him.

Waymark fine tuned his binoculars and moved them steadily across the townscape of Kesa. There was hardly any traffic in the streets and only a few pedestrians were to be seen. There was no sign of any defences and it was clear the Crown Prince's Regiment had not yet arrived.

'The plum's ripe for the picking,' he said. 'We'll go straight in to the centre. Occupy the Presidential Palace, the King's residence, the Assembly building and the rail station. If you can find them, seize the President and the King and get them to our back area. Then you will move into the northern outskirts and prepare a defensive line against the arrival of the Crown Prince. Choose whatever line you think most favourable. We can push it forward when our main force comes up if that seems desirable.'

The assault commander needed no second bidding. His light armour and rapid troop carriers positively leapt forward, throwing up clouds of dust as they did so. When they reached the surfaced streets, it subsided and Waymark could see his troops advancing rapidly towards the centre of the city, which they soon reached without opposition. The commander radioed back that he had occupied the central public buildings and was moving up with the balance of his force into the northern outskirts. Everything was going as planned. The only disappointment was that the Presidential Palace, the King's residence and the Assembly building were all deserted. There were no high level prisoners to consign to the bag.

Waymark turned round and looked south. His binoculars told him that the clouds of dust he could see with the naked eye were indeed the van of his follow-up force. He reckoned that within an hour he would have seven or eight thousand men in Kesa and that in another two hours his strength there would have grown to nearly twenty thousand. If the Crown Prince had caught him in the open, his position might have been perilous. As it was, the initial battle would be within the city or, in other words, as he had got there first, under conditions of Waymark's choosing. A built up area as a battlefield, Waymark knew well, tended to favour the defence. If the Crown Prince intended to regain control of Kesa, he would have to attack.

The Field-Marshal ciphered a signal to the Leader in Atlanta City.

'Our Expeditionary Force has this evening captured Kesa. Opposition negligible. We dine tonight in the Presidential Palace. I now intend to crumble the Crown Prince's Regiment if he gives me the opportunity by engaging in fighting within the city area. As my strength here is adequate, suggest second troop convoy should land second wave at Bogotown. Waymark F/M.'

The Leader responded, 'Most hearty congratulations. The nation is proud of you and your gallant troops. Second wave will land at Bogotown. Do you know whereabouts of President and King?'

To this last question, the Field-Marshal had regretfully to reply that he did not, but his dinner in the Presidential Palace that night did indeed take place. The Crown Prince had pulled up short of the northern suburbs and seemed undecided as to his next move. Meanwhile, Waymark's troops flooded into the city and, before the meal was over, their position seemed to be impregnable.

* * *

At the dinner in the Presidential Palace, Waymark sat in the centre of a long elegant table made of that splendid Treskan hardwood regarded by many as superior to mahogany. There were thirty-three officers present in addition to the C-in-C. Many were of his staff and the rest were those fortunate enough to be off duty at this time. Bottles of very fine Treskan claret, which had been brought up from President Tamu's cellar, were ranged along the table. The cutlery and glass matched the quality of the table and wine, but the food did not. There was no sign of the President's kitchen staff or indeed of any of his staff whatsoever. So the officers dined off standard army rations, which looked incongruous in such a setting.

Various toasts were drunk, starting with the Leader's health, but it was noticeable that the Field-Marshal allowed the wine no more latitude than the merest touch of his lips. In fact, though he enjoyed offering alcohol to his guests, he never took the stuff himself, being fond of saying that, as they would get drunk, he would be sure to win the argument. This time, however, as everyone foresaw, it was not the argument he was about to win; it was the war.

'There will be some stiff fighting in the next few days,' the Field-Marshal told the company, 'but the enemy has fallen into our trap and once we have crumbled the Crown Prince's Regiment, there will be no effective military opposition to our occupation and control of the country.'

He was just embarking upon an outline of how the crumbling battle would be fought when all the lights went out and the dinner party was plunged into total darkness.

Looking out over the city, it became apparent that the power failure was not just in the palace; it engulfed the whole town. Then, as suddenly as the darkness had fallen, the scene was lit by a series of vivid leaping flames all over the city. Radio reports from the street patrols soon revealed that most of these flames came from troop carriers and armoured vehicles that had been set on fire by some kind of incendiary device. The patrols were reinforced and ordered to sweep the streets in a search for the saboteurs. None was found but the fires were extinguished and, after a time, the electric supply was restored. Here and there, however, there had been gun fights and Waymark's army suffered its first battle casualties. Eleven men were killed and six more wounded. Thirty-eight military vehicles were destroyed or damaged irreparably by fire.

Though order had been quickly restored, it did not seem very secure. There was no sign of any saboteurs. There was no explanation of what had happened. The street patrols were further reinforced, mainly at the expense of those troops that had been stood down to rest, but also partly at that of the force that had been moved up to meet the Crown Prince's expected attack.

Of course an episode of this character was not likely to cause Field-Marshal Waymark undue concern. That pockets of resistance had remained in the city was not surprising; it was merely rather annoying. He did not deem it necessary to send any amendment of the signal he had earlier despatched to the Leader. He was not to be distracted by a few saboteurs from his fixed aim of crumbling the Crown Prince's Regiment.

* * *

In Atlanta City, Mr Belling was now exerting all his authority and a good many threats to speed up the sailing of the five troopships that were to disembark their passengers at Bogotown. He considered it crucially important to get them away before the King's fleet arrived on the scene. If those ships were indeed equipped with weapons that could shoot down Swifts, the convoy might be denied air cover and become vulnerable to sinking by surface vessels. If, on the other hand, the troopships got through and landed the follow-up force, Waymark would be able to bring the war to a rapid and victorious conclusion. He might even be able to do this without the follow-up force, but to be sure, Mr Belling thought, it was necessary to be very sure.

There were, however, two exasperating obstacles. One was that it had so far proved impossible to discover exactly where the King's fleet was. The Swift radar reconnaissance patrols had been ordered to keep their distance from the King's naval vessels until the question of what armament they carried had been resolved, but there should have been no difficulty in locating the ships by radar at safe ranges. This, all the same, had not happened and, as they got to within radar range of Portugese waters, the Swift radar screens had gone blank. Whether this was due to freak electrical storms, of which there had been several, or to Portugese jamming or to something else, had not been established. This was disquieting. Even so, elementary navigational calculation showed that the King's fleet could not yet be other than well short of the possible scenes of action.

Mr Belling saw all this as a further argument in favour of the speedy despatch of the troopships, which is why he found the second obstacle particularly exasperating. He was told that one of the troopships was threatened with engine trouble. There was wobble on one of the turbines. As yet, this would not cut the ship's maximum speed by more than ten to twelve knots, but if the defect was not remedied, it was likely to get worse and might reduce speed from sixty to less than twenty knots. In such a situation, the Commodore of the convoy would have the alternatives of detaching the limping ship or slowing the others to its speed. He was anxious to avoid having to make that choice and advised that the sailing date should be postponed until the necessary repair work had been completed. That would take four to five days.

The Leader's first response was to withdraw the defective ship and get the other four under way. But it was explained to him that this would seriously unbalance the force. Most of the troop carriers had been embarked in the ailing ship. The Engineer component was on board as also was the Signals company. To redistribute the embarked troops and equipment now would take several more days than those required to repair the damaged turbine.

The Leader decided that the convoy must put to sea forthwith and proceed at the best speed it could make. Even with successive reductions in speed from sixty to twenty knots, there was still a more than reasonable chance that it would be out of the danger zone before the King's fleet could intercept it. It was a safe assumption that Admiral Fiskin would rely on his destroyers to attack the troopers and would risk neither his cruisers nor his carriers. That meant that, at least in the opening phase, the troopers at over fifty knots would outpace the destroyers with their maximum of forty-five. The Leader was also far from convinced that the naval attack Swifts would, in the event, be unable to inflict a 'Brazilian' on the King's fleet.

If slightly reluctantly, the Chief of the Naval Staff and the Chief of the Air Staff endorsed this view. The Chief of the Army Staff said it was the only possible course of action in the circumstances. Within an hour of their meeting with the Leader, the convoy of five troopships sailed, making an initial speed of fifty-one knots. The entire Swift attack force was placed on standby and reconnaissance flights were stepped up and concentrated on the waters that lay between the convoy and the supposed position of the King's fleet. As a further precaution, the original plan for the convoy to steer a south-easterly course directly for Bogotown had been changed. Initially, it steered south south-west with the object of placing more distance between it and the possible position of the King's fleet. Having achieved that, Commodore Wilkins intended, in two changes of course, to swing round onto a nearly easterly heading for Bogotown. As it turned out, by one of those curious twists of fate that do from time to time occur in maritime warfare, the Atlantan convoy, seeking to evade the King's fleet, was now heading directly into the path of the Brazilian troopships and their two escorting destroyers, also bound for Bogotown and not yet spotted by the Atlantans.

*　　*　　*

At about the same time that Field-Marshal Waymark sat down to dinner in the Presidential Palace, its former occupant, President Tamu, sat down to his in the Hotel Fairview in the centre of Pennon. Dining with him were the King, General Attagu, the Crown Prince, four of the Treskan Ministers, Count Connors and Commander Holland of Rear-Admiral Fiskin's staff. General Attagu openly admitted that his battle plan had been frustrated by Waymark. The loss of Kesa was a serious blow. Waymark would now be able to garrison the city with perhaps a third of the force he now had in it and then he would be able to move off with the other two-thirds to link up with the second wave of the invading force.

'But,' said General Attagu, 'my first plan has been defeated, so I now make a second plan.'

The Crown Prince was not to attempt to enter Kesa, which Waymark would certainly expect him to do. Instead he was to move from his position to the north of it and take up one to the east. Here he was to wait until, as inevitably would happen in the course of time, Waymark, having garrisoned Kesa, moved his troops out to link with the second wave of reinforcements. He would be very unlikely to seek battle to the east of Kesa, where the country was afforested and devoid of surfaced roads or rail links. He would, in any case have, as his priority, a junction with the second wave and therefore probably would wish to evade the Crown Prince's Regiment until he had achieved it and gained an overwhelming superiority in numbers. His only feasible exits from Kesa would therefore probably be southwards or, less probably, northwards. He would not wish to go westwards and cross the River Treska whose bridges from Kesa were all blown. The Crown Prince would then have the opportunity of attacking Waymark's flank, forcing him to turn and expose his rear to the river.

The Crown Prince thought this was an ingenious plan.

'But suppose,' he said, 'Waymark doesn't come out of Kesa. Suppose he waits for his second wave to come up and join him there. Would it not be better that I should attack him in the city before he has regrouped his forces and before his reinforcements arrive?'

'No,' General Attagu insisted, 'it would not. That's what he hopes you will do. The splendid qualities of your Regiment would not shine in offensive street fighting. In street fighting, the advantage goes to the one who is in the street first and that, unfortunately, is not you.'

While this dinner was in progress, a message was brought in. It was a covert cipher from Nick Hardy courtesy of Mr Hindley. It read:

'Convoy of five trooping liners sailed from Atlanta Port

20.10 hours today. Rumoured, repeat rumoured, destination Bogotown. Understand 20,000 plus troops and much equipment aboard. No naval escort. Swift aircraft spotted but not in direct vicinity of ships. Believe them naval attack version.'

Everyone round the table looked at Commander Holland. He shook his head.

'We've missed them,' he said. 'They'll make up to sixty knots. We can't catch them. We planned on them being in port another two days.'

The next one to speak was neither a sailor nor a soldier. 'What about the Brazilians?' Count Connors asked.

'Very doubtful,' Commander Holland replied. 'At sixty knots the troopers'll be in Bogotown before the Brazilians are on the horizon.'

* * *

In war the best laid plans and the most ingenious deductions often prove to be imprecise to the point of being downright wrong. At 23.14 hours, about two and a half hours after Commander Holland had made his assessment of the situation, the leading destroyer of the Brazilian convoy, using its newly acquired Swift radar, picked up Commodore Wilkins's five troopships at a range of thirty-eight nautical miles and closing the course of the Brazilian ships at the surprisingly low speed of twenty-four knots. Without a moment's hesitation the Brazilian destroyer Captain ordered both his ships to clear for action and turned towards the Atlantans, leaving his own troopships to fend for themselves for the time being.

Increasing speed to their maximum of forty knots, the Brazilian destroyers were soon closing the Atlantan troopships at a combined speed of nearly sixty-five knots, but not for long. Within five minutes the pattern on the radar screen began to break up.

'What's happening?' the destroyer Captain demanded of Air Lieutenant Smith, who was up on the bridge with him operating the equipment.

''They're turning away sir,' Smith said. 'They've probably picked us up on their radar.'

'Damn the devil,' the Captain exclaimed.

'They're on a reciprocal now,' Smith continued, 'and they're increasing speed. Let's have a closer look.'

Smith switched the angle and the scope of his search along various options.

'They're drawing away at, heavens above, at almost sixty knots.'

'So we can't catch them,' the Captain said. 'The most we can do is forty.'

He was on the point of going about when Smith let out a sudden yell.

'Look at this sir. You see those dots at the top of the screen. Now if I bring those into detail you can see quite clearly there are four ships making high speed away from us. Four ships. Now look at this. You see that dot there. That's the fifth ship and it's hove to.' Smith gave a nervous smile. 'Is that the right phrase sir?'

'It'll do very nicely. You mean it's stopped,' the Captain said, as he peered at the fifth dot and then watched Smith bring it into detail on the screen. There it was: the fifth ship, dead in the water.

Not many minutes later, the Captain picked up the fifth troopship, brilliantly lit by moonlight, with his binoculars. He ordered the front four-inch turrets of both destroyers to be trained onto it and he continued to close at high speed. As soon as the range was right, he opened fire, deliberately aiming the first round a hundred yards ahead of the stricken ship and the second the same distance astern. He then signalled the ship with his forward searchlight calling upon it to surrender on pain of being blown out of the water. Immediately the trooper struck its colours.

'What are you carrying?' the Brazilian Captain enquired.

'Four thousand eight hundred troops and a crew of two hundred and fifty,' came the answer.

'What armaments do you carry?' was the next question.

'Four thousand two hundred and twenty rifles, three hundred and eighty light machine-gun cars, twenty-five light tanks and a hundred and fifty armed troop carriers,' the troopship signalled.

'Quite a prize,' the Captain remarked to Air Lieutenant Smith. 'Pity we don't get the money. They used to you know,' he added.

He then flashed a warning to the troopship that in the event of the slightest sign of disobedience it would instantly be sunk. This was acknowledged. The two destroyers continued to close their prize until the range was suitable to board. They then lowered two boats and put five armed marines from each and two of their bridge officers aboard the trooper. The Captain of the second destroyer was ordered to escort the trooper to Bahia at the best speed it could make and the first destroyer turned to resume the care of the Brazilian convoy of troopships.

'I had no idea of the size of their troopships,' Air Lieutenant Smith remarked to the Captain. 'They're enormous.'

'Indeed they are,' the Captain agreed. 'They were built as cruise liners I believe. Must be at least a hundred and fifty thousand tons, maybe two hundred thousand,' he added.'

'So it's quite a thing to have captured one,' Smith said.

'Yes, and I expect they'll miss those troops and the equipment in Treskania,' the Captain concluded.

His mind, however, was now on his own destination. It certainly could not be Bogotown. The four troopships that had got away would be there long before he could make it.

Smith continued to ponder the extraordinary action he had just witnessed. When he joined the Air Force, it had not occurred to him that one day he would see a naval action, especially one of this kind. How strange it was, he reflected, that the troopships had come out so far west on their way to Bogotown and given the Brazilians their chance of capturing one. He also wondered how it was that the destroyer Captain knew they were bound for Bogotown. He assumed Admiral Fiskin or General Attagu must have an efficient spy in Atlanta City.

Chapter 26

Air Lieutenant Smith was right in assuming that the Treskans had an efficient spy in Atlanta though, in fact, there were two: Nick Hardy and Laura Blick. Up to now, their pose as South African travel agents had been very successful and they had been able to move about the country, ostensibly examining buildings and sites as potential tourist attractions, but actually keeping their eyes open for anything that might be of interest to General Attagu, the Crown Prince and Admiral Fiskin. Thus, they had noticed the time of departure of the convoy of troopships and, from information they got from Beth Roberts, the fact that their probable destination was Bogotown. It had been their good fortune that Captain Fenton, virtually in sole charge of the Department of Security Services, had gone over to the King's cause, together with his assistant. Not only had Captain Fenton and Beth Roberts passed on numerous important secrets to them, but they had also screened them from the attentions of Belling's Police. Mr Hindley's covert communications system was the means by which Nick's and Laura's information was passed to Treskania. Now, however, this extraordinary run of luck and success was about to hit the buffers.

Nick and Laura, in the guise of Mr and Mrs van Ploeg, walked into the reception hall of the Department of Security to make one of their routine calls on Captain Fenton. The ostensible purpose was to consult about historic buildings they thought of viewing, to see if there were any security objections. As on previous occasions, the actual purpose was to compare notes about the development of Belling's plans for the conduct of the war.

They proceeded to the reception desk where the girl, known in the office as the Bombshell, was on duty. This very well endowed gorgeous creature had the reputation of not having any great amount of brain power, but her presence was thought to be good for the morale of the Department, especially the male members of it, and certainly she attended to this aspect of her duties with diligence. Her blonde hair had constantly to be brushed aside from her face, none of her variously coloured skirts did more than just about cover her bottom and her tops were always stretched to the limit, emphasising rather than concealing what the normal observant man liked to see.

Nick and Laura were by now on quite familiar terms with the Bombshell and they had always found her cheerful and helpful. On this occasion they were therefore surprised to find her looking unaccustomedly serious and disquieted.

'We've come to see Captain Fenton,' Nick said.

'Haven't you heard?' the Bombshell whispered. 'There's been a disaster and he's been killed and Beth Roberts too.'

'How perfectly dreadful,' Nick exclaimed. 'What happened?'

'Nobody seems quite to know,' the Bombshell said, 'but it seems a car bomb blew them up as they left the office last night.'

'How dreadful,' Nick repeated.

'And I'll tell you what,' the Bombshell continued, gesturing to Nick to bring his ear close to her mouth, 'the same thing's planned for you two or something like it. They found things in Ed's flat and more in Beth's. They know you're not travel agents and the only reason they haven't picked you up is they're watching to see who else you talk to. I get to know these things because people do talk to me.'

Suddenly the conspiratorial whisper changed to normal voice volume.

'So I'm afraid I can't help you,' it said.

Nick glanced over his shoulder and saw that another visitor had arrived at the desk and was well within hearing range.

'Well thanks anyway,' Nick said as nonchalantly as he could manage.

Nick and Laura turned and walked out of the Department. As they did so, they noticed a Belling's Policeman saying something into a mobile phone.

'We'd best get into a crowd,' Laura said. 'That's our best bet.'

They headed as quickly as they dared without appearing to be in a hurry for Government Square tube station, which was now full to capacity with the rush hour crowd. Never had the seething mass of humanity been more welcome; the fugitives were, for the moment, as anonymous as they could hope to be. They travelled four stops down the line and got out at Commerce Centre. They emerged into the land of banks, insurance institutions, building societies and suchlike. They entered one of the largest bank buildings, which Laura remembered was open until a late hour, and sauntered across to a display of leaflets about banking facilities. They were confronted by a young man in a shiny black suit whose hair had somehow been trained into a series of waxy stalks.

'How are you this evening?' he asked them. 'Have you had a good day?'

'We're fine,' Nick assured him.

'So how can I help you?' the young man enquired.

'We're buying a flat,' Nick said. 'My father's putting up half the cost and we can do the deposit. I wondered if

239

your bank would do a mortgage for the rest.'

Laura thought this a very good ploy. Whatever things Belling's Police might expect them to do, negotiating to buy a flat would hardly be among them.

'Yes sir, I'm sure we could offer you excellent terms. If you follow me, I'll introduce you to one of our personal mortgage managers.'

'Thanks, but I think we'd like to have a look at the rates first. Have you a leaflet?'

'I'm sure we have sir. I'll find our leaflet assistant.'

'This seems to be what we need – in the first instance you know,' Nick said, taking a glossy leaflet marked 'Mortgage rates that will astonish you' from the rack. 'We'd like to look through this first and think about it a bit. And I'd need to get onto my father. Is there somewhere we could go?'

'Oh yes sir, we have a quiet room. Would you like me to call our quiet room supervisor?'

'Well, I think we only need to sit down with our calculator and have a bit of a think and then I could call my father on my mobile. I don't thing we really need a supervisor, not yet anyway.'

'I understand sir. That's no problem. The only problem is you need the supervisor to show you to the room.'

'Oh right, I see,' Nick capitulated.

'So have a nice day tomorrow,' said the young man with the waxed hair as he withdrew in search of the quiet room supervisor.

Eventually a rather tired looking young woman with straight blond hair turned up.

'You're the quiet room couple are you?' she asked in a tone that rather suggested she thought they wanted it for the purpose of copulation.

'That's right,' Nick told her.

And so Nick and Laura were shown into a small room

equipped with masses of leaflets, a table and a few swivel chairs.

'Press this bell, if you need help,' the supervisor told them.

Nick logged on to Mr Hindley's code and printed, 'Rumbled. What do you suggest? AT6A and AT6B'.

Within minutes the reply came, 'Fish and chips 21 Copper Street. Immediate. Give codes.'

'Copper Street?' Nick wondered, 'Where's that?'

'I remember it,' Laura said. 'It's cheap fish restaurants and that sort.'

'Yes but where is it?' Nick persisted.

'Not all that far from here,' Laura told him. 'We could walk it in twenty minutes or so. Or we could get a taxi.'

'Better walk it,' Nick suggested.

He pressed the bell and the quiet room supervisor appeared.

'Got what you wanted?' she said.

'Yes thanks,' Nick replied, 'or not quite. I couldn't get through to my father, so we'll have to come back another day.'

'Your father?' the girl said.

'Oh sorry, I suppose we didn't tell you.'

'No problem,' the girl assured him. 'Have a nice day.'

As they walked out, they were once more challenged by the man with the waxy hair.

'Found what you wanted?' he enquired.

'Yes thanks,' Nick told him. 'We'll be back.'

'No problem,' he said. Take care. Have a nice day.'

Nick and Laura hurried along towards Copper Street. It was comforting to note the light was beginning to fade. They felt less conspicuous.

'There's more to Bombshell than meets the eye,' Laura remarked.

241

'I know,' Nick agreed, 'and you'd hardly think there could be would you?'

'She's really about the last person I would have expected to risk her life for our cause,' Laura said. 'She doesn't look the part.'

'She looks all right to me,' Nick offered.

As Laura had expected, Copper Street proved to be cheap restaurants and number 21 proved to be one of them. But who would be waiting for them there?

'Seventy-five to twenty-five it'll be one of ours; twenty-five to seventy-five it'll be one of Belling's,' Laura suggested.

'Suppose I go in first and see what the score is,' Nick proposed.

'Certainly not,' Laura said. 'The last thing we should do is get separated.'

They walked in. There were only three or four people there. Nick and Laura went over to a table in the corner and sat down. A waiter with a thin black moustache and a shiny apron approached.

'Did you make a booking?' he asked.

'Um, did we?' Nick replied, looking to Laura.

'Yes, we did,' she said. 'The reference was AT6A and AT6B.'

'Oh yes,' said the waiter, 'we were expecting you. I'll bring the menu.'

This was contained in a cheap leather-bound folder. On top of it there was a sheet of closely typed paper – rice paper, the now not inexperienced agents noticed. Nick and Laura read it together.

'Your message anticipated. We heard of Fenton's and Roberts's death and put two and two together. You must leave at once. Golden opportunity has presented itself. This justifies risk of plain language message. EAT IT AS SOON AS READ. Order meal and spin it out at least an hour to an hour and a half. Car will call for you. Waiter will advise its arrival. It will be marked "Spanish Cruises Courtesy Car". It will take you to Westport docks where you will board Spanish cruise liner *Spanish Crystal*. Driver will hand you documentation – cruise tickets, Australian passports, currency etc. Luggage with clothing and living requirements will be on board. Ship has excellent shops. Study your documentation on car journey. *Spanish Crystal* will visit several South American countries but NOT Brazil. Make your own way home. Meanwhile, telephone Hotel Luxe. Say you will be away for the night but wish your room to be kept. Offer to pay for six more nights with credit card. Thank you for excellent work. Good luck. Have a nice cruise. See you again one day. Best wishes, one of your friends.'

Laura tore the sheet of paper in two and scrunched up the halves into balls. She swallowed one, Nick the other. It was the ink that tasted nasty and the waiter was very slow in bringing the fish and chips to take it away.

The news started up on a TV just above their heads. Some of the other customers, who had now somewhat increased in number, came across to watch it. A girl screeched out that Captain Fenton, an important security officer, had been assassinated. The police were looking for the criminals who had committed this outrage and, from forensic evidence, already knew who they were. They would shortly release photographs of a man and a woman, after which they would appeal to the public to report any sightings. It was vital that these Royalist criminals should be found and brought to justice, the girl shouted.

'A sad business,' said the waiter,' but I'm sure they'll catch the Royalist bastards.'

'Of course they will,' a rotund chap, standing practically on top of Laura, said. 'As soon as the photographs come out that is,' he added. 'But they'll have their reasons for keeping them in the dark for the moment. They'll be looking for others as well, but they'll get them all in the end. You'll see.'

'Of course they will,' Nick assented.

Chapter 27

Events at sea were beginning to place Field-Marshal Waymark and his troops encamped in Kesa in a difficult position. While four troopships with nearly twenty thousand reinforcements had reached Bogotown, a fifth, with more than four and a half thousand men and much equipment on board, had been lost and was now limping across the South Atlantic towards Bahia. Moreover, his reinforcements at Bogotown had been reduced to the status of infantry, since their troop carriers and armoured cars were on board the fifth ship. Waymark's original plan of moving the bulk of them up to Kesa so that he could confront the Crown Prince with overwhelming strength had to be abandoned. The distance from Bogotown to Kesa was over six hundred miles. An infantry march of that distance meant that the reinforcements would not be in time to be of any use in Kesa. Waymark decided they should stay in Bogotwn from where they might eventually open a second front. He would have to tackle the Crown Prince with the resources he had in Kesa.

A second difficulty confronting Waymark was the arrival of the Brazilian contingent at Portville, about seventy miles to the south of Bogotown. This was only a small force of just over two thousand men, but it was highly mobile and well armed and armoured. It had moved off without delay and seized the road bridge over the River Treska. It was now advancing rapidly in the direction of the oil fields, where it would certainly outclass the occupation troops Waymark had left there before advancing on Kesa.

There was also a third difficulty. There were large numbers of Attagu's guerrilla troops in Kesa – many more than Waymark had at first estimated. What was worse was that they seemed able to move in reinforcements and supplies and evacuate their casualties more or less at will. To a great extent they operated from underground, exploiting the old city sewer, now disused as such, but which had originally discharged into the River Treska. This provided access and egress which the guerrillas had succeeded in controlling. They were also making use of cellars and connecting tunnels between them. In this kind of warfare, they had a marked superiority over Waymark's modern mechanised formations.

Finally, Waymark's appeal for an air strike against the Crown Prince had been turned down. The much vaunted Swift squadrons, indeed, were proving to be much more a shadow than a substance. Most of the force had been dedicated to naval attack, but it had proved ineffective because the radar did not work as expected for reasons that were still not understood. And now the Swift force had suffered a very serious blow. Under cover of a radar blackout, Admiral Fiskin had moved one of his carriers to within Hawk range of Atlanta. Though the Hawks were obsolete, being sub-sonic, they were capable, if undetected, of launching damaging bombing attacks and this they had now demonstrated. Four of them turned up out of the blue over the main Swift operational base. Five Swifts were destroyed on the ground and others were damaged. Simultaneously, four more Hawks bombed the National Aircraft Factory at Greenbridge. It appeared from photographs that substantial damage had been done and that, at the very least, the delivery of new Swifts would be delayed. Two Hawks were lost, but the other six landed safely on their carrier, which then steamed off at high speed, still enveloped in the radar mist.

All the circumstances pointed to the need for urgent and effective action against the Crown Prince. Once his Regiment was shattered, the field would be Waymark's. The guerrillas would present problems but their resistance would gradually be worn down. Treskan morale would not survive the occupation and control of all the administrative centres and military and naval bases in the country. Kesa would have to be abandoned, but when the Crown Prince's Regiment was knocked out, it could soon and easily be reoccupied. Waymark, in fact, was by no means downhearted.

* * *

Almost exactly as General Attagu had forecast (he did not wish to be known as a Field-Marshal until after the war was won), Waymark's army advanced in battle order southwards out of Kesa. It was four o'clock in the morning. Visibility was poor owing to mist and low cloud, but the Crown Prince could see, or thought he could see, that here was his chance to strike Waymark's flank, force him to turn and expose his rear to the River Treska. What the Crown Prince failed to observe was that Waymark's force was not advancing in the conventional column order of battle; it was, so to speak, side-stepping. His machine-guns were on his left flank ready to act as his front; his artillery on the right could quickly become his rear. This meant, in effect, that when he engaged, the Crown Prince was not, as he believed, attacking Waymark's flank; he was attacking his front and the manoeuvre cost him dear.

Within ten minutes of the start of the Crown Prince's attack, four hundred of his assault force were mown down by Waymark's heavy machine-guns. Having made the mistake, however, the Crown Prince was quick to recognise it. He ordered an immediate withdrawal and this most difficult of military manoeuvres was accomplished with remarkable speed, though not without further heavy casualties. As he watched the tide turn, Waymark was for a moment tempted to counter-attack, but discretion soon told him that to follow the Crown Prince into rough afforested country would be hazardous in the extreme. Instead, he ordered his artillery to pound the area in the hope that the morale and material damage on top of the battle casualties already inflicted would destroy the cohesion of the Regiment.

After an hour of this, Waymark's artillery ammunition began to run low. He ceased fire and despatched foot patrols to investigate. None returned. The Crown Prince's rifle companies were positioned in open order and well under cover of trees and hillocks. They picked off Waymark's patrols with ease. The Field-Marshal had lost the initiative; the Crown Prince had extricated himself from a near disaster.

Meanwhile, General Attagu called in his guerrilla troops from the countryside to the north of Kesa, concentrated them and entered Kesa, making a junction with the guerrillas already there. His guerrillas to the south were directed to remain dispersed and to harass Waymark, and especially his lines of communication, by all the means in their power. He ordered the Crown Prince to move north and then to enter Kesa from the west. Thus, the capital was recovered, the President returned to the Presidential Palace and something like normal life was resumed. Field-Marshal Waymark was left outside to contemplate his next move.

His options were now drastically reduced. He had dented but not destroyed the Crown Prince's Regiment, enemy guerrillas were all around him and the Brazilians, on their way to the oil fields, had intercepted and wrecked a supply convoy that was bringing up food, fuel and ammunition from Waymark's dump near his original landing place in

Sudka. He concluded that his best course would be to fall back on Bogotown where he could join up with his reinforcements and benefit from the supplies that he hoped would have come in with them. Despite having lost many of his troop carriers during his occupation of Kesa, his force was still reasonably mobile and the drive of six hundred odd miles, though not an attractive prospect, appeared to be a feasible one.

As soon as it became clear to General Attagu that Waymark was heading south-westwards, presumably for Bogotown, he ordered the Crown Prince to follow at a safe distance. He was to avoid an engagement until Waymark was further starved of supplies. Should Waymark turn to challenge him, the Crown Prince was to withdraw, maintaining his distance. Eventually, General Attagu believed, conditions would change in favour of the Crown Prince's Regiment and the time to engage in a battle of destruction would arise. This, he stressed, would have to be before Waymark could effect a junction with his reinforcements in Bogotown.

The key to effecting such a junction seemed to be the road and rail bridges over the Treska about seventy miles east of Bogotown and a similar distance from Portville. If Waymark was indeed heading for Bogotown, he would have to cross the Treska. If the bridges were blown, he would have to reinstate them, but obviously it would suit him better to occupy them and prevent their destruction. General Attagu could have blown them and, later, the Brazilian contingent could have done the same, but Attagu had ruled that out in the light of intelligence reports showing that Waymark had extensive and sophisticated bridging equipment in his Sudkan depot. Now, he was glad of that decision because he foresaw that to cross by the bridges would force Waymark to abandon his battle order and regroup into extremely thin files. That, he

249

hoped, would give the Crown Prince a second opportunity to strike a decisive blow. For this reason, he took no action to prevent Waymark's advance parties in Bogotown from moving out to capture the bridges.

Waymark had also, of course, identified the bridges as the key to the unfolding situation and when his rear reconnaissance told him that the Crown Prince was following at a discreet distance, he guessed Attagu's intentions with exactitude. He considered the possibility of reversing the junction plan by ordering his reinforcements to advance eastward over the river from Bogotown so that he could mass an army of thirty-five thousand men to engage the Crown Prince's seventeen to eighteen thousand. On reflection, however, he discarded that idea. The reinforcements, stripped of their mobility, would be slow-moving and difficult to regroup when they reached the east bank of the river. He preferred a different plan.

He instructed his staff to prepare to detach the heavy machine-gun troops and, under cover of darkness, to move them to the van of his march. When they came to within three miles of the river, they were to deploy into a defensive arc covering the approaches to the bridgeheads and dig in. The main force, travelling at maximum speed, would then pass through these positions and start crossing by the bridges. The success of the plan depended, in the first instance, upon the main army getting to the west of the machine-gunners before the Crown Prince realised what was happening and had time to come up. The second condition was that the machine-gunners would then have sufficient firepower to hold up the Crown Prince while the river crossing was completed by the rest of the force.

Waymark's plan was a bold one, though it did involve high risks but, had General Attagu and the Crown Prince been aware of it, they would, no doubt, have thought it masterly. As it was, they, of course, did not know of it.

Nor did they suspect it. But they too had a ploy which was equally unsuspected by Waymark.

* * *

The outside world had some knowledge of these events. A remarkably astute and no less brave Portugese war correspondent had penetrated to the heart of the war zone and had picked up an amazing amount of information. On the basis of what he heard and what he observed, he concluded that the balance of the war was tipping against Waymark and in favour of Attagu and the Crown Prince. In a series of dramatic despatches to Lisbon, he highlighted the importance of Waymark's failure to draw the Crown Prince into a battle of destruction at Kesa. He reported:

'So long as the Crown Prince's Regiment retains its fighting efficiency, it plays the role that a fleet in being fulfils in naval warfare. It ties Waymark's hands and prevents him from proceeding to his ultimate purpose, which is the control of the governance of Treskania. Waymark's every move is dictated by his need to be on constant alert against attack by the Crown Prince's Regiment. His apparent superiority in numbers is less convincing than it seems. Half his force has been deprived of its mobility and all his troops are beginning to suffer from a lack of supplies. Atlanta's failure to command the sea will ultimately prove fatal to its war aim.'

General Attagu's comment on this report was that he wished it was exactly true.

'All the same,' he said, 'if we play our cards correctly, it may become just that.'

Mr Belling also read the report which he found shocking. None of his advisers were talking in anything like those terms. Everyone he spoke to seemed quite confident of success. Field-Marshal Waymark's communiqués remained wholly optimistic. The reinforcements had got through, or the greater part of them had. Waymark's army greatly outnumbered the Crown Prince's and there was no need to be bothered about Attagu's rabble. True, the Air Force Swifts had failed but, as the Royal fleet had not dared to intervene and the troopships had delivered their passengers, that didn't really matter. That's what the Chiefs of Staff said. That's what Silk said. That's what everyone said. And yet, was it possible that he was not being told the truth? Was it possible that this Portugese fellow knew more than his Chiefs of Staff, more than his C-in-C in the field? An awful gnawing doubt entered the Leader's mind. He sent for the Chiefs of Staff.

'What d'you make of this?' he demanded, slapping down a copy of *The Illustrated Lisbon News* on the desk top that divided him from them.

'I don't think we need pay attention to these newspaper Johnnies,' the Army Chief averred.

'Well I am paying attention,' the Leader blasted. 'What d'you make of it?'

'Propoganda,' the Army Chief said. 'If there was anything in it, we'd have heard from Waymark.'

'Is he running short of supplies?' the Leader asked.

'We've no reason to think so,' the Army Chief said. 'He's got what he needs in his depot in Sudka.'

The discussion turned to Waymark's next moves. None of the Chiefs expressed any undue concern about anything, but Silk, who had refrained from contributing any opinions, thought the Leader was far from convinced by what they had said. The Portugese war correspondent had got to him and his confidence had been shaken. Silk resolved to keep himself on full alert for what might happen next. There would come a moment when he would have a word with Offenbeck, but that moment was not yet, not quite yet.

Chapter 28

Air Lieutenant Smith, having completed his mission to the Brazilian Navy by instructing it in the use of the Swift radar system, was airlifted off the destroyer that, at a low speed, was escorting the captured troopship to Bahia, because his services were urgently required elsewhere. On arrival at Bahia, he was ordered to fly his Swift back to Kesa, where he would get a further briefing. It was explained to him that his aircraft, which had been in a reconnaissance mode, had now been modified to a fighter role. It was equipped with Brazilian air-to-air missiles in a ready to fire condition. He was also to carry a substantial stock of these lethal weapons from which it was intended to arm the Swift already at Kesa.

His flight was trouble free and on landing he was instructed to get some shut-eye so as to be on the top line for strenuous duty the following day. On that following day, he and his comrade, Air Captain Marshall, were called at 05.00 hours for briefing at 05.45. They were then told that their task was to cover the King's fleet, which was now moving into the war zone and heading in the direction of the waters off Bogotown and Portville. The initial part of this movement would take Admiral Fiskin perilously close to the Atlantan mainland and expose him to the risk of visual detection, against which his blanket radar would of, course, be useless. During this critical phase, Marshall and Smith were to fly in tandem, ready to engage any Atlantan aircraft that might threaten the fleet. They would be supported by Hawks flown off the carriers but, if enemy Swifts appeared, only they would be capable of effective action.

At 06.30 the two pilots shot off at twice the speed of sound on track to rendezvous with the King's fleet. They were both firmly resolved to do their duty to the utmost despite the naturally unwelcome fact that this might well involve shooting down former comrades. Fortunately, however, no former comrades turned up and, after three hours on patrol, Smith was ordered to return to base and to rest. Marshall remained with the fleet for another three hours and then followed Smith back to base. The bulk of Fiskin's fleet was now past the most dangerous zone and it was still undetected. The fact, unknown to the Atlantan Air Force, that Fiskin was equipped with Swift radar and covered to a considerable extent by Swift aircraft was proving fatal to Belling's hope of neutralising the King's fleet. Worse was to follow.

At 18.30 hours on the day after Marshall's and Smith's first sortie, the Crown Prince's outposts saw the rear of Waymark's march turn to face them. Shortly afterwards they reported a group of armoured vehicles advancing head-on. The Crown Prince called in his outposts, halted his march and gave orders for a withdrawal, thus, as he had been told to do, maintaining his distance. But, within a short time and seeing that Waymark's attack was in surprisingly slight strength, the Crown Prince deduced that this was a faint, probably designed to increase the distance between his Regiment and Waymark's army for some tactical purpose. He therefore decided to disregard his instructions, to turn again and counter Waymark's oncoming armour.

Having quickly got the range, the Crown Prince's anti-tank guns soon began to play havoc with Waymark's light armour. What survived of it broke off the engagement and sped back to the rear of Waymark's march. The

Crown Prince had won a miniature victory but, more important than that, the distance between his Regiment and Waymark's army had not been increased.

As night came on, the Crown Prince calculated that Waymark's van must now be approaching the Treska bridges and would be forming into narrow files. His opportunity, he reckoned, was now at hand. He signalled Admiral Fiskin to stand by for his part in the operation and then ordered his assault force to close up and engage the enemy. Alas, instead of coming up against thin files in poor battle order, this attack was met by entrenched heavy machine-gun fire which caused grievous casualties and forced the Crown Prince to turn away.

Survivors from the assault force now reported that Waymark's army was ahead of the machine-gunners and was, in fact, crossing by the bridges in strength. The Crown Prince sent a second signal to Admiral Fiskin consisting of the single word 'GO'. Three coastal motor torpedo boats that had been marshalled in the mouth of the Treska, shot off upstream at speeds of more than eighty knots. The sound of their engines was drowned by the roar of aircraft overhead, forty Hawks to be precise. These Hawks began to strafe what they took to be Waymark's troops but which, in the darkness and river mist, often proved to be the Crown Prince's. Yellow flares had to be fired to tell them to lay off. But as that happened, there were three startling explosions, the centre piers of both bridges collapsed and the central spans canted into the river together with the unfortunate men who happened to be on them at that moment. If the Hawks had been neutralised by the poor visibility, the coastal motor boats had not. They had achieved a stunning success; Waymark's army was literally cut in half and in the confusion that followed the Crown Prince spotted his chance of pinning his half of it against the now bridgeless river. He brought up his heavy tanks and, using them as cover, moved his infantry through the enemy machine-guns and into direct contact with Waymark's thin files, now in serious disarray and unable to use their armament in any effective manner. Waymark watched the state of disarray develop into one of utter chaos. He recognised that he had been totally defeated and that he was left with only one course of action. He ran up a white flag and had it illuminated by searchlight.

The Crown Prince ordered a ceasefire, but neither commander could instantly gain control of the battlefield and sporadic firing continued for some time. At last this died down and Waymark and the Crown Prince came face to face. The Crown Prince demanded that his opponent should order all his troops on both sides of the river and those further back towards Bogotown to lay down their arms and evacuate their vehicles. Waymark argued that his surrender should be confined to the troops on the east side of the river, but the Crown Prince was adamant. He required the surrender of the whole army on pain of launching a full-scale offensive against the stranded troops on the east side and calling for an air strike against those on the west side together with a naval bombardment. He pointed out that there was a large fleet of the King's ships not many miles off the coast fully capable of enforcing a blockade that would quickly starve Waymark to death, even assuming that his army survived that long.

Waymark asked for time to consult his staff, to which the Crown Prince agreed, subject to the time being not more than twenty minutes. Waymark then saw that he had got to the end of the road. He signed a capitulation. The Battle of the Bridges was over; the war in Treskania was over. The problems now confronting the two commanders were concerned with the collection and treatment of the wounded, the burial of the dead, the collection of surrendered arms, the administration of thirty thousand prisoners of war and other scarcely less complicated matters. What was clear beyond argument was that Belling's war had met a hugely more disastrous fate than that of Paul Reynolds's earlier invasion.

Chapter 29

Just after 23.00 hours Mr Belling was woken by his Personal Assistant and told reports were coming in from Treskania that seemed to be of great importance. He dressed and went to his office where the State Secretary was already in attendance.

'What's going on?' he asked.

The State Secretary produced three signals that had come in over the last hour from Field-Marshal Waymark. The first one stated that the Expeditionary Force was beginning to cross the River Treska in order to effect a junction with the reinforcements based in Bogotown. The manoeuvre was going well but there was a serious threat from the Crown Prince's Regiment which, despite diversionary measures, had retained an uncomfortably close proximity to the rear of the Expeditionary Force. The second signal said that an attack by the Crown Prince had been successfully repulsed with heavy losses and that the crossing of the river continued to proceed according to plan.

'So why have I been called at this hour?' Mr Belling asked. 'This could have waited till morning.'

The State Secretary made no reply, but handed over the third signal.

This read:

'Waymark for Leader. Most urgent. Top secret.

Both bridges blown by unknown means. Half of army across. Other half still on east bank. Enemy has infiltrated our lines. Hand to hand fighting in progress. Situation critical. Message ends. Waymark F/M.'

Mr Belling turned a horrible shade of white and clutched his heart.

'Fetch the Chiefs of Staff. Fetch Silk and Offenbeck,' he shouted at the State Secretary.

'I've already taken that step, sir,' the State Secretary replied.

'Then why aren't they here?' Mr Belling demanded.

'They say they'll come as soon as they've concluded an important meeting sir,' he was told.

'How can they be having an important meeting when I'm not present?' the Leader yelled.

'That, sir, they did not explain,' the State Secretary informed him.

In the midst of a convulsive explosion on the part of Mr Belling, a fourth signal from Field-Marshal Waymark arrived.

'Waymark for Leader. Most urgent. Top Secret.

Regret to report have had no alternative other than to sign capitulation. Battle situation hopeless. Further resistance would have resulted in pointless loss of life. Am assured of full Geneva Convention Prisoner of War status for all troops. Repeat no alternative available. Conduct of our troops has been exemplary throughout campaign. Message ends Waymark F/M.'

At this moment, Silk and Offenbeck, followed by the three Chiefs of Staff, entered the room and lined up opposite the Leader's desk, behind which, Mr Belling stood, hands shaking, ashen-faced, but jaw jutting.

'No surrender. There's to be no surrender,' he shouted. 'If need be, the men must die at their posts. There must be no surrender. Place Waymark under arrest. Appoint a new C-in-C. The fight must go on.'

'The fight can't go on,' the Army Chief said with a touch of truculence that had not been heard from him before. 'The battle's lost. There's no getting away from it.'

'The fact we had no naval strength to confront the King's fleet was a fatal flaw in our strategy,' the Chief of the Naval Staff contributed. 'You can't fight a war overseas without sea power,' he added.

'That was to have been dealt with by the Air Force,' Mr Belling retorted.

'The Swifts were forced into service too soon,' the Chief of the Air Staff said. 'I distinctly remember saying we needed two years development time. We never got it.'

'There's to be no surrender,' Mr Belling repeated. 'Signal that to the new C-in-C.'

'There is no new C-in-C,' the Army Chief said. 'Waymark is the C-in-C and he *has* surrendered.'

'So it's come to this has it?' Mr Belling muttered. 'Am I to take it that you're all traitors? You've betrayed me. You've betrayed Atlanta. You've betrayed our historic mission.'

Major Silk stepped forward.

'On the contrary,' he said, 'it's you who have betrayed us.'

'Silk!' Mr Belling blasted, 'you're under arrest.'

'On the contrary Mr Belling,' Major Silk replied, 'it's you who are under arrest.'

He came up to the desk and pressed the Leader's audience bell. Four of Belling's Police entered the room, pinioned the Leader's arms and removed him from the Residence.

'That, gentlemen,' Major Silk announced, 'was a *coup d'état.*'

'What'll be done with him?' the Naval Chief asked.

'Oh come come, Admiral, we never discuss that sort of thing,' Major Silk told him. 'The point is he's deranged, lost his reason. He has to be restrained. He's a threat to the State. Surely it's enough if we all take note of that.'

There was a sort of murmur, though whether of approval or disquiet was hard to guess. Major Silk asked the company to be seated, but he himself remained on his feet.

'We need a new government,' he said. 'I've talked it through with Dr Offenbeck whose immense experience and great wisdom we all appreciate. He and I are agreed on all points. We think there are three immediate steps we must take. First, we must form an Emergency Council of State, which we suggest should consist of those here present now. Second, we should resolve to rule through the appropriate heads of department in the Civil Service. Third, we must have a Head of State who can present a proper face to the outside world and who will not ... who will, er, understand that the executive power lies with the Council of State.'

'A figurehead?' the Army Chief enquired.

'Exactly,' Major Silk confirmed, 'and one who has no connection with the Belling regime.'

'I suppose we're all guilty, or a bit guilty, on that score,' the Air Chief said.

'Perhaps,' Major Silk agreed,' but with an independent Head of State, we'd be covered.'

'Covered?' said the Air Chief.

'Yes, I mean he'd be the public face of the government, see the ambassadors, make the speeches and all that, and would be prepared to say what the Council of State decided should be said. Dr Offenbeck and I concluded that we'd be a lot safer ... I mean it would be more appropriate for us to be out of ... well, not quite in the front line.'

Everyone nodded. This proposal really did meet with unanimous approval.

'So, who have we got in mind?' the Naval Chief asked.

'Dr Offenbeck and I thought Mr Waterman would do very well,' Major Silk submitted.

'Waterman?' the Air Chief recollected. 'Wasn't he President in Paul Reynolds's day?'

261

'Indeed he was,' Major Silk said, 'and technically still is, I suppose. Belling seemed to forget about him and he's still living in a flat in the Royal Palace. We could just announce that he is the legitimate President.'

'That would be quite convenient,' the Air Chief said. 'Is he pliable? I mean is he willing to serve?'

'Oh yes, we've sounded him. He'll do it,' Major Silk said.

As the meeting broke up for a brief pause for refreshments, the State Secretary muttered to Dr Offenbeck, 'It's all a bit makeshift isn't it?'

'Yes, said Dr Offenbeck. 'but it'll do for the present. Later of course we'll have to get the King back.'

* * *

It so happened that at almost exactly the same time that Mr Belling was roused from his bed, President Tamu was also awoken from his. General Attagu wished to speak to him.

'He wouldn't ring at this time of the night unless he had something very important to say,' the President remarked to Madam Tamu. 'Put him on,' he told his scrambled-communications operator.

General Attagu reported that signals were coming in to his HQ from the Crown Prince in the field.

'It seems to me,' he said, 'that an action that will be decisive for the war is imminent. At any moment decisions may have to be reached that only you, Mr President, can make.'

'All right,' said the President, 'I'm awake and alert. Go on.'

'All details to follow later,' General Attagu told him, 'but the immediate gist is this. The Crown Prince has pinned Waymark against the River Treska. The bridges are blown and half his army has been trapped.'

'Splendid,' the President responded. 'What about the other half?'

'They've got across the river and could now join up with the reinforcements in Bogotown. That would make an army of at least thirty thousand men, albeit deprived of a good deal of their mobility. Now the point is this: the Crown Prince wants to demand a capitulation that will include all these men as well as those on the east bank for whom there is no escape. If Waymark accepts, the war will be over. If he refuses, we will kill or capture ten to twelve thousand of his best troops and much of his remaining mobility, I mean his troop carriers and so on. But Waymark may succeed in regrouping on the west side of the river. The war would go on and it will not be easy for the Crown Prince to cross now the bridges have gone. There's a political decision here. Shall we stake all on ending the war now or shall we fall back on a continuation of the campaign and present demands that Waymark is more likely to accept?'

'My expectation is that Waymark's beaten whichever course we take,' the President said. 'Even if the Crown Prince can't get across the river, the naval blockade will finish him. It's only a matter of time. But that's going to cost more and more lives and involve more and more suffering. My ruling is that the Crown Prince should be authorised to demand a full capitulation.'

'Thank you Mr President,' General Attagu said. 'That's what I hoped you would decide. After all, the Crown Prince is on the spot and can gauge better than either of us the extent of his grip of Waymark.'

'Precisely,' the President assented.

* * *

The war, indeed, was now over. The Crown Prince had prevailed upon Field-Marshal Waymark to surrender almost forty-five thousand men. General Attagu's troops were rounding up stragglers and the Brazilians had captured another two thousand at and around the oil fields. The main problem for the Treskan government, and certainly its most urgent one, was the administration of this huge number of prisoners of war.

In Atlanta, Major Silk and his Emergency Council of State fully recognised the defeat they had suffered. They did not think it was any disgrace to Field-Marshal Waymark. They were realist enough to see that he had had no alternative. Once the Air Force had failed to neutralise the King's fleet, the fate of the Expeditionary Force was sealed. As the Chief of the Naval Staff had told Belling, an overseas war cannot be fought without command of the sea. Mr Belling, of course, did not agree with this, but what Mr Belling thought had suddenly become of no importance. He was, in fact, already on his way to Prison Island in a police helicopter.

The immediate problem facing Major Silk and his cabal was what to say to the country and what to say to the Treskan government. They first grappled with the problem of what to say to the country. In the end, they decided to announce that the Leader had suffered a heart attack and had been taken to hospital for emergency treatment. In his absence, the President of the Republic, Mr Waterman, had assumed the full powers of government. He would be supported by an Emergency Council of State. On the strongly emphasised advice of Dr Offenbeck, it was, however, decided to say nothing about who was to sit on this Council. It was further decided to announce that the military situation in Treskania had 'deteriorated' and that 'for humanitarian reasons' an armistice had been sought between Field-Marshal Waymark's forces and those of the Crown Prince and General Attagu.

As to what President Waterman should say to President

Tamu, there was prolonged discussion without the emergence of any clear consensus. Ultimately, following a proposal by the Army Chief, it was resolved that Dr Offenbeck and Mr Waterman should be charged with the production of a statement that would then be accepted by the Council without further discussion.

Major Silk thought this was a very odd solution, but it was now becoming clear that his influence was waning rapidly, waning in fact, as rapidly as that of Dr Offenbeck was waxing. The result was an address by President Waterman to President Tamu recognising the capitulation of the Expeditionary Force and proposing that negotiations for a peace settlement should be initiated.

Thus, the people of Atlanta were left without a very exact picture of what had taken place. Even so, there was an immediate shift in the focus of public perception. So far, the man in the street had seemed to believe that victory in the war would be won and that Mr Belling was the man to win it. Beside this belief, domestic issues had seemed of comparatively small consequence. Now, there could be no question of victory in the war and Mr Belling, well, he wasn't there any more. The whole business had collapsed in disaster, an even worse disaster than Paul Reynolds's efforts had produced. What the man in the street now began to notice was the truculent behaviour of the police, the soaring rate of inflation, the increasing dominance of the black market, the shortage of fuel and the duplicity of the government. Dr Offenbeck, for all his self-effacement, possessed antennae that enabled him to gauge to an extraordinary extent what the man in the street thought. It was almost as though he could induce the man in the street to think what he thought.

*   *   *

President Tamu and his advisers were nowadays in almost permanent conference with the King and his. Now restored to the ranks of the latter were Nick Hardy and Laura Blick. They had an exciting tale to tell. Forced to leave Atlanta in a hurry, they had managed to secure a passage in a Spanish cruise liner to the Argentine, whence they had made their way by air to Portugal and eventually, by a roundabout route, they had arrived back in Kesa. Here, they provided the President and the King with an up-to-date briefing on conditions in Atlanta which, even before Waymark's capitulation, they had judged to be deteriorating rapidly.

Putting two and two together, it was apparent to President Tamu and the King that the Atlantan government, such as it was, no longer had any negotiating strength. President Tamu could dictate whatever terms he chose. But President Tamu was a far-sighted statesman. His aim was to secure a situation that would rule out, as far as humanly possible, a third invasion of his country. If the outcome of this war was bitterness and humiliation in Atlanta, a second Belling might arise and a third invasion might be attempted. His solution was the restoration of the monarchy and the re-establishment by the King of civilised government in Atlanta.

'You should now return,' he suggested to the King. 'That would safeguard good relations between our two countries and it would save your people from a sense of humiliation.'

'No,' said the King. 'I will not return unless I am invited to do so. And, If I am invited, I will accept only subject to certain fundamental principles being agreed beforehand.'

'But invited by whom and accepted by whom?' the disappointed and slightly irritated President asked.

'We would have to think about that,' the King replied.

That, the President thought to himself, was typical of his friend the King. He was very strong on right and wrong, on the principles of things, but not quite so good on how to achieve them. Something to do with his background and upbringing, he assumed.

'Yes,' he said, 'we'll have to think about that.'

Field-Marshal Attagu, as he was now happy to be ranked, asked and received permission to speak.

'We have nearly fifty thousand prisoners of war on our hands. It's largely a citizen army. So we have nearly fifty thousand Atlantan citizens facing the humiliation of being prisoners of war in an African country. Suppose we release them. Suppose we offer them the chance of being reunited with their former comrades now serving in the Crown Prince's Regiment. Suppose they accept, or suppose the vast majority of them do, might they not perhaps be persuaded to petition their government for the return of His Majesty?'

'And might not that petition be backed up by similar petitions from Mr Hindley's Rings in Atlanta?' Nick suggested.

'That's worth thinking about, is it not?' the President put to the King.

'I suppose it might be,' the still somewhat reluctant King conceded.

Field-Marshal Attagu's proposal might not have borne fruit had not a similar idea been forming in Dr Offenbeck's head. He suggested to President Waterman that Field-Marshal Waymark should be asked to resume his loyalty to the King.

'I see our prisoners of war in Atlanta as a bridge,' he said. 'By that route we may be able to escape the worst consequences of military defeat. The men will rally to the King if they see that as a means of early repatriation. The Treskan government will be relieved to be shot of the problem of trying to accommodate and feed a foreign army of prisoners.'

267

'But how could we advocate that?' the startled Mr Waterman asked. 'We're supposed to be a republic. What would happen to me?'

'Neither the republic nor you Mr President are likely to last very long. The people see the revolution has been a failure. The whole Idealist wave has perished on the battlefields of Treskania. People will turn back to the King. The republic is as good as dead already.'

Dr Offenbeck allowed these words to sink in and then resumed. 'If you were to invite the King to return and if you were seen as instrumental in raising support for him in the country, I do not doubt that an appropriate reward would be found for you, a pension perhaps, or a ceremonial office.'

'Do you really think they'd do that for me?'

'I have no doubt of it,' Dr Offenbeck confidently asserted.

In Kesa, the King's communications system at his Residence was clogged with messages affirming loyalty and imploring him to return to Atlanta. Carloads of letters saying the same thing arrived in a seemingly endless stream and in the waiting rooms people were jostling one another in the hope of securing an audience. Count Connors and the King's valet fought a losing battle against the resulting chaos and confusion, but both wore the smile of a Cheshire cat.

Among the aspirants was Field-Marshal Waymark, released for the purpose by the express order of Field-Marshal Attagu. Count Connors managed to steer him through the milling crowd and into the silence and composure of the King's office.

'The Crown Prince permitted me to retain my sword,' the Field-Marshal said. 'I now have the honour to surrender it to Your Majesty.'

He drew the sword and held it before the King. The King touched it and said, 'Thank you. I am glad to return this sword for your retention.'

Chapter 30

Three weeks had now passed since Field-Marshal Waymark had been received in audience and the day of the King's broadcast to the Atlantan people had arrived.

'After the tumult of recent years I am at last able to speak to you all,' he began, 'and I now do so from the city of Kesa in the friendly country of Treskania. In the last few weeks I have been inundated with expressions of loyalty from all over the country and from those of us who are at present in Treskania. These have lifted my spirits and touched my heart. They have also inspired my decision to return to our dear country and resume my functions as your King, which I am now convinced is your wish.

'At this, the dawn of new opportunity, I wish to assure you that I will return firmly resolved to introduce a rule of peace and reconciliation. Past misdemeanours against the state or against my person will be expunged from the record. There will be no witch-hunts; there will be no vengeance; there will be, for everyone, the chance of a new start.

'Future misdemeanours will be dealt with only by the proper processes of our long-established code of law. There will be no special tribunals; there will be no so-called summary justice and people will once again enjoy the right of free speech.

'My first duty to you is to bring peace and the spirit of reconciliation to our country. My second duty is to restore to our government its historic constitutional

269

components under which the will of the people will once more be expressed by universal suffrage within the balance of a House of Representatives and a Senate. To ensure that our system is adjusted to the requirements of these changing times, I will appoint a Constitutional Commission to report upon such revisions as may be required. After that and in its light, we will proceed to the election of Representatives and Senators.

'Meanwhile, I will appoint a provisional government and charge it with responsibility for seeking post-war resettlement and orderly life at home, peace abroad and the foundations of a new prosperity.

'At this hour of liberation, I express my profound gratitude to President Tamu and the great country of Treskania, as I also do to President de Farius and the people of Brazil, who have fought with such gallantry and suffered so much in our cause. Our country is bound in the indissoluable links of friendship by a mutually supporting and non-aggressive alliance with Treskania and Brazil.

'Let us now go forward with confident step and heads held high. May God bless you all.'

As the King stepped away from the TV cameras, he was buttonholed by his Valet.

'Time to dress Your Majesty,' the steadfast loyalist said.

'Good God, is it time already?' the King exclaimed.

'Yes Your Majesty, the President's banquet starts in fifty minutes.'

'Fifty minutes. Good God. What did you make of the broadcast?'

'Of course Your Majesty speaks in the old style, but I think people will like that. They'll see it means we'll be getting back to proper orderly life. And I'll tell you another thing Your Majesty. People will know you mean what you say. You can tell that by listening and I think they'll like that too.'

'Ah well, but of course you're prejudiced,' the King said.

'I'm not prejudiced Your Majesty. As Your Majesty knows, I know what's what and I'm telling Your Majesty that if Your Majesty doesn't hurry up and dress, Your Majesty will be late for the President's banquet and then we've got the ball after that.'

'All right Fred,' the King said. 'Then get on with your slave-driving.'

The banquet was a grand occasion but the ball that followed was yet grander. President Tamu and Madame Tamu took their seats on a dais at the head of the huge ballroom. On their right, sat the King and on their left, the Ambassador of Brazil. The President, the King and the Ambassador all wore the same stars; those of the Orders of Treskania, of Atlanta and of Santa Maria of Brazil. The President's tail coat was crossed by the light blue sash of the Order of Atlanta, the King's white uniform of a Fleet Admiral, with the scarlet of the Order of Treskania and the Ambassador's diplomatic uniform, with the green sash of the Santa Maria. Flanking the dais there were, on either side, lines of chairs on which the principal Treskan Ministers and dignitaries sat together with many other distinguished guests from the three countries, including Field-Marshal Attagu, the Crown Prince, Field-Marshal Waymark, Admiral Fiskin and the startlingly attractive and elegant daughter of the Brazilian Ambassador. In this group, there was also another guest who had travelled from Wales and whom few in the great concourse recognised. This was Miss ap Llewellyn of Dolgellau Hall.

Those on the dais and on the flanking chairs rose and the three national anthems were played. The King and Madame Tamu then led off the dancing, if such the King's performance could be called. He moved stiffly, as though following the instructions of his first ever dancing master.

271

Madame Tamu, however, moved with that particular grace and sense of rhythm that are the special province of the Hurnot people. What the King lost by comparison, as far as dancing was concerned, he made up by his affability and unaccustomed vivacity. He and Madame Tamu obviously found each other's company congenial.

Following closely on the heels of the opening pair, President Tamu descended from the dais, proceeded across the floor to one of the flanking rows of chairs and invited Miss ap Llewellyn to partner him. That turned all heads and not only because of their elegant movement, but because nearly everyone wondered who the lady was. They were followed by the Brazilian Ambassador, who handed Madame Attagu onto the floor. The next to join the fray were the Crown Prince and the daughter of the Brazilian Ambassador. They too turned all heads, but this time on account of the dazzling beauty of the young girl with the dark eyes, the long black hair and the chic of a lamé evening dress cut to display her perfect figure and litheness of movement.

More and more couples followed until, when the floor was quite crowded and the President, the King and the Ambassador had regained the sanctuary of the dais, Nick and Laura felt it would be in order for them to join in.

They moved along in perfect unison, enjoying the familiarity and compatibility their bodies had for each other. Laura hummed the tune and seemed unaffected by her august surroundings. Suddenly she stopped humming.

'Let's get married,' she said.

'You do choose the oddest moments to say things,' Nick replied.

'Oh I don't know,' Laura said. 'A dance seems quite the appropriate occasion.'

'This is not a dance,' Nick told her. 'This is a state ball.'

'OK, it's a state ball, but what's wrong with a state ball?' Laura went on.

'Nothing much. I suppose,' Nick said. 'So why don't we?'

'Why don't we what?' asked Laura.

'Get married,' Nick explained.

'I take it that's a proposal,' Laura said.

'You take it quite right Mrs Hardy,' Nick assented.

'Great,' said Laura. 'Miss ap Llewellyn will be so pleased.'

'What's Miss ap Llewellyn got to do with it?' Nick asked.

'She was keen we should,' Laura explained.

'Oh I see,' said Nick.

At midnight, the President and the King, accompanied by the Ambassador, withdrew from the ball and were driven to Kesa airport. Here, they assembled in the VIP lounge where refreshments were served and farewell good wishes exchanged.

'I liked your phrase about going forward with confident step and heads held high,' President Tamu remarked to the King.

'Well,' said the King, I will try to follow my own precept, but make no mistake, things are going to be very difficult in Atlanta. This revolution has done terrible damage to the national mind and it has inflicted wounds on the national body that will be hard to heal.'

'I understand that fully,' the President said. 'We in Treskania even now are scarcely more than convalescent from the years of civil war we endured. Atlanta will need time.'

'True,' said the King. 'Time and reconciliation.'

With Count Connors, his valet and others of his immediate entourage and his guest, Miss ap Llewellyn, the King then boarded the presidential helicopter and took off for

273

Bogotown. Others of his staff and several of his principal supporters were taken out to a fleet of six rather rackety looking old aircraft bound for the same destination.

As they boarded one of them, Laura asked Nick what sort of an aircraft it was.

'It's a Dakota,' he told her.

'Ah', said Laura, 'I've heard of those. I think they were used in the Third Crusade.'

At Bogotown, the royal party embarked in the massive carrier commanded by Captain Willis on which they joined more than three thousand former Atlantan prisoners of war who, like the King, were on their way home.

At 08.00 hours the carrier sailed for Atlanta City Port. The restoration of the monarchy in the person of King Arthur IX was underway.